Going Home

Judith Keim

BOOKS BY JUDITH KEIM

The Talking Tree (The Hartwell Women –1)
Sweet Talk (The Hartwell Women – 2)
Straight Talk (The Hartwell Women – 3)
Baby Talk (The Hartwell Women – 4)
The Hartwell Women Series – (Boxed Set)
Breakfast at The Beach House Hotel –1
Lunch at The Beach House Hotel – 2
Dinner at The Beach House Hotel – 3
Christmas at The Beach House Hotel – 4
Fat Fridays (Fat Fridays Group – 1)
Sassy Saturdays (Fat Fridays Group – 2)
Secret Sundays (Fat Fridays Group – 3)
Finding Me – A Salty Key Inn Book – 1
Finding My Way – A Salty Key Inn Book – 2
Finding Love – A Salty Key Inn Book – 3
Finding Family – A Salty Key Inn Book – 4
A Christmas Star – A Seashell Cottage Book – 1
Going Home – A Chandler Hill Inn Book – 1
Coming Home – A Chandler Hill Inn Book – (Late 2019)
Winning BIG – a little love story for all ages
For more information: **http://amzn.to/2jamIaF**

CHILDREN'S BOOKS BY J. S. KEIM

The Hidden Moon (The Hidden Moon Series – 1)
Return to the Hidden Moon (The Hidden Moon Series – 2)
Trouble on the Hidden Moon (The Hidden Moon Series – 3)
Kermit Greene's World
For more information: **http://amzn.to/2qlqKMI**

PRAISE FOR JUDITH KEIM'S NOVELS

THE BEACH HOUSE HOTEL SERIES

"Love the characters in this series. This series was my first introduction to Judith Keim. She is now one of my favorites. Looking forward to reading more of her books."

BREAKFAST AT THE BEACH HOUSE HOTEL is an easy, delightful read that offers romance, family relationships, and strong women learning to be stronger. Real life situations filter through the pages. Enjoy!"

LUNCH AT THE BEACH HOUSE HOTEL – "This series is such a joy to read. You feel you are actually living with them. Can't wait to read the latest one."

DINNER AT THE BEACH HOUSE HOTEL – "A Terrific Read! As usual, Judith Keim did it again. Enjoyed immensely. Continue writing such pleasantly reading books for all of us readers."

CHRISTMAS AT THE BEACH HOUSE HOTEL – "Not Just Another Christmas Novel. This is book number four in the series and my introduction to Judith Keim's writing. I wasn't disappointed. The characters are dimensional and engaging. The plot is well crafted and advances at a pleasing pace. The Florida location is interesting and warming. It was a delight to read a romance novel with mature female protagonists. Ann and Rhoda have life experiences that enrich the story. It's a clever book about friends and extended family. Buy copies for your book group pals and enjoy this seasonal read."

THE HARTWELL WOMEN

"This was an EXCELLENT series. When I discovered Judith Keim, I read all of her books back to back. I thoroughly enjoyed the women Keim has written about. They are believable and you want to just jump into their lives and be their friends! I can't wait for any upcoming books!"

"I fell into Judith Keim's Hartwell Women series and have read & enjoyed all of her books in every series. Each centers around a strong & interesting woman character and their family interaction. Good reads that leave you wanting more."

THE FAT FRIDAYS GROUP

"Excellent story line for each character, and an insightful representation of situations which deal with some of the contemporary issues women are faced with today."

"I love this author's books. Her characters and their lives are realistic. The power of women's friendships is a common and beautiful theme that is threaded throughout this story."

THE SALTY KEY INN SERIES

FINDING ME – *"I thoroughly enjoyed the first book in this series and cannot wait for the others! The characters are endearing with the same struggles we all encounter. The setting makes me feel like I am a guest at The Salty Key Inn...relaxed, happy & light-hearted! The men are yummy and the women strong. You can't get better than that! Happy Reading!"*

FINDING MY WAY- *"Loved the family dynamics as well as uncertain emotions of dating and falling in love. Appreciated the morals and strength of parenting throughout. Just couldn't put this book down."*

FINDING LOVE – *"I waited for this book because the first two was such good reads. This one didn't disappoint.... Judith Keim always puts substance into her books. This book was no different, I learned about PTSD, accepting oneself, there is always going to be problems but stick it out and make it work. Just the way life is. In some ways a lot like my life. Judith is right, it needs another book and I will definitely be reading it. Hope you choose to read this series, you will get so much out of it."*

OTHER COMMENTS

"Always love books written by Judith Keim. From these strong women who go through lots of difficulties and adventure to the Florida beach hotel books. Every book is entertaining and fun to read with plenty of excitement and surprises.

"I was first introduced to Judith Keim's books with her Beach House series and since then look forward to each new book from this author. Her stories draw you in so you become invested in the lives of her characters and want to know what comes next."

Going Home

A Chandler Hill Inn Book - 1

Judith Keim

Wild Quail Publishing

Wild Quail Publishing
PO Box 171332
Boise, ID 83717-1332

ISBN# 978-0-9992448-6-9

Dedication

This book is dedicated to Wayne Bailey, his wife, Nicolette Nickolau, and the staff at Youngberg Hill for their kindness and hospitality

CHAPTER ONE

Some people's lives unfold in the most unusual ways.

In 1970, the only things Violet Hawkins wanted for her eighteenth birthday were to escape the Dayton, Ohio, foster-care system in which she'd been raised and to make her way to San Francisco. There, she hoped to enjoy a mellow lifestyle and find the love that had always been absent in her life.

Though she made it to San Francisco easily enough, she soon discovered she couldn't afford a clean, safe place in which to settle down. At first, it hadn't seemed to matter. Caught up in the excitement and freedom of living in a large city where free love and openness to so many things reigned, she almost forgot about eating and sleeping. One couch, one futon was as good as any other as long as grass or other drugs were available, and others didn't mind giving her a place to sleep. But after spending four months there, the dollars she'd carefully saved, which had seemed so many in Dayton, were nothing but a mere pittance in a city where decent living was too expensive for her. She took to wandering the streets with her backpack until she came upon a friendly group willing to give her a sleeping space inside or a bite to eat.

One June day, feeling discouraged, she'd just sunk down onto the steps outside a row house when a young man emerged. He smiled down at her. "Tired?"

She was more than tired. She was exhausted and hungry. "Looking for work. I need to eat."

He gave her a long, steady, blue-eyed look. "What's your name?"

"Violet Hawkins. But call me Lettie."

His eyebrows shot up. "With all that red hair, no flowery name for you?"

She shook her head. She'd always hated both her hair and her name. The red in her hair was a faded color, almost pink, and the name Violet indicated a delicate flower. She'd never had the luxury of being the least bit frail.

He sat down beside her and studied her. "You don't look like the hippie type. What are you doing in a place like this?"

"On my eighteenth birthday, I left Dayton, Ohio, to come here. It sounded like a great plan—all this freedom."

"How long have you been here?"

"Four months. I thought it would be different. I don't know ... easier, maybe."

He got to his feet. "How about I fix you a sandwich, and then I'll tell you about a job, if you want it. It's at a vineyard in Oregon. I'm heading there later today."

Her glance slid over his well-built body, rugged facial features, and clean, shoulder-length, light-brown hair. He didn't fit into the usual crowd she'd been with, which made her cautious. "Who are you? And why would you do this for me?"

"Kenton Chandler." His lips curved into the same warm smile he'd given her earlier. "I'm heading to Oregon, and, frankly, I could use the company. Keeps me from falling asleep."

"Yeah? And what is this vineyard?"

He shrugged. "A couple of years ago, my dad bought a small inn with 75 acres in the Willamette Valley south of Portland. He's planted most of the land with grapes. He doesn't know that much about making wine and wants me to learn. That's why I'm in San Francisco. I've been working at a vineyard in Napa Valley just north of here, learning the ropes." He grinned. "Or maybe I should say, learning the vines."

"What kind of sandwich?" she asked, warming toward him and his wacky humor. Her stomach rumbled loud enough for them both to hear it.

"How does ham and Swiss sound?" he said, giving her a knowing look.

"Okay." Lettie didn't want him to think she couldn't manage on her own. That was dangerous. She'd learned it the hard way, fighting off a guy who thought he could have her just because he gave her a puff of weed. She'd been careful ever since to stay away from situations and guys like that.

"Well?" He waved her toward the door.

Lettie checked to see if others were within hearing range if she needed them. Plenty of people were hanging around nearby. Thinking it was safe, Lettie climbed the stairs behind Kenton. He didn't know about the knife tucked into one of the pockets of her jeans.

Inside, she found the same kind of contrast between this clean house and others she'd been in. It wasn't sparkling clean, but it was tidier than most.

He led her into the kitchen. "Sit down. It'll only take me a minute to make your sandwich." He handed her a glass of water. "Mustard? Mayo?"

"Both," she replied primly, sitting down at a small pine table in the eating area of the room.

She sat quietly, becoming uncomfortable with the idea that he was waiting on her. She wasn't used to such a gesture. She was usually the one waiting on others both in her foster home and at the church where she'd spent hours each week attending services and events with her foster family. Thinking of them now, a shiver raced across her shoulders like a frightened centipede. It had been her experience that supposedly outstanding members of a church weren't always kind to those they'd taken into foster care primarily for the money.

"Ready!" said Kenton, jarring her out of thoughts of the past. He placed a plate with the sandwich in front of her and took a seat opposite her.

She lifted the sandwich to her face and inhaled the aroma of the ham. Keeping her eyes on Kenton, she bit into the bread, savoring the taste of fresh food.

He beamed at her with satisfaction when she quickly took another bite.

"Who lives here? Lettie asked.

"A friend of mine," said Kenton. His gaze remained on her. "You don't look eighteen."

She swallowed, and her breath puffed out with dismay. "But I am."

"And you're not into drugs and all the free-love stuff everyone talks about?"

Lettie shook her head. "Not really. I tried weed a couple of times, but it wasn't for me." Her strict upbringing had had a greater influence on her than she'd thought.

"Good. Like I said, if you want to ride to Oregon with me, there's a job waiting for you at the Chandler Hill Inn. We're looking for help. It would be a lot better than walking the streets of Haight-Ashbury. Safer too."

She narrowed her eyes at him. "And if I don't like it?"

He shrugged. "You can leave. One of the staff recently left for L.A. That's why my father called me to ask if I knew anyone who could come and work there. You're my only choice."

Lettie's heart pounded with hope. Acting as nonchalant as she could, she said, "Sounds like something I'd like to try."

###

The ride to Oregon was mostly quiet as an easy camaraderie continued between them. Kenton answered any questions she had about him, the inn, and the way he thought about things. Lettie was surprised to learn he hadn't joined in a lot of the anti-war protests.

"My best friend died in 'Nam. He believed in serving our country. I want to honor him," he said to Lettie.

"A boy in my high school was drafted. His parents weren't happy about it."

"Well, if I'm drafted, I'm going," Kenton said. "I don't want to, but I will. I don't really have a choice."

As they talked, they agreed that John Wayne was great in the movie *True Grit*.

"And I love the Beatles," said Lettie.

"Yeah, me too. Too bad they just broke up."

"And what about the new group, The Jackson 5?" Lettie said.

"They're great. And I like Simon and Garfunkel and their music too."

At one point, Lettie turned to Kenton. "Sometimes you seem so serious, like an old man. How old are you, anyway?"

He gave her a sheepish look. "Twenty-two."

They shared a laugh, and in that moment, Lettie knew she'd found a person with whom she could be herself.

Lettie woke to someone shaking her shoulder. She stared into the blue-gray eyes of a stranger and stiffened.

"Lettie, we're here," said a male voice.

As she came fully awake, she realized Kenton was talking to her.

"Here at Chandler Hill?" she asked, rubbing the sleep from her eyes.

She looked out through the windshield of the Ford Pinto and gaped at the huge, white-clapboard house sitting on the top of a knoll like a queen overlooking her realm.

Lettie scrambled out of the car and stood gazing at the clean lines of the two-story building. Across the front, four windows offset by green shutters were lined up with identical windows below. Beneath a small, protective, curved roof, glass panels bracketed a wide front door, welcoming guests. To one side, a two-story wing had been added to the house.

Green, leafy bushes offset by an assortment of colorful flowers she didn't recognize softened the front of the building. As she walked closer, she realized between the main house and the addition a small, stone patio and private garden had been installed.

"Come on in," said Kenton. "There's a beautiful view from the back porch."

Feeling as if she were Alice in a different kind of Wonderland, Lettie entered the house. As she tiptoed behind Kenton, her gaze darted from the polished surfaces of furniture to gilt-edged mirrors to a massive floral bouquet sitting on a large dining-room table. It all seemed so grand.

Kenton led her to a wide porch lining the back of the house. Observing the rolling land before her and, in the distance, the hills crouching in deepening colors of green, Lettie's breath caught. The sun was rising, spreading a gold topping on the hills like icing on cake.

"Nice, huh?"

Lettie smiled and said, "I've never seen anything so beautiful, so peaceful."

At the sound of footsteps behind her, she whirled around.

A tall, gray-haired man with striking features similar to Kenton's said, "Welcome home, son."

They shook hands, and then the older gentleman turned to

her. “And who is this?”

Shy, she stared at the man who seemed so familiar to her.

Kenton nudged Lettie.

Minding her manners, Lettie held out her hand as she’d been taught. “Lettie Hawkins. I’ve come for a job.” A niggling feeling kept her eyes on him longer than necessary. When she could no longer stop herself, she blurted, “Aren’t you Rex Chandler, the movie star?”

He smiled kindly. “Yes, I am. But I’ve changed professions.”

Lettie held back a chuckle of delight. A friend’s mother had privately adored him.

“Why don’t the two of you come into the kitchen,” said Rex. “Mrs. Morley will want to talk to Lettie, and I need to talk to you, Kenton.”

As Lettie followed the men into the kitchen, a woman hurried toward them, crying, “Kenton! Kenton! You’re home at last!”

Laughing, Kenton allowed the woman to hug him. “You’d think I’ve been gone a year, Mrs. Morley.”

“You almost were,” she said, smiling and pinching his cheek. “And look at you! More handsome than ever.”

Looking as if he couldn’t wait for her to focus her attention elsewhere, Kenton said, “Mrs. Morley, I’d like you to meet Lettie Hawkins. She’s here for a job.”

Mrs. Morley’s gaze settled on Lettie. “So, you like to work?”

“She likes to eat,” said Kenton, bringing a smile to Mrs. Morley’s full face.

“By the looks of it, Lettie, you could use more food,” said Mrs. Morley. “Let’s you and I talk about what kind of jobs you could do around here. I’m short-handed at the moment.”

Kenton and Rex left the kitchen.

Mrs. Morley waved Lettie over to a desk in a small alcove

in the kitchen. After lowering her considerable bulk into a chair, Mrs. Morley faced her. Her green eyes exuded kindness as she studied Lettie. Her gray-streaked brown hair was pulled back from her face and banded together in a ponytail, giving Lettie a good look at her pleasing features.

"Have a seat, dear."

Lettie sat in the chair indicated for her and clutched her hands. After seeing the small inn and the beautiful countryside, she desperately wanted the job.

"Where are you from, Lettie? And why in the world do you want to work here in the country? I'd think a pretty, young girl like you would want to be in a city having fun."

Lettie paused, unsure how to answer her. She'd thought she'd like living in the city, being free to do whatever she wanted. But after four months of doing just that, the excitement had worn off. She liked to know where she was going to sleep at night and when she'd next eat.

"Maybe I'm just a country girl at heart," she answered lamely. Her two best friends at home would scoff at her, but right now, that's how she felt.

"Well, that's what you'll be if you stay on. A lot of activity is taking place around here, what with people buying up turkey farms and the like, turning them into vineyards, but it *is* country. I hope it always will be." She leaned forward. "Know anything about cooking? Cleaning?"

"Yes," said Lettie. "I used to do both in my foster home. I was the oldest of eight kids there."

"Eight? My land, that's a lot of kids to take in," said Mrs. Morley.

"It's a lot of money," Lettie said, unable to hide her disgust. "That's why they did it."

"I see," said Mrs. Morley, studying her. "So how long have you been on your own?"

"Four months," she replied. "I was in San Francisco when I met Kenton."

"Such a good, young man. I've known him for a while now," Mrs. Morley sighed with affection. "You're lucky he found you. Why don't we start in housekeeping, see how it goes, and then maybe you can give me a hand in the kitchen."

"Okay," Lettie said, jumping to her feet. "Where should I put my things? I need to get them from the car."

Mrs. Morley gave her an approving look. "I like your eagerness. Let me show you to your room and then I'll give you a tour."

The north half of the front of the house consisted of a large, paneled dining room she'd seen earlier. The long mahogany table that sat in the middle of the room held seats for twelve. A summer flower arrangement consisted of pink roses and pink hydrangeas interspersed with white daisies and sat in a cut-glass vase in the middle of the table. Along one wall, above a service counter, an open cupboard made of dark wood stored coffee mugs, extra wine goblets, and water glasses. A coffee maker and a burner holding a pot of hot water sat on the marble counter. A bowl of sugar, a pitcher of cream, and a dish of lemon slices were displayed nearby. At the other end of the counter, a large plate of homemade, chocolate-chip cookies invited guests to take one.

"How many guests do you usually have?" Lettie asked.

"We have six guest rooms, so we have as many as twelve people for the breakfast we serve. During the day, people come and go on their own, tasting wine at nearby vineyards or sightseeing. We offer a simple dinner to those not wishing to travel to restaurants at night." A look of pride crossed Mrs. Morley's face. "Sometimes my husband, Pat, grills out, or Rita Lopez cooks up Mexican food. Guests like these homestyle meals. In fact, we're becoming known for them."

Lettie's mouth watered. It all sounded so good.

Mrs. Morley led her to a sideboard, opened its drawers, and gave her a smile. "Let's see how well you polish silver."

Later, after being shown how, Lettie was working on the silverware when Kenton walked into the kitchen.

"Well? Are you going to stay?" he asked.

"Yes," Lettie said with determination. The whole time she'd been cleaning the silver she'd been able to gaze at the rolling hills outside. This, she'd decided, is where she wanted to be. It felt right.

CHAPTER TWO

That night, Lettie lay in bed thinking how lucky she was to have met Kenton. Most of her life, luck had eluded her. Being here made up for it all. Her room on the ground floor behind the kitchen was the nicest one she'd ever had. And it was hers alone.

The Morleys lived in a house down the hill. Kenton explained to her that if no guests requested dinner, Mrs. Morley left by five o'clock. On nights she cooked dinner, Mrs. Morley left after guests had been served their meal. Depending on the schedule, it would be up to Lettie to fill in where necessary, making sure guests had what they needed for a comfortable night.

Lettie rolled over onto her side and pulled a blanket closer to her neck, reveling in the clean smell of the sheets, the warmth of the blanket. She'd taken a shower in her private bathroom and now rubbed the blanket's softness against her skin feeling grateful to be given the chance for a job like this.

At the sound of tapping, Lettie awoke with confusion. It took her a moment to realize someone was knocking at her door. She checked her bedside clock. Six thirty.

Groaning, she got out of bed and went to answer it.

She cracked open the door and faced Mrs. Morley. "What is it? It's still dark outside."

"Time to get up. We've got fresh muffins to make. Hurry now. Our four guests are leaving this morning, and they need breakfast by eight."

"Be right there," said Lettie, closing the door.

After quickly dressing, she hurried into the kitchen to find Mrs. Morley measuring ingredients into a glass bowl. She looked up and smiled at Lettie.

"Well, now ... Good morning!"

Lettie bobbed her head. "Good morning."

"Why don't you go about setting the table? We'll need six placemats. Rex and Kenton will be joining the guests for breakfast."

At the surprised look Lettie gave her, Mrs. Morley continued, "It's good for the guests to know their host. Brings in more business."

"I see," said Lettie. She'd forgotten that the inn, small as it was, was a way to bring in money.

In the dining room, she opened a wide drawer in the sideboard and counted out six wine-colored placemats and six matching napkins. She'd done enough waitressing to know what she needed.

She placed the mats and napkins in front of the seats at one end of the long table, added the appropriate silverware, moved the flower arrangement closer, and stood back to admire her work.

Mrs. Morley came up behind her. "Okay, now set juice glasses, water goblets, and coffee cups at each place. Salt and pepper shakers need to be in the middle of the table, along with the butter dish, which is in the kitchen."

Lettie hurried to the kitchen to get the butter and bumped into Kenton. "Sorry."

He grinned at her. "No problem. Later, when you're finished your chores, I want to show you the vineyard."

"Really? I'd like that." There was something about the land with its rows of growing vines that gave Lettie a sense of comfort. She knew it was crazy, but it was as if she'd been waiting all her life for the day she could be in this very place.

Mrs. Morley watched from a corner of the dining room as Lettie brought in food from the kitchen and served it to the guests and the Chandler men. She'd been given instructions to serve from the left and take away from the right. Her hands shook when she poured the first cup of coffee into a mug, but then she felt more at ease. And it was nice to overhear pleasant conversation from people who were far more interesting than the people back home.

After breakfast, Mr. Morley appeared at the inn to help guests with their luggage. Left with cleanup duty, Lettie cleared the dishes from the dining room and carried the placemats and napkins to the laundry room.

Mrs. Morley checked on her. "Okay, wipe down the table and then you can do the dishes. It being the middle of the week, we don't have guests registered for tonight. After you clean the two guest rooms that were used and help straighten the public rooms, you may have some free time to explore. I'll take care of the family's private rooms. When we're really busy, Paloma Sanchez, a young woman about your age, comes in to help us. She's away with her kids right now visiting relatives in California for the summer and won't be back until sometime this fall. Her husband is in the military and serving in Vietnam.

"Oh? I hope he'll be all right," said Lettie.

Mrs. Morley smiled at her. "Keep up the good work. It already feels as if you belong here."

Lettie's heart warmed at the words. *So, this is what it feels like to belong.*

After doing the dishes and then cleaning the guest rooms with Mrs. Morley's approval, Lettie wandered into the library to make sure everything was tidy, and then went to the living room to fluff pillows.

"Tomorrow," Mrs. Morley announced, "we'll give these rooms a proper cleaning. Go now and have some fun!"

Lettie couldn't remember ever having someone say that to her. Impulsively, she gave Mrs. Morley a quick hug and left the room before acting like a complete fool and crying.

Outside, Lettie breathed in the warm June air and studied the trees around the inn. She wasn't sure what kind they were, but their leaves formed mosaic shadows on the ground below. Some of the bushes near the foundation of the inn were in bloom lending color to the scene. Lettie's breath caught as a golden butterfly rested on a plant momentarily and then fluttered away.

Looking for Kenton, Lettie walked toward a barn in the distance. She couldn't help humming as she crossed the grounds. Country living was suiting her just fine.

She'd almost reached the barn when Kenton emerged with another young man.

Kenton waved and called to her.

Lettie lifted her hand and quickened her steps.

"Free for a while?" Kenton asked.

"Yes. Work is done for the day."

Her attention veered to the tall, young man standing beside him, and her breath left her in a rush. With his straight black hair, brown eyes, tanned skin, and strong features, he was the most handsome guy she'd ever seen.

He studied her with an intensity that quickened her pulse. As he continued to gaze at her, emotions ran wild inside her. This person, whoever he was, had reached deep inside her to where she hid her innermost thoughts, making her feel so vulnerable she wanted to run away.

As if he knew what she was thinking, the pleasant smile that crossed his face reassured her of his kindness.

"Hey, you two! Stop staring at each other and say hello," teased Kenton, turning to her. "This is Rafe Lopez. Rafe, this is Violet Hawkins from Ohio. You can call her Lettie. She's the new girl at the house."

"And what do you do?" Lettie asked Rafe, curious to know as much as she could about him.

"My father is the grape grower. I help him," Rafe said.

"In time, we'll have a winemaker," said Kenton. "But we're not quite ready for that yet. C'mon, we'll show you around."

As they walked into the barn, Lettie noticed the limp in Rafe's left leg. "What happened to you?" Realizing it might seem rude, she felt heat creep into her cheeks.

"Tractor accident a few years ago," Rafe said smoothly.

Kenton turned to her. "He's been turned down for military service, though he can shoot the feathers off a hawk."

Rafe gave Kenton a playful push. "Says who?"

"I've seen you shoot, and you're good," said Kenton. "The best." He turned to her. "Rafe might be upset he can't go to war, but I'm not. I've already lost one best friend."

They walked on.

Kenton indicated the area around them with a wave of his arm. "My father studied organic farming. We've set up the vineyard to be sustainable, which means having a full circle of nature maintain it." He pointed out a few stalls in the barn. "We even have some cows on the property so that fertilizer is available. We use only natural products for fertilization."

"There's a lot to learn about putting together a vineyard," said Rafe. "Bet you don't know why most vineyards plant their rows running north and south here in the Willamette Valley."

Intrigued by his enthusiasm, she shook her head.

"It's to take advantage of the sunlight equally on both sides of the grapes," Kenton said.

"That makes sense," she conceded, glancing from one man

to the other.

“And there’s no irrigation required for the vines. Know why?” said Kenton.

Aware it was a rhetorical question, she waited for him to continue. “The soil consists of marine sedimentary deposits and volcanic rock. It’s light in color because of the clay and the naturally crushed volcanic rock. Grapes don’t do well in poorly drained soils. That’s why the hills around the valley are good for grape growing. The pulverized rock doesn’t hold water but allows drainage.”

Lettie followed the guys outside to where a row of grape vines had been planted. She scooped up a handful of the soil, studied it, and rubbed her fingers through it. It seemed odd to talk of volcanic soil. She’d never given it much thought. Dirt was dirt.

Kenton said, “I’ve done some research, and within the vicinity of Portland alone, close to fifty volcanoes erupted more than half a million years ago. Cool, huh?”

She laughed. “Very cool.”

“Okay, enough ‘wine school’ for today,” said Rafe. “Let’s try some California wine.” He turned to Lettie. “Red or white?”

Lettie gazed at him wide-eyed. “I ... I ... don’t know.”

“Okay, we’ll start with a light chardonnay,” said Rafe. “We keep a stash of wine at the cabin for tasting and analyzing.”

Behind the barn and nestled among a clump of trees, a wooden structure peered out at her. Clapboard siding painted red matched the color of the red-brick chimney rising above the roof line at one side.

“Who lives here?” Lettie asked.

“I do sometimes. And when we have a full-grown harvest, a few of us will bunk in here,” said Rafe. Lettie thought of the westerns she’d seen on television and wondered what the inside of this bunk house would look like.

When she followed the men inside, the scent of burned wood greeted her. She gazed at the two maple bunk beds that lined a windowless wall opposite the fireplace. Their colorful blankets brightened the beige and brown of the braided rug placed nearby. In front of the fireplace, two comfortable-looking, green-plaid chairs sat angled at either end of a couch. The surface of the couch must have been a soft brown leather in earlier days. Now, cracks in the leather showed its age.

At the back of the cabin, the door to the bathroom stood open. Golden pine cabinets lined the back wall on either side of an old electric stove and a refrigerator covered with handwritten notes stuck to the front of it.

A worn maple table sat in the middle of the kitchen area, surrounded by four matching chairs.

"Not bad, huh?" Kenton said.

"Nice," said Lettie, impressed. The interior had a homey feel.

Kenton checked his watch. "We have a couple of hours before we're expected at the main house for dinner." He turned to Rafe. "Let's open that bottle of chardonnay and introduce Lettie to one of the reasons winemaking is so important."

Rafe laughed and saluted Kenton. "Aye, aye, sir."

Kenton turned to Lettie. "In this state, you're legal for wine at eighteen."

He pulled a bottle out of the refrigerator and uncorked it. Taking three glasses out of the cupboard, he turned to Lettie. "This is a good way to start. Chardonnay can be smooth with a hint of fruit and depending on how long it ages in oak barrels, it can be called buttery."

Rafe poured a little wine into the three glasses and handed one each to Lettie and Kenton.

Lettie watched as Rafe and Kenton swirled the wine in their

glasses, sniffed it, held the glass up to look through the wine, and then took a sip.

"Nice legs on this one," said Kenton. "See how the wine forms lines and seems to cling briefly to the glass in sheets on the inside of the glass?"

"Good nose," added Rafe.

After swallowing, they looked at each other and grinned.

"Nice," said Kenton. "Not too oaky, with a touch of fruit."

"Some pineapple, perhaps?" added Rafe.

Lettie stared at the liquid in her glass. *Pineapple? Were they crazy?*

"Go ahead, Lettie, and take a sip," urged Kenton.

Lettie swirled the wine in her glass, sniffed it, and held it away from her. It didn't smell sweet at all.

"Well?" Kenton said.

She took a sip and swallowed. Her tongue curled in confusion as it tried to sort out the taste of the wine.

"I don't know what I'm supposed to say," Lettie said, feeling awkward. "If I had to guess, I'd say I tasted some melon."

Rafe grinned at her. "Good. I think we're going to find you have a good palate."

She gave him a questioning look.

"A good palate is having the ability to taste the different nuances in the wine. And, like I said, I think you do."

By the time she'd had her share of the bottle of wine, her cheeks felt warm. She leaned back against her chair and let out a sigh of contentment. No wonder people liked wine. Once she got past the surprise of the initial taste in her mouth, it was pleasant.

Rafe put a cassette tape into a player, and the sound of the Beatles filled the air. Here in the cabin with Kenton and Rafe, the music sounded much better than what she'd heard on the streets of San Francisco. Lettie closed her eyes and let the music pour through her.

She wasn't sure how much time had passed before Kenton announced, "Time to go to dinner."

Her pulse pounding with alarm, she jerked to a sitting position. Part of her job was helping Mrs. Morley in the kitchen.

"See you up there," she said to Kenton. "Thanks, Rafe. I've gotta go help in the kitchen."

After running back to the main house, Lettie arrived breathless and hurried into the kitchen. "I'm here to help with dinner."

Mrs. Morley studied her with a raised eyebrow. "With it being just family, I have things under control. But, next time, you need to be here to help me. Understand? You're a member of the staff, not the family."

Reality hit her. The camaraderie she'd just shared with Kenton and Rafe evaporated in a gut-wrenching moment. "Yes, Mrs. Morley," she said, politely, hiding the bitter taste of disappointment. She'd thought she'd found a comfortable situation with two new friends.

Lettie quickly set the table for two, and then, after Mrs. Morley had dished up the lasagna Kenton had requested, Lettie carried the plates into the dining room and served them to Rex and Kenton.

Kenton studied the plates and frowned. "Why aren't you eating with us?"

"Like Mrs. Morley said, I'm just a member of the staff."

Kenton faced his father sitting across the table from him. "Dad, when no other guests are here, can't Lettie eat with us? It would mean a lot to me. She's becoming a good friend."

Rex looked with surprise at Kenton and turned to her. "Well? Would you enjoy that?"

Lettie hesitated and then spoke from the heart. "I would love it."

"Then set a place for yourself, go to the kitchen for your food, and join us. It will be nice to have a feminine voice at the table. Besides, I'm interested to know more about you."

Lettie hurried to do as he'd told her. Within a few minutes, and after receiving a disapproving frown from Mrs. Morley, Lettie sat beside Kenton at the dining room table.

"How did you like your first day at the Chandler Hill Inn?" Rex asked her.

"It was good. Mrs. Morley is very nice. And after my work was done, Kenton and Rafe showed me around."

"What do you think of the vineyard? Did you check out the vines?"

Remembering the overwhelming feeling of finding her rightful home when viewing the vines, Lettie clasped her hands together in an almost prayerful gesture. "I love the land, the rolling hills, the fact that volcanoes and marine sediments made the dirt, the look and feel of the vines, everything. The soil even smells good when you lift it to your face." Suddenly aware of what she must sound like, Lettie clamped her mouth shut.

Rex continued to stare at her with surprise.

Wishing she'd given a simple answer, Lettie squirmed in her chair.

"And, Dad, we tested her. She has a good palate for wine," said Kenton.

"I understand from Mrs. Morley you're from Ohio. Have you ever been to Oregon before?" Rex asked her.

Lettie shook her head. "I'd never been anywhere but Dayton, Ohio, until I went to San Francisco."

"So, tell me again why you like Oregon," Rex said, leaning forward and studying her.

Her cheeks aflame with shyness, Lettie said," I don't know about other parts of Oregon, but the land around here is beautiful. The hills roll on and on like folds of fabric striped with grape vines. It makes me think I'm looking at a big, beautiful, green quilt."

Lettie noticed the looks of amazement Kenton and Rex were exchanging. "Did I say something wrong? I probably shouldn't have spoken. I've been told that I sometimes say things in a crazy way. My foster parents hated when I talked like that."

"No," said Rex quietly. "Your way of speaking is delightful. It's obvious you love the land. Nice. Very nice."

Embarrassed, Lettie stood. "May I get either of you something more? If not, I'll clear the table."

Lettie quickly gathered the empty plates and carried them into the kitchen.

"Who wants dessert?" Mrs. Morley said. "I've made Mr. Rex's favorite pie. Apple."

"I'll ask," Lettie said.

Moments later, she returned. "Both Kenton and Rex want pie."

Mrs. Morley gave her a warning look. "*Mr. Rex* to you, Lettie. Remember what I told you."

"Okay," Lettie said politely. "If you want, I'll carry dessert into them."

"Aren't you going to have any dessert?" Rex asked, when she placed a plate of warm apple pie in front of him.

Lettie shook her head. "No, thank you."

Uncertain whether she should stay or go, she quietly slipped out of the room.

CHAPTER THREE

The next day after Lettie's chores were done, Mrs. Morley said, "Remember, you must keep an eye on the house. We have four guests arriving this afternoon. We want to make sure they have everything they need, like we talked about. Understand?"

Lettie bobbed her head. It was a nice day. The sun was shining, and the temperature was in the low 70s. She was anxious to get outside, walk the land, and settle her thoughts.

She stood outside the house and surveyed her surroundings. In the distance, a tractor moved. Curious, she headed that way. As she walked, she inhaled the fresh air and wondered what the next months would bring. The last few days had been the best of her life.

As she was walking down the knoll, she noticed Rafe working on a piece of machinery by the barn and waved.

He waved back and headed in her direction. "Where are you going?" he called to her.

She pointed toward the tractor.

"Hold on," he said.

She stopped and waited for him to reach her.

"Why are you going all the way down there?" he asked. "It's just the tractor guy doing his work."

"I know, but what is he doing?" Lettie asked. "I want to know everything about growing grapes. It's fascinating."

A grin broke out on his face. "I've never met anyone like you. Your hair. Is that what you call strawberry blond? And your eyes aren't just blue, but a kind of green."

Lettie scuffed her feet in the loose dirt, unsure if he was giving her a compliment or teasing her, as had happened so often at home.

"Hey! I'm sorry if I made you uncomfortable," said Rafe. "I like the way you look."

Their surroundings faded away as she returned his gaze. His dark hair formed a curl over his right eyebrow. She studied his straight, proud nose, the cleft in his chin, the fullness of his lips. But it was his brown eyes that drew her in.

"I like the way you look too."

He chuckled happily. "I can't wait to get to know you better, Lettie." He checked his watch. "I'd better get back to work."

Before he left, he gave her a wink.

Lettie waited for her heartbeat to slow before moving on.

"Hey there!" called Kenton as he hurried her way. "What's up? Where are you going?" He looped an arm around her shoulders.

At his easy-going manner, she smiled at him. "I'm on my way to check out a tractor. I want to see what it's doing."

"Pretty boring, but I'll go along. And then later, maybe we can taste some more wine."

Lettie shook her head. "Not today. We have four guests coming in, and Mrs. Morley wants me to make sure I'm around to help her check them in."

"Too bad," he said, grinning. "If you married me, you wouldn't have to worry about the guests."

Shocked, she stopped and looked at him. "You don't even know me. Why would you say something like that?"

"Just teasing. My dad asked me about our relationship, and I told him we were just friends, but that I liked you a whole lot and maybe more than that."

"Oh." Lettie hid her surprise. She'd thought they were just friends. A worrisome thought struck her. "I don't want him to think I'd ever skip out on my job. It's the best one I've had for the last four months, if ever."

"Deal," said Kenton, and they smiled at each other.

After watching the tractor mow the grass that grew erratically between the rows of grapes, and talking briefly with the driver, who Kenton said was Rafe's father, Joe, Lettie and Kenton headed back to the inn.

"Rafe's dad seemed nice," Lettie commented.

"Joe's a good guy," said Kenton. "My dad trusts him. He's what we call the grape grower. In time, after we hire a winemaker, I'd like to learn to do both."

Lettie gave him a thoughtful look. She was learning that it took a lot of work from a lot of people to produce a single bottle of wine.

Winemaking was forgotten as guests arrived. As instructed, Lettie delivered pitchers of cold water and fresh cookies to their rooms and told them about the happy hour in the library starting at five o'clock.

Since both couples were opting to go into McMinnville to Nick's Italian Café for dinner, Mrs. Morley left for home early, leaving instructions for Lettie to serve the meal for Mr. Rex and Kenton—a simple casserole of chicken, broccoli, and a lemon sauce. That, a tossed salad, fresh bread, and fruit would serve them well.

This time, Lettie happily set three places at the pine table in the kitchen. Mrs. Morley had told her that sometimes Rex chose to eat with guests in the dining room, but that most times he was content to live a quiet life in his separate wing. Curious, Lettie was eager to find out more about the Hollywood legend that women used to swoon over. He was still a handsome man.

"Well, this is cozy," said Rex as he sat in a chair at the kitchen table. He inhaled and smiled. "Nothing like some of Mrs. Morley's cooking."

Kenton raced into the room and slid into a chair opposite Rex. "Sorry, I'm late."

Rex raised his eyebrows but said nothing.

Lettie ate quietly, waiting for conversation to begin. Rex was a puzzle to her. On the screen, he was a smooth-talking hero who always saved the day. At home, he was a quiet man who liked to read. He met others in town for social times, but not too frequently. "Are you sorry not to be making movies?" Lettie finally asked him.

Rex laid down his fork. "Yes, and no. I got tired of the same old roles. But, I suppose, if an interesting part comes along, I may take it. Right now, I'm trying to get the vineyard off to a good start along with this inn. I hope someday to expand the inn and to make wine from our own grapes. It'll take time, but I believe we can do it."

"I'm glad you decided to do this, Dad," said Kenton. "Other people are seeing how good the land is for growing grapes and are coming in, taking over farms, and turning them into vineyards. We're lucky you were able to get good vine cuttings a couple of years ago and planted them. We might be among the first to make wine here."

"When is that going to happen?" Lettie said.

"It would be great if we could harvest enough grapes next year to test our yield," said Rex. "With your love of the land and interest in the grapes, I thought it might be fun for you to join Kenton and me when we talk with one of the grape growers from California, who's been training Kenton. He's planning to visit us after the harvest in a couple of months to see how the vines here are coming along. And when things start to happen, we're going to need all the help we can get."

"Ben Kurey is really nice," Kenton said to her. "He might even consider moving here if things take off. He's a good winemaker."

"Is there a reason why women can't be winemakers too?" Lettie asked.

"There are several women in the valley who are interested in winemaking. Someday, you might like to be one, too," Rex said to her.

"I'd like that," said Lettie, feeling as if her entire future were in his hands. It felt good to have new possibilities.

"Great idea, Dad. That would make us unique. Even Gloria Steinem would approve."

Rex laughed. "Ah, yes. That women's lib thing."

When he was through eating, Rex wiped his mouth with his napkin and stood. "I'm going into town to see a few people. I'll be back later."

After he left, Lettie cleared the table. Kenton hung around while she did the dishes. At one point, she turned to him. "Your father seems lonely. Where's your mother?"

Kenton's laugh was bitter. "My mother is now on her third husband since my parents got divorced. Dad has never remarried. Said he didn't want to go through that shit again. A lot of women have tried to change his mind, but he isn't interested in marriage, and they get tired of trying. He returns to California less and less." He waved her forward. "C'mon, let's find Rafe. He's staying in the cabin tonight, and I've got an idea for some excitement for us."

As Lettie followed Kenton out of the house, she thought of her foster parents. They'd fought often, but they'd stayed together out of what? Fear of reprisal from their church? But theirs hadn't been a happy marriage or a happy home life. All of the foster kids had known this—especially she, as one of the oldest. And when, on rare occasions, alcohol was introduced to the volatile mix, there'd been times when she'd feared for her life.

Kenton was marching ahead of her with such angry steps Lettie wondered if he was still thinking of his mother. She'd never known hers. She'd been dumped into foster care as an infant and had never escaped. It wasn't all bad, but she wouldn't want any child of hers to live through it. The feeling of being unwanted, unloved lingered in her mind.

Kenton knocked on the door and walked into the cabin. Lettie followed.

Rafe was lying on the couch, listening to music. He scrambled to his feet. "Hey! What're you two doing here?" He smiled at her. "Thought you had to take care of guests, Lettie."

"They're in town for dinner. I'll check on them later," she said, plopping down into one of the chairs.

"I thought maybe the three of us could drive into town," Kenton said to Rafe. "There might be something going on at the hotel bar."

Rafe shook his head. "You go ahead. I've got to get up early tomorrow. I'm helping the guys at White Hills with pruning."

"I'd better stay here," said Lettie.

"You guys are no fun," Kenton griped. "Guess I'll go on my own."

"See you later, man," said Rafe.

"You all right on your own?" Kenton asked her. "I'll leave all the lights on at the inn."

"I'll walk her over there," said Rafe. "Don't worry. She's safe with me."

Lettie liked the way his words made her feel.

After Kenton left, Rafe said, "Want anything to drink? Smoke?"

Lettie shook her head firmly. She wanted a real friendship with him, not one laced with alcohol or grass or worse.

She sat down on the couch with him, leaving a comfortable space between them.

"Kenton tells me you, along with the rest of us, are going to meet with Ben Kurey to discuss how things are going here at Chandler Hill. What's that all about?"

"I'm not sure, but I'm excited about it. Rex knows I love learning about making wine and says he's going to need all the help he can get."

"Yeah, winemaking gets into your blood. There's a lot to learn. It's still quite new in the valley, and the pinot noir grapes can be tricky." He smiled. "I'm as hooked on the land as you are."

Lettie's insides warmed. They'd make a perfect couple.

He studied her for a few heart-pounding moments, and then, as if he did this every day, he leaned over and kissed her.

His lips, warm and soft on hers, sent waves of heat through her. Lost in sensation, she lifted her arms to draw him closer. His tongue entered her mouth, and, unsure how to respond, she started to pull away and then succumbed to the rhythmic thrusts.

"Hmmm," he murmured, drawing her even closer.

Lettie opened her eyes, sat back, and felt herself swimming in his brown gaze.

He cupped her face in his strong, rough hands. "You're so beautiful."

"So are you," she said, meaning it.

He chuckled. "I wanted to kiss you the first time I saw you. Have you had a lot of boyfriends, gone all the way before?"

"No," she said. "Once, at a party in San Francisco, some guy tried, but I didn't really like it, and I definitely didn't like him."

"Ah, I see." He sat up straight. "Uh, oh. I'm pretty sure I heard a car driving up the hill. Come on, I'll walk you to the inn."

Disappointment coursed through her. But not wanting to appear to be too eager, she got to her feet and straightened her clothes.

Rafe rose and brushed a strand of her hair behind her ear. “My sweet little friend, you have no idea how much I want you to stay.”

He went to the door and opened it.

“Thanks, but I’m okay on my own.” Then, before Lettie could change her mind, she hurried past him and ran as fast as she could to the inn.

CHAPTER FOUR

A few days later, as was her usual routine following the evening clean-up in the kitchen, Lettie stepped out onto the back porch. This time of evening enchanted her with the sights and sounds of the land and its creatures coming to rest at the end of a summer's day.

She stopped in surprise. Rex was standing at the porch rail reciting a poem from the Robert Frost book she'd once noticed in his office. He ended the poem and turned to her.

"Will my reading aloud bother you?"

"Oh no! I love hearing your voice, and poems are special to me."

He gave her a wide smile. "A voice is like a musical instrument. I like to practice like this in order to keep my vocal chords exercised."

"I won't interrupt. I promise," she said, thrilled with the idea of sharing this special moment with him.

Rex's deep, velvet voice was like music as it soared around her. She sank into a rocking chair, curled her legs up, and leaned back, drinking in the sound of the words.

After another two poems, Rex closed the book and sat in a chair nearby. "I'm glad you enjoyed this. You said poetry is special to you. Tell me, did you do well in school?"

"Yes," she answered shyly. "But I knew I couldn't go to college. That was one reason I left for San Francisco as soon as I turned eighteen. I doubled up on courses and graduated high school in January."

He gave her a thoughtful look. "Did you know I never got a

degree from college? There's no reason you can't succeed without it, though I believe it's important to get as much education as you can."

"That's why I want to learn everything about growing grapes and winemaking," she said and then covered her mouth for her boldness. "I'm sorry, I shouldn't have ..."

His dark eyes drilled her. "Shouldn't have what, Lettie? Shouldn't have spoken from your heart?" His voice was soft with understanding.

Too embarrassed to utter a word, she simply nodded.

"Do you have any idea how refreshing it is to talk to you? After all the phoniness in Hollywood, your honesty is welcome." He leaned back in his chair and stared out at the scene in front of them. In the distance the sun was slipping below the horizon, spreading fingers of light and orange color as if grabbing onto the sky for as long as it could.

"Amazing isn't it?" Rex said. "The days and nights come and go in a regular pattern. Makes me wonder about bigger things."

"Like where the stars come from and if we're alone in the universe," said Lettie.

"Exactly." Rex smiled at her. "I see we have much to talk about. Feel free to come sit with me anytime." He rose. "Thank you, Lettie."

She jumped to her feet. "No, thank you, Rex. I mean Mr. Rex."

"Rex will do nicely," he said, and left her on the porch alone, filled with an inner joy she couldn't contain. "Good night, everyone!" she shouted, and then as her words fell to the land, she laughed at herself and went indoors to the privacy of her room where she could relive every moment of this unforgettable encounter. No one had ever treated her with such respect and kindness, engaging her in a way that was new to her.

That evening was the first of many discussions with Rex over that summer. Sometimes he read aloud; other times they sat quietly and talked about nothing and everything. Lettie knew if she could have chosen any man to be her father it would be Rex. He understood her need to know things, and though she was just a young woman, he respected her, even when she asked silly questions.

As he'd promised, Rex arranged for her to meet Ben Kurey when he came to the vineyard.

On this early fall day, Lettie stood in the field with Rex, Kenton, Rafe, and Rafe's father, Joe, while Ben Kurey let a handful of dirt sift through his fingers.

"Nice soil with both the marine sediment and volcanic stone. You're making this vineyard an organic one?"

At Rex's nod, Ben issued a sigh of satisfaction. "Very good. Now let's walk along the vines so I can see how you're treating them."

Lettie listened as Ben remarked on the wiring of the arm of the grapevine to the wire trellis that formed each row. He turned to her. "The cordon or arms extend from the trunk and are the part of the plant where additional arms and eventually leaves and grape clusters extend."

She fingered one of the arms.

"Look at these shoots." He knelt down. "They are hardening and changing color, becoming what we call canes. Come winter, you trim the canes off." Ben straightened and shook hands with Rex. "Your grape grower, Joe here, is doing a fine job. Congratulations! Looks like you'll have a good crop next year."

"This calls for a celebration," said Rex. "I realize it's only eleven o'clock, but a taste of a nice California pinot noir is in order. In a few years, Lord willing, it will be a Chandler Hill wine."

"I'll drink to that," said Ben, grinning.

As the men headed up the hill, Lettie paused.

"Go ahead," said Kenton. "I'm staying here with Joe and Rafe."

Lettie walked quietly behind Rex. At the mention of her name, she leaned forward to hear better.

"What is Lettie doing here working at Chandler Hill? With her looks, she should be in Hollywood," said Ben.

Rex chuckled. "She's a stunner all right, but I'd never encourage her to go there. Those people would eat her alive. Besides, I have other plans for her."

Lettie jerked to a stop. *Stunner?* Not according to her foster mother, who'd constantly told her that with her odd-colored eyes and almost pink hair, she'd have a hard time finding a decent, church-going man. *And what plans did Rex have for her?*

She hurried to catch up to them.

Their conversation was all about a couple of other vineyards that had emerged.

Ben was now saying, "It's going to be big, this pinot noir crop in the Willamette Valley. I predict in a few years, people will be asking for it."

"At the moment, a lot of guys can't even give their wine away," Rex said.

"No worries. As we get to know the ins and outs of the pinot noir grape here in the valley, things will improve," Ben assured him.

Listening to them, Lettie filled with excitement. The Chandler Hill Vineyard and Inn was on the brink of something wonderful. She could feel it in her bones.

All her excitement evaporated when Mrs. Morley greeted her. "Now that your meeting is over, better get to work. Mr. Kurey is leaving this afternoon. We're going to serve him lunch and then his room will need to be cleaned. After that, you can help me prepare dinner."

"Okay, Mrs. Morley," said Lettie. "But like Mr. Kurey says, things are going to get busier and busier around here."

"Is that right?" Mrs. Morley said, giving her an indulgent smile.

Lettie's lips curved. "Wait and see."

The next few weeks sped by as Lettie became more involved with the inn. She now handled the guest rooms on her own, taking care of cleaning and refreshing them every day. Both she and Mrs. Morley did the laundry, working the two washing machines and two dryers in the large laundry room behind the kitchen near Lettie's room.

Sometimes, on days Lettie liked best, she worked with Mrs. Morley in the kitchen. She'd seen the enjoyment Kenton and Rex got out of Mrs. Morley's cooking and wanted to do the same for her own family one day—the family she dared to dream of having with Rafe. Not that she'd ever tell him. They hadn't had any time alone together since that one evening in the cabin. But she could dream, couldn't she?

At night, Lettie lay in bed replaying that evening over and over in her mind. Rafe's kiss had made her want to do things she'd only heard about. And when she'd told him about her one experience, he hadn't laughed or made fun of her. She could still remember the way his eyes had flickered with concern when she'd told him she hadn't liked it.

She and Kenton spent a lot of her off-hours together. Like his father, he was someone who respected her and gave her the freedom to be herself. The same corny sense of humor that had attracted her to him in San Francisco gave her reason to groan at his jokes. But Kenton was a serious young man with high principles. Though she knew he wanted to kiss her in the same way as Rafe, he did nothing more than give her a few playful kisses on the cheek. She liked him so much.

As the third week in November approached, Rex came into the kitchen to speak to Mrs. Morley and her.

"Kenton and I are going to L.A. for the holiday. Therefore, Mrs. Morley, you may have the time off. Lettie, I'm hoping you'll agree to stay here at the inn. Rita Lopez has asked you to join her family for Thanksgiving dinner, but otherwise, it would be helpful to know someone is keeping an eye on the inn. Do you mind?"

"No, not at all." And, in fact, she didn't. She'd been looking at the books in the library and would love the opportunity to enjoy reading some of them. A new one had been added to the collection, and she had her eye on it. *Rich Man, Poor Man.* She'd always loved to read. Though she'd had to cram it in between her duties at the foster home, reading had been an escape for her.

"I'll make sure to leave enough food here for you," Mrs. Morley said to her. She turned to Rex. "When do you expect to return?"

"We'll be back the Sunday following Thanksgiving. I promised a friend we'd stay with him for the duration."

"I see. Well, it'll be a nice break for you," Mrs. Morley said.

"And for the both of you, I hope," Rex said, smiling at each of them. "It's a quiet time for the vineyard, and we don't have any reservations lined up for the holiday, so it's perfect."

After Rex left the room, Lettie turned to Mrs. Morley. "He mentioned a friend. Doesn't he have any family? He's never spoken of one."

"From what I've learned, he and Kenton are all alone. No relatives. Each is an only child. Sort of sad, if you ask me, but that's how some families are." Mrs. Morley's eyes rounded. "Oh, Lettie, I'm sorry. I forgot ..."

Lettie waved away Mrs. Morley's concern. "It's all right. It wasn't as if you were teasing me like some of the kids used to do."

Mrs. Morley pulled her into a bosomy hug. "Such a shame, especially when you couldn't help your situation." She smelled of talcum powder and a rose-scented perfume.

Lettie nestled in for a moment and then pulled away. "Now that you have the time off, will you go visit your daughter in Seattle?"

Mrs. Morley's face brightened with excitement. "Why, yes! That's exactly what we'll do. Wait until I tell my husband. Pat has missed her, being the last to leave the nest."

On the day before Thanksgiving, Lettie lay on her bed reading one of the books she'd chosen for the long weekend. Even though the house was eerily quiet, she wasn't afraid. Either Joe or Rafe would be around before dark to check the property and take care of the cows and other livestock.

She was deep into her book when she heard knocking at the front door. She got up to answer it. When she opened the door, Rafe greeted her with a smile.

"Just doing my duty and checking up on you like Mr. Rex asked me to," he said, his dark eyes gleaming.

"Come on in." Her pulse raced at the thought of them being alone without any interruption.

"Are you sure you want me to?" Rafe asked.

She knew he was asking much more than this simple question. She held the door for him. She was attracted to him and wanted to experience the kind of love everyone was always talking about.

"Would you like something to eat? Mrs. Morley left all kinds of food for me."

"How about a cup of coffee? It's getting chilly out there."

In the kitchen, she went about setting up the coffee maker, glad for something to keep her busy. She wanted nothing more than to run into his arms and continue the thrilling moments she'd had with him a few months ago in the cabin. From the way he kept staring at her, she was pretty sure he wouldn't mind at all.

After the sound of the percolator stopped, she poured him a mug of coffee and sat down at the kitchen table opposite him.

"Be sure to thank your mother for including me for your Thanksgiving dinner," she said, trying not to let her gaze rest on him too long.

"Mom loves having a big crowd for the holidays, and she's happy to have you. She hasn't done one of her special Mexican meals for the inn since you've been here, but they're the best."

They chatted about some of her cooking. Lettie admitted she hadn't tried much Mexican food beyond tacos.

Rafe finished his coffee and set the mug down. "What are you doing this evening?"

She shrugged as nonchalantly as she could. "Not much. I'm reading a good book."

His gaze remained steady, and then he stood. "Maybe I'd better go."

"Don't," she said, surprising herself. She got to her feet. "I mean ... we could watch television or something."

"Or something?" His gaze settled on her.

Her cheeks grew hot. She glanced at him and then away. She didn't know how to tell him that he brought out new feelings in her, urges that needed to be satisfied.

"Come here." He drew her to him. "Is this what you want?" he whispered, his voice hoarse with desire. He pressed his lips to hers.

At the touch she'd yearned for, Lettie closed her eyes and let herself be carried away by the desire that pounded inside her.

His kiss deepened. She fitted her body up against his and felt his arousal. Even new as she was to this, she felt a sense of satisfaction at her power to make him feel this way.

He withdrew his lips from hers and hugged her. She lay her head against his chest, loving the feel of him, the smell of him. Her breath caught as his hands caressed her breasts, sending a fresh rush of need through her.

He pulled away, and, face flushed, studied her. "Should I go before it's too late?"

Her gaze locked onto his. "Please, stay." She couldn't bear the thought of his leaving now.

Later, lying beside Rafe, she placed a hand on his strong chest and felt the racing beat of his heart begin to slow.

He rolled onto his side and beamed at her. "Wow!"

She laughed, pleased with herself and him. She'd easily followed his guidance, giving them both pleasure.

"So, you liked it this time?" His grin indicated he already knew the answer, but she told him anyway.

"Oh yes," she said. "All I needed was the right man."

Chuckling, he cupped her cheeks in his broad hands. "Those beautiful eyes, your body, the way you respond are all part of a package that's something amazing."

At his kind words, her eyes filled.

"Are you okay?" he asked, giving her a worried look.

She nodded, too overcome with emotion to speak. He made her feel so lovable, so worthy of tenderness—something she'd missed her entire life.

Rafe turned to look at the bedside clock. "I'm sorry, but I have to leave. My family is expecting me, and I don't want anyone to get the wrong impression of you."

"I wish you could stay," Lettie said.

"I'll bring you home after dinner tomorrow and spend the night in the cabin, so you have someone around. All right?"

"Okay," she said, wondering how she could wait that long.

While he dressed, she slipped on a white terry robe that had been in her room when she'd first arrived. They offered robes like this to all their guests for use at the inn.

Lettie walked Rafe to the front door.

"I'll see you tomorrow," she said, unsure what else she should say. Thank you seemed wrong.

Rafe gave her a tender smile. "I'll pick you up by two o'clock. Someone, I'm hoping not me, will take care of the animals here early tomorrow morning." He gave her a kiss on the cheek. "Until tomorrow."

She watched him walk away and felt the urge to cry. Maybe he didn't feel the same way about her as she did about him. Otherwise, why would he leave? Maybe, like so many times before in her life, she wasn't good enough.

He turned around, saw her standing in the doorway, and waved.

She waved to him and then closed the door. Leaning against it, she let out a trembling sigh.

CHAPTER FIVE

Thanksgiving Day dawned gray and cold. A drizzle wept from the sky like the forlorn lovers in her dream. Restless, feeling out of sorts, Lettie got out of bed and headed for the kitchen, thinking a cup of hot coffee might do wonders for her.

She was standing in her pajamas sipping the hot liquid when she heard a vehicle climbing the hill. Curious, she wandered over to the window in the living room and looked out with surprise at Rafe's truck. Instead of going to the barn, he pulled up in front of the house.

Watching him get out of the truck and head her way, she felt a surge of excitement. She set down the coffee cup on a table and went to open the door.

"Good morning! I didn't expect to see you!" she said brightly.

His smile didn't meet his eyes. "I need to talk to you."

Her stomach plummeted to her feet. "Is everything all right?"

"Yes, and no. Before you come to my house for dinner, I want to set some things straight. May I come in?"

A numbness traveled through her body, making it impossible for her to do more than step aside.

"About last night," he said, entering and facing her.

Tears sprang to Lettie's eyes. "Oh, God! You didn't like it. You were faking the whole time." Her teeth began to chatter. "I'm so embarrassed."

"Whoa!" he said, looking at her with concern. "Where is all of this coming from? No part of what you're saying is true. Sit down and let me explain."

Lettie went into the living room and folded her shaking legs into the couch. She waited for Rafe to take a seat in a nearby chair.

"At the Thanksgiving dinner at my house, you'll meet my family and some of our friends. Maria Mendoza will be among them."

"Maria? Who's she?" He hadn't mentioned her name before this.

"She's my old girlfriend, who still thinks I'm going to marry her."

"Marry her? How old are you?"

"I'm twenty-four, and for several years our families have wanted us to marry. I've tried to tell my parents that though I like Maria a lot, I don't want to marry her or anyone else right now."

Taking in all this information, Lettie sat back against the cushions of the couch and studied him. "I see," she finally said, though she wasn't sure what all of this meant. She'd never had a family that cared about her, while he had to answer to his.

He reached over and clutched her hand. "Lettie, I care for you. I really do. But I'm not able to make a commitment to anyone. I have family issues to take care of, and after the Christmas holidays, I'm moving to California for a year to study viticulture." He squeezed her fingers. "In so many ways, you're an innocent. I don't want to be the one to break your heart. Understand?"

Tears filled her eyes. "So, later, you're not going to spend the night?"

"I don't think I should."

"But I want you to!" she burst out. Then, before she could make a bigger fool of herself, she got up and ran from the room.

Rafe followed her to the door of her bedroom. "I'll pick you up at two. See you later."

Lettie lay in bed staring at the ceiling while conflicting thoughts raced through her mind. Rafe was just trying to do the right thing, wasn't he? He'd called her an innocent, but for the first time she was aware of the awesome things her body could do with a man she might already love. Maybe, she thought, glumly, he was telling her politely that she was no good at making love or not good enough, period.

A large part of her wanted to call his family home and tell them she wouldn't come to dinner. But she decided not to allow herself that bit of cowardice. Besides, she wanted to see what kind of family he had and what kind of woman Maria was.

The short ride in Rafe's truck from the inn to the Lopez home was awkwardly silent. Lettie couldn't talk about what had happened between them, and he, apparently, wouldn't.

But as they pulled into the driveway of a rambling two-story house, Rafe turned to her.

"Lettie, my talk with you this morning has everything to do with how much I wish I could be with you, not the other way around." His brown eyes bored into her.

Before she could respond, he climbed out of the truck, walked around behind it, and opened the door for her.

As she stepped onto the ground, she gazed up at him. "It's too late, Rafe. I think I'm already in love with you."

She breezed by him and headed to the wide porch along the front of the house.

He hurried to catch up to her. "You can't know that. There hasn't been enough time for you to be sure."

Before she could answer, the front door was thrown open

and a woman stood there looking at them.

Rafe gulped and said, “Hi, Mom. This is Lettie.”

“Hi, Lettie. I’m Rita Lopez.” Dark eyes above a smile flashed with interest as her gaze traced Lettie’s body from top to toe. “Come in. Rex called to ask if I’d like to include you in our family meal. I’m so glad you agreed to come. We like introducing others to our family, don’t we, Rafe?” Lettie heard both pleasure and caution in her voice.

“Yes,” Rafe answered, avoiding eye contact with either of them.

Lettie followed his mother into the house. The living room was crowded with people, mostly men. Some looked up at them; others continued their loud conversations. Rita led her into the kitchen where a group of women had congregated.

“Ladies, say hello to Lettie Hawkins, the young woman who’s working at the Chandler Hill Inn. We’re happy to have her here with us today.”

Staring into a sea of brown faces, dark eyes and dark hair, Lettie felt every strand of her unusual-colored hair. Automatically, she looked away and down to the floor, as she’d been forced to do so often in her youth when she’d been teased about her looks.

She felt a hand on her arm and glanced up.

A pretty, young woman smiled at her. “Hi, I’m Paloma Sanchez. Nice to meet you. Where did you get hair like that? It’s beautiful.”

Lettie blinked in surprise. “Really?”

“Yeah,” Paloma laughed. “Really.”

The women gathered around her, introducing themselves. All the names seemed a jumble until a stunning young woman said, “I’m Maria Mendoza.”

Though they greeted one another pleasantly, Lettie’s stomach curled with dismay. Rafe would never choose her over Maria.

"Here, Lettie. Have a glass of white wine," said Rita.

Lettie accepted the glass Rita handed her and took a sip. It was a nice, light wine.

As conversation among the women resumed, Lettie looked around the kitchen. A massive pine table dominated the room. Lettie got the impression from its worn edges that it was often filled with guests.

"Rita is the best cook in the neighborhood," said Paloma, coming to stand beside her. "Several of us often meet here for social occasions."

"How many children are in the family?" Lettie asked, watching several of them racing around outside.

"Rita and Joe have five of the older ones, the rest of us each have a couple."

"You're married?" Lettie asked, surprised because they seemed the same age.

Paloma grinned. "My husband is in the service. Our Mikey is three, and little Isabel is just one. She's in the bedroom with my mother." Her gaze settled on Lettie. "Rex Chandler must like you a lot to make sure you have some family for the holiday."

"It's been the best job ever. Mr. Rex and Kenton have been wonderful to me."

Paloma gave her an impish grin. "And Rafe?"

Lettie didn't know where to look. She knew she couldn't face Paloma without giving herself away.

"It's all right," Paloma whispered to her. "I've seen the way Rafe looks at you when he thinks no one is watching."

"But Maria ..."

Paloma shook her head. "She demands much more from him than he wants to give. She thinks she can talk him into moving to southern California, but he has dreams of becoming a landowner here in the valley."

"Hey! What are you two talking about?" said Maria, approaching them carrying a glass of wine.

"I'm just filling Lettie in on the families," said Paloma. "She couldn't believe I'm married with kids."

Maria laughed. "I swear, Paloma, you've always been married with kids." Still smiling, she turned to Lettie. "She and her husband have been in love since third grade. Isn't that right, Paloma?"

"Afraid so. It happens like that sometimes." Paloma's eyes filled. "I'm just hoping Manny comes home to me."

Since coming to Oregon, Lettie had pushed thoughts about the war aside as she'd adjusted to her new life. She reached over and patted Paloma's arm. "I hope so too."

"Okay, everybody, dinner's ready. Come help yourselves," Rita announced.

While Lettie had been chatting, a buffet had almost magically been set up on the long kitchen counter.

Paloma left Lettie and went to help a cute little boy fill a plastic plate with food.

Rafe came over to her. "You're in for some treats. Mom's known for her chorizo stuffing for the turkey. And Aunt Sophie's pumpkin empanadas are the best."

"That's right," said a woman, smiling at him. "My regular pumpkin pie is pretty darn good too."

"What about my apple pie?" said another woman, elbowing him.

Watching the way members of the group teased each other, Lettie thought back to her past Thanksgivings and realized how empty they were of fun, how bland the food had been. This kitchen, filled with happy people and tantalizing aromas, was delightfully different. After she'd loaded her plate with food, Lettie found a place to sit in the living room near

Paloma. The conversational noise that had filled the house disappeared as people dug into their meals.

"When are you going to get off your arse and ask Maria to marry you, Rafe?" said a gray-haired man. "Don't wait too long. I want to be able to dance at her wedding, like I promised her."

Lettie set down the fork she'd lifted to her mouth and held her breath.

"Ah, you know that was just a childhood dream. Maria wants to leave here. I'm going to northern California for a year, and then I want to come back and set up my own business in the valley."

"There's no reason the two of you can't work something out," said Rita. "Maria can try California with you. She'll see that home is where family is."

A small child's voice broke into the silence. "Can I have pie now?"

The mood instantly changed.

"For those who aren't ready for dessert, there's more food in the kitchen," said Rita.

"I'll put on the coffee and set out the desserts," Paloma offered, rising to her feet along with two other women.

The conversation changed to different topics. People came and went, filling their plates with seconds of the main course or with pie, cake, or other tempting desserts.

"How about you, Lettie? Ready for dessert?" Maria asked.

Lettie stood. "Thanks. I'm going to try to make room for some pie. Maybe if I help in the kitchen it will settle my meal."

Inside the kitchen, women were working together to get dishes scraped and washed.

"What can I do?" Lettie asked Rita.

Rita handed her a dish towel. "Why don't you help Connie dry?

Lettie gave her a grateful smile and went to work. It felt good to be part of this congenial group of women.

When the bulk of the dishes were done, the women stopped and helped themselves to dessert. Sitting at the table with their plates and cups of coffee, the women relaxed while their men did the same in the living room. Lettie was amused by the snores that emanated from that room.

Rita turned to her. "Tell us a little about yourself, Lettie. We were so busy getting dinner on the table we didn't have a chance to talk."

"There's not much to tell. I'm from Dayton, Ohio. I was in San Francisco when I bumped into Kenton Chandler. He told me about a job, and I came here to the valley to work at the Chandler Hill Inn."

"Mabel Morley is a good woman," said Connie. "If you're a hard worker, she'll be good to you."

"Mr. Rex has taken a liking to you," said Rita. "My Joe tells me Rex wants you to learn about grape growing. How do you feel about that?"

"It's very exciting. I love the land and what it can produce with work and care. Joe knows how to do it right. Rafe, too. And Kenton is learning how to make wine."

"Seems odd to me that he's taken such an interest in you," said a woman Lettie knew to be Paloma's mother.

Lettie's cheeks grew hot. "I don't know why he has. I think he's pretty lonely." The minute she said the words, her whole body felt hot. "I don't mean ... I never would ..."

Rita placed a hand on her arm. "It's okay. I know Rex Chandler well enough to know he would never play games with an innocent like you."

Lettie could only nod numbly.

"Are you planning to stay a long time? The last person who worked there lasted only through the spring," said a woman whose name Lettie couldn't remember.

"I'd like to stay forever," Lettie said honestly. "The first time I stood on the back porch of the inn and looked at the countryside, I felt like I'd come home, you know?" At the silence that followed, Lettie quickly said, "I know that sounds silly, especially from someone who was raised in a foster home, but I knew I wanted to be here."

Rita's smile brightened her face "No wonder Rex likes you. He said the very same thing after he came to look at the inn."

"The view and Mrs. Morley's cooking convinced him to stay," said Connie.

"Your cooking too, Rita," said Paloma, joining them with a baby in her arms.

Everyone laughed.

"I've got to take off," said Paloma. She kissed Rita on the cheek. "Thanks for everything. Enjoy my leftovers. I'll get my dishes later."

Lettie stood. "I guess I should be going too."

As the group broke up, Rafe came into the room. "Ready to go?" he asked Lettie.

"Do you want me to ride with you?" Maria asked.

Rafe shook his head. "No, I'm spending the night at the cabin to take care of the animals."

Maria gave him a steady look. "I see." She turned to Lettie. "Make sure he takes good care of them, okay?"

"Sure, I'll try, but I'll be busy. I've got things to do at the inn for Mrs. Morley."

Rita walked Lettie and Rafe to the front door.

"Thank you for having me," Lettie told her. "It was very nice. Very yummy."

Rita returned her smile. "I'm glad you could join us. I'm sure I'll be seeing you at the inn."

"See you tomorrow, Mom," said Rafe.

"Be good," she said, and turned away.

Outside, Rafe gave Lettie an apologetic look. "Sorry for the bit of grilling you got. Everybody's been curious about you. Especially Maria."

Silent, Lettie got into the truck and waited for Rafe to join her.

He slid behind the wheel, and they headed for the inn.

"Maria is beautiful," Lettie said. "I can see why you'd be so perfect together."

Rafe slammed on his brakes and pulled off to the side of the road.

"Don't you get it, Lettie?" He rubbed a hand through his dark hair, forming peaks of despair. "After being with you, I never want to think of being with anyone else."

Lettie's breath came out in a gasp of surprise. And then she began to cry.

CHAPTER SIX

What's the matter?" Rafe's voice quickly changed from one of frustration to one of concern. He wrapped an arm around her, and she nestled against his chest, trying to control the sobs that felt as if they'd never stop. She'd been so scared that he never wanted to see her again, a thought that had threatened to rip her heart apart.

When she was able to lift her head and look at him, she blurted out, "I thought ... I thought ..."

His lips met hers, stopping her words. She responded to his kiss, desperate to show him how much she cared. They'd only come together once, but it had been so much more than sex for her. She'd felt as if their souls had touched.

As Rafe pulled the truck back onto the road, Lettie straightened in her seat and sat quietly, lost in thought.

The inn appeared before them. Even though it had seemed to take forever, Lettie realized the trip that should have taken fifteen minutes had taken just ten.

Her nerves tingled with anticipation as she climbed out of the truck. Now that she knew how Rafe felt about her, she couldn't wait to show him the love she felt for him. He'd worried that she hadn't had enough time to know her true feelings, but the first time she'd seen him, she knew he was special. And when they'd kissed, she'd felt her body fill with a longing she'd never known. It was true that she hadn't had much experience because of her strict, church-going foster parents, but her body and mind had applauded that kiss.

Inside the inn, Rafe drew Lettie to the couch and settled

her into his lap. "What am I going to do about you?" he murmured before lowering his lips to hers.

A deep sigh of satisfaction welled within her. This is where she wanted to be, with Rafe. Even though life in San Francisco encompassed free love, she'd never participated in it. She knew from books and movies how intense passion could be, and she'd decided to wait for the right time, the right person.

Rafe stretched out on the couch and tugged Lettie up beside him.

Lettie suddenly realized how inappropriate it was to make love there. She scrambled to her feet. "We'd better go into the bedroom. It's more private."

She started toward the door to her room and squealed with surprise when Rafe caught up to her and pulled her against him. "Can't get away from me," he growled playfully.

"Don't you get it?" she said, mimicking his earlier statement. "I never want that to happen."

"Me neither."

Lettie placed her arms around his neck and lifted her face for a kiss.

Fingers of early morning light entered her room through the blinds and shone in rosy stripes on the wooden floor. Lettie lay in bed wishing them away. She didn't want the day to begin. Not if it meant that Rafe would leave her bed and her life. Their lovemaking last night had been as fabulous, as exciting, as fulfilling as the night before.

Beside her, Rafe stirred.

She turned to face him. "I want it to stay like this forever."

His smile was sad. "Wish we could." He checked the bedside clock. "The cows are waiting for me. I can't let them down." His kiss lingered on her lips, playing a teasing game with the desire that quickly built between them. “Ah, Lettie, if I could magically make things different, I would choose to stay right here.”

He stood outside the bed. “Mind if I take a quick shower?”

“Go ahead. I’ll put on coffee and mix up some scrambled eggs.” Lettie reluctantly got to her feet, wrapped her robe around herself, and left the room.

In the kitchen, Lettie, too, wished she had magical powers. But, like the cold floor beneath her feet, reality chilled her. Others may consider her too young, too inexperienced to know what real love was all about, but something unbelievable had happened between Rafe and her. If their relationship didn’t work out the way she wanted, she had nobody to blame but herself. Though Rafe had made his feelings for her clear, he’d been honest about being unable to make a commitment to her.

Sighing at what she couldn’t control, Lettie went about putting together breakfast.

Later that morning, while Rafe worked with his father, Lettie cleaned the kitchen cupboards, wiping down the shelves and replacing the contents in a more organized way.

In the afternoon, Rafe and his father, Joe, came into the kitchen for a cup of hot coffee. Some of the work outside at this time of year, she’d learned, was tedious.

Glad for the company, she handed each of the men a mug of coffee and offered cookies that Mrs. Morley had made before she left.

Their cheeks flushed from the cold, both men bobbed their thanks and took seats at the kitchen table.

“How’s it going?” she asked them, trying desperately not to make a fool of herself with Rafe in front of his father.

"Pretty well," Joe said. "Checking the leafy canopies, making sure vines were not damaged by the harvest of grapes is time well spent come spring."

She fixed herself a cup of coffee and sat down with them. "I guess it's going to be pretty slow at the inn for the next couple of months."

"What are you going to do for the holidays?" Joe asked her.

"I'm going to stay here." She sighed. "I really don't have any other place to go."

Joe studied her openly. "I heard you were raised in a foster home. That didn't work out so well?"

She shrugged in what she hoped was a casual way. "It wasn't as bad as some. My foster mom didn't really like me or the way I look. She told everyone I was her cross to bear. My foster dad wanted me to marry a boy from the church to fulfill my duty as a young woman."

"What?" said Rafe. "Was he part of a cult or something?"

"Pretty much," Lettie admitted. "That's why I had to get out of there."

Joe glanced at Rafe and got to his feet. "C'mon. We'd better get back to work. Then you can go home and help your mother put up the holiday decorations. I'll take care of the animals tonight and tomorrow morning, so you don't have to worry about them. Understand?"

"Yes." Rafe stood. "Go ahead. I'll be right there. I need to talk to Lettie."

After Joe left, Rafe turned to her. "I'm sorry, Lettie."

"What's going on?" At his serious expression, Lettie got to her feet and grabbed hold of the edge of the table for support.

"I can't see you anymore. What we had was very special, but I've got a commitment to my family and community that I can't ignore. I wish things were different, but they're not."

"But ..."

Rafe's eyes were moist as he shook his head. "There are no buts ... it's over. Even though I tried, I can't change things. It's out of my hands." He studied her for a moment, the pain on his face unmistakable. Then, back stiff, he turned and followed his father out of the house.

Watching them leave, Lettie collapsed into a chair. She should've known it wouldn't last, that it was another person in and out of her life. She dabbed at her wet cheeks with a napkin. Why, she wondered, did nobody want her enough to fight for her?

The Sunday following Thanksgiving was filled with getting the inn ready for Rex and Kenton's return. Mrs. Morley wouldn't be back on the job until Monday morning, so it was up to Lettie to prepare a meal for them. She searched through recipe books to find one that contained ingredients they already had on hand. She finally settled on an easy chicken-and-noodle casserole. As she was growing up, casseroles to feed a large family had been a staple.

She was looking forward to the company. Rafe had remained out of her sight since Friday, making it very clear that their short relationship was over. Though it hurt, she told herself that she had to move on, that it was never meant to be.

The sound of a car pulling up to the house caused Lettie to clutch her hands nervously. She'd dusted and vacuumed the entire inn, had the casserole ready to slide into the oven, and had even put together an appetizer tray to serve to Rex with his normal evening cocktail.

Rex and Kenton came into the house together.

First Kenton, and then Rex gave her a quick hug hello.

She treasured the feeling of their arms around her, their warmth and caring. She realized this kind of accepting love was what she really needed.

"Mmm, something smells good," said Rex.

"Just some cheese toasts to go with your cocktail," she said.

"Thanks," said Rex, beaming at her. "Good to be here."

Kenton took off for their wing, carrying both Rex's and his suitcases.

Rex stood in the living room and glanced around. "Seems as though you've been busy. Everything looks good, Lettie."

She bobbed her head. "I wanted it to be nice for your return."

He gave her a steady look. "Would you rather run the inn than become involved with grape growing and winemaking?"

"Oh, no," she quickly said. "I hated doing all that work." She clapped her hand to her mouth and looked at him wide-eyed. "I didn't mean that the way it sounded. I like being part of the inn, but I'm more excited to learn about the winery itself."

"Good, because I've hired someone to replace you in the inn come spring, when we'll begin trimming the canopy."

"Oh?" Lettie wasn't sure how she felt about that. "I can still help Mrs. Morley, if you need me to do that."

His smile was wide. "I know how much you love the land, and I'm eager to help you learn the business. I've been told a woman's palate is very important to the process of making wine, and I'd like to see you become part of the growth at Chandler Hill."

Kenton walked into the room with a grin. "Well, are you two going to stand there and talk, or is it time for a glass of wine?"

"Let's go into the library where we can light the fireplace. We'll talk there," Rex suggested.

"I'll get the appetizers," said Lettie.

Kenton followed her into the kitchen. As she put the little

cheese toasts on the plate, Kenton came up behind her and put his arms around her. “I missed you, Lettie.”

Surprised by his actions, she turned to face him. “I’ve missed you and your dad too.” She realized how true it was and gave him a warm smile. He was her best friend, someone she could count on.

Kenton’s eyes glowed with affection as he bent to kiss her. At the touch of his lips, the taste of him, the sweet feelings that rose in her surprised her. When he wrapped his arms around her, she felt an overwhelming sense of feeling at home there.

His kiss deepened.

Filled with a wholeness she’d never known, she responded, wanting more.

When they stepped apart, she stared up into the smile on Kenton’s face, confused by the deep feelings he’d set racing through her. She wondered why this kiss, so different from Rafe’s, felt so right. Maybe this kind of love was what she’d been searching for all along. She knew Kenton well enough to know he’d never let her down.

“I’ve been thinking about you a lot,” said Kenton, caressing her cheek. “I want the chance to get to know you in a different way. I’ve waited until I was sure before telling you, but I can’t wait any longer.”

She continued to gaze into the face of the person she’d once thought of as her best friend and didn’t know what to say. She wasn’t thinking of just friendship with him anymore.

“C’mon, like Dad says, we can talk in the library,” said Kenton, wrapping an arm around her and leading her to the library.

The library was her favorite room in the house. When they walked inside, the room was filled with soft lighting from above and the flickering, orange glow of wood burning in the fireplace. A large, green-patterned Oriental rug spread across the floor, enhancing the look of the old pine floors around it. The stone fireplace filled a large portion of the outside wall. Where walls were free of built-in bookcases, wood paneling gleamed with the richness of polished walnut.

Rex was sitting in one of the two green-leather, wingback chairs on either side of the hearth. On a table next to his chair sat an open bottle of red wine and three glasses.

Lettie placed the plate of appetizers next to the wine glasses and took a seat on the small settee facing the fireplace. Kenton settled in the other wingback chair.

Rex poured a small amount of red wine into one of the glasses, lifted it to the light of the fire, swirled it, sniffed it, and took a sip.

"Very good," he said. "Lettie, will you have a taste?"

Feeling very grown up, she nodded. The drinking age for liquor was twenty-one. Beer and wine, with a smaller percentage of alcohol, were allowed at eighteen.

After Rex had poured the wine into all three glasses, he lifted his. "Here's to my son, Kenton. I wish him all the luck as he enters the next phase of his life. I pray for his safety."

Lettie swiveled her attention to Kenton. "Does this mean you've joined the service?"

"More like they've joined me. I've been called to serve. A notice was waiting for me at our house in L.A." He sighed. "I don't like it. Especially after meeting you, but like I told you early on, I'll do my duty and go."

Lettie felt sick to her stomach at the thought of Kenton being killed in combat. "Is there anything you can do to make sure you don't go into battle?"

"I've thought a lot about it," said Kenton. "I'll take my chances like everyone else. I'd like to be a medic, but I don't know. I have to take some tests, and it may not be the right thing for me. I'm due to show up for induction and basic training right after Christmas."

Lettie's gaze flew to Rex. He looked as unhappy as she felt.

"I could try to intercede, but Kenton asked me not to," Rex said. "Our hope is for something safer to show up as a possibility from the testing the army does."

"Between now and then, I want to enjoy as much as I can," said Kenton. "I've spoken to Dad, and he's agreed to allow me time off to take you to the beach for a holiday."

Rex smiled at Lettie. "I've arranged with a friend of mine for the two of you to stay at his beach house in Malibu. Kenton wanted this very much. I hope you do too."

"What about the inn?" Lettie said.

"We'll close it for the time being. We don't have any reservations for the holidays anyway," Rex explained. "Once the inn gets better known, that won't be the case. For now, it's fine. I've yet to start building the addition I've planned. We'll start sometime in the spring. Might as well wait until after the major project is done before doing much advertising."

"Will Mrs. Morley be okay with this?" Lettie asked.

"I'm certain she will be," Rex said. "She knows I have plans for you to become a bigger part of the operation here. When you and Kenton get back from your trip, I'll talk to both of you about some of the things I have in mind."

"Okay," said Lettie, loving the feeling of being included.

"So, you'll go with me?" Kenton asked her. "We'll be gone for a total of three weeks."

Still reeling from his kiss in the kitchen, Lettie said, "Yes." Rafe had told her she hadn't had enough time to know if she was in love. She'd thought she loved him, but what she felt for Kenton was so different. When Kenton had talked to her about his feelings for her and then kissed her, she knew how much he really meant it. He was looking at her now with such vulnerability, she never wanted to hurt him.

Their gazes met, and Lettie felt nervous tension ease out of her body. Kenton was the one who'd brought her to the inn. He was the one with whom she felt the safest. He was the one who was asking to spend time with her.

Wanting to learn much more about him and about being together, she returned his smile.

CHAPTER SEVEN

As Lettie packed her suitcase for the trip to Malibu, she realized she needed more and better-quality clothes—especially if she was to be with Kenton. He was used to the finest things. She definitely wasn't.

Maybe, she thought, she could find a nice thrift store in California. The shopping in the small towns and cities of the valley and in the countryside was almost non-existent. Most people, she assumed, went into Portland, almost an hour's drive away from McMinnville. In the months she'd been at Chandler Hill, she hadn't ventured there.

Kenton knocked on her door and poked his head inside the room. "Ready?"

"As ready as I'll ever be." She sighed. "But, Kenton, I'll have to do something about my clothes. They're not right, at all."

He chuckled. "Don't worry about it. We'll take care of that. Come on. We have to get on the road. It's going to take a couple of days for us to drive there."

"Malibu? I can't wait."

He grinned at her. "And I can't wait to have all this time alone with you."

She gave him her best smile. The words were sweet to her ears. Maybe she wasn't the ugly, weird-speaking child of the past. Maybe he saw something better in her.

The next two days passed in blissful companionship, broken in the middle by a brief stay in a motel during which

Kenton had kissed her and looked at her longingly, but had kept his distance.

Riding in the car, listening to music, snacking on treats, she felt as if she were in a vacuum where nothing else in the world mattered except her time with Kenton.

As they drove into Malibu and down to the beaches lining the shore, Lettie sighed with contentment. The houses on stilts and the wide sandy beaches were every bit as wonderful as she'd seen in pictures. She stared at the young people stretched out on towels atop the sand talking, reading, or simply soaking up the sun. Out on the water, a few people were trying to surf.

She rolled down the window and inhaled the salty air, feeling as if she'd entered a picture postcard.

"Groovy, huh?" said Kenton grinning at her. "And nice that a friend of my father's is letting us stay at his house. Better than staying in Beverly Hills."

"It's wonderful!" Lettie said. She impulsively leaned over and kissed him on the cheek.

He grabbed hold of her hand. "*You're* wonderful! Let's get unpacked, change into bathing suits, and take a walk on the beach."

"Uh, I don't have a bathing suit," Lettie reluctantly admitted. "But I do have a mini skirt and sleeveless top. I'll wear that."

"Okay, but tomorrow we'll get you a proper bathing suit. Maybe a bikini." He gave her a leering grin that made her laugh.

"My foster mother would drop dead of a heart attack if she ever saw me in a bikini, but why not?"

"She's not here, and you're going to look great in one," Kenton assured her.

He drove down a road and pulled to a stop in front of a

white-clapboard house on stilts. From the outside, it looked like the others nearby—genuinely beachy.

They carried their suitcases up the wooden stairway and into the house.

"Wow!" said Lettie, staring at a huge picture window overlooking the beach. She hurried over to it and peered out.

The beach lay in front of them, a sandy welcome to the area. Beyond it, the Pacific rolled toward them in white-crested waves. A surfer balanced on a board, riding the crest of a wave for a few seconds before toppling into the water.

"What is he wearing?" Lettie said, watching the surfer emerge from the water wearing a black, tight-fitting suit of some kind.

"That's a wet suit. They're really neat. When the water is this cold, it keeps someone warm by absorbing a small amount of water into the sponge-like material and then using their body heat to keep them warm. C'mon, let's get changed and go outside. I want to get some rays of sun."

She grinned. "Okay, where do we put our suitcases?" Though she knew he'd like to do much more than share a few kisses, he'd done nothing about it.

"Let's see."

They walked from the living room to a back hall. A large bedroom, obviously the master, sat on one side of the hallway. Two smaller ones sat across from it.

"What do you think?" Kenton asked her. "Okay, if we take the big room together?"

Lettie drew a deep breath and studied Kenton, knowing exactly what sharing that room with him would mean. His kindness, his caring, his sweet kisses were things to treasure. Maybe it was time to see what kind of relationship they really had. Especially with his going to war.

"We'll share the room." The thought of his being injured in

war, or worse, was terrifying. She wanted to be here for him now. Though the attraction to him was different from what she'd felt for Rafe, this was even better, deeper, and more tender. To her, that meant a lot.

They got things settled in the bedroom and quickly changed their clothes. Kenton was kind enough to leave the room to allow Lettie privacy.

When she stepped out of the bedroom, Kenton grinned. "Even in a mini-skirt and a halter, you're a knock-out, Lettie. Before we get out in the sun, though, you need to put on some suntan lotion. There's some in the bathroom. I'll help you."

"Thanks." With her fair coloring, she'd need it.

After dabbing lotion on her face, arms, and legs, she turned to Kenton, who'd watched her. "Can you help me with my back?"

He jumped up out of his chair and gave her a sexy grin that sent goosepimples across her skin. "I've been waiting to do this." He accepted the tube of lotion she handed him, put some on his hands and palmed it across her back in soothing strokes.

At his touches, shivers traveled across her shoulders. His fingers, so gentle on her skin, held a strength she appreciated.

He gave her back a pat. "There. More than a little dab, but that will do it."

She chuckled and turned to face him. "You sound like the Brylcreem ad. You know ... 'a little dab will do ya.'"

He laughed in response. "You're adorable, you know." He drew her to him and lowered his lips onto hers. The shivers that filled her this time had everything to do with the sexual response he aroused in her. She knew then that she couldn't deny her feelings for him. They were so much more than friends. With him, she felt treasured.

When he pulled away, he stared at her with a deeper color

to his blue eyes. “Should we stay here or go on down to the beach?”

“You choose,” she said, suddenly shy.

He grinned. “Okay, us now. Beach later.”

Kenton kissed her again—kisses that sent a pulsing need through her. His hands palmed her back in comforting circles and then moved to her breasts. She moaned softly at his touch.

Wordlessly, Kenton took her hand and led her back into the bedroom. With one sweep of his arm, he yanked the bedspread down.

They lay together atop the bed, facing one another.

Kenton cupped her cheek and studied her with an intensity that added a brightness to his blue eyes. “Lettie, do you have any idea how I’ve fallen for you? Seeing you sitting on the steps of that condo building in San Francisco, I wanted to pick you up and wrap you in my arms. Figured I’d better start with a sandwich.”

Tears stung Lettie’s eyes. After being the “unwanted one,” even as recently as the incident with Rafe, Kenton’s words, spoken with emotion, caressed her like silk on her skin.

She reached for him.

Later, she rested beside Kenton, who was lying on his back and snoring softly. Lettie studied him. He was such a kind, generous man. His lovemaking didn’t have all of Rafe’s wild intensity, but Kenton had made sure she was satisfied before he allowed himself that same pleasure.

He sensed her looking at him, opened his eyes, and turned to her. “I love you, Lettie. I think I have since that day I met you.”

At his words, her heart filled with joy. She reached over and caressed his cheek, needing that touch to know she hadn't dreamed that moment. In all her life, she'd never been told she was loved.

She met his lips, eager to show him just what he meant to her. Not only was he sexy and handsome, Kenton was the sweetest guy she'd ever met.

Outside on the sandy beach, Lettie lifted her arms to the sky. Even at this holiday time of year, the sun gave a welcome warmth to the salty air that wrapped around Lettie like a soft woolen shawl.

She and Kenton walked briskly next to the water's frothy edge and then jumped out of the way when a wave rolled in with unexpected energy.

He laughed when she almost fell, caught her hand, and swept her up into his arms. "There! I've got you now."

"Don't let go," she said.

With love shining in his eyes, he tightened his embrace. "I have no intention of ever letting go. You'll always be safe with me."

Knowing he meant what he said, she laid her head against his chest, hearing his heartbeat, wondering how she could be so lucky. The emotional moment was shattered when a seagull squawked loudly and dipped down toward them.

Kenton waved his arm and shouted, "Go away!"

The seagull gave him a beady-eyed stare and flapped its wings with as much dignity as it could. As they walked down the beach, the seagull landed on the sand behind them and followed from a distance.

"What's with this bird?" Kenton complained.

"I think it's hungry. I have a piece of cookie in my pocket. Should I give it to him?" Lettie asked, coming to a stop.

"Okay but be prepared to run. All hell will break loose when they notice one of their own getting food."

Lettie pulled the cookie out of her shorts pocket and threw it as hard as she could toward the gull. "Here you go!"

A whole flock of birds descended, crying for their share.

Lettie grabbed hold of Kenton's hand and, squealing, ran down the beach with him. After leaving the birds behind, they slowed their steps and walked as far as the pier, where they found seats on a bench and spent time watching surfers riding the waves.

When the sun showed signs of beginning its nightly descent, Kenton said, "We'd better get back to the house. Besides, I'm hungry. Aren't you?"

She grinned. "Yes. I'm ready for dinner anytime."

He laughed. "I'm so glad you're not one of those girls who wants to look like Twiggy. They might think guys like that, but we don't."

Lettie placed her hands on her hips in mock horror. "Are you calling me fat?"

Kenton shook his head. "Absolutely not. You've got the perfect body. Can't wait to see it in a bikini."

Her cheeks turned warm. "Oh, right. You're taking me shopping tomorrow."

"Yeah. Even though I like you best with no clothes on, I know you need some new ones."

She laughed and took a moment to study the setting sun. The yellow orb was beginning to sink below the horizon sending shards of gold, orange, and red into the sky like pieces broken off a rainbow. The waves rolling into shore were tipped with the colors making her feel as if she were standing at the edge of a painting. She breathed in the salty air and sighed. It was so lovely.

They strolled side by side down the beach to the house

where they were staying. Lettie's gaze kept returning to the setting sun to the west and the way the orange and red glow in the sky was reflected on the water, making each wave shimmer with color.

"Nice, isn't it?" Kenton said, breaking into their silence.

"Oh yes," she murmured. "I've never experienced anything like this. The beach is beautiful. The people here are too."

"Malibu Barbies," said Kenton, casting an admiring glance at a tall, leggy blonde striding from the water wearing a black bikini.

Lettie had already noticed girls in mini-skirts and maxi-skirts and had decided she'd get one of each. Excited now at having the chance to get some new clothes, she squeezed Kenton's hand.

"Having fun?" he asked.

"Yes, but tomorrow is going to be fun too."

Lettie awoke and stretched in bed. Thinking of the day ahead, she felt as if Christmas was coming early. Today, she and Kenton would go shopping, and then maybe she'd look like she belonged with all the beautiful people.

Quietly, so as not to disturb Kenton, she climbed out of bed, put on a robe she'd found in a closet, slipped out of the room, and stepped onto the deck that overlooked the beach. The air was chilly against her skin, but she didn't mind. Wrapping the robe tighter around her, she sat in one of the deck chairs and gazed out over the water. She loved the sight almost as much as she loved the rolling hills of the Willamette Valley, where she felt entirely at home. Here, she was merely a visitor.

She heard the glass door slide open behind her and smiled up at Kenton. "It's going to be a wonderful day."

He bent down and kissed her on the cheek. "Any day with you is wonderful. Come back to bed."

At the sexy look he gave her, she eagerly followed him into the warm room, dropped her robe and slid beneath the covers. Home, she thought happily. Kenton had led her to the inn where she'd found a new home, and now, she'd found a spiritual, loving home with him.

Several hours later, inside one of the trendy stores, Lettie whirled around in front of Kenton. He sat in a chair outside the dressing rooms. "What do you think?"

"You look great," he said. "Does that about do it?"

She laughed. "Yes, I can tell you're ready to leave, and I am too. I'm going to go ahead and wear these bell bottoms, along with the T-shirt and sweater, so you'll have to wait while I cut off the tags."

"Okay," he said, standing. "Man, you look good."

Lettie flung her arms around him, surprising both Kenton and her. She was so used to being self-contained that, for a moment, it seemed strange for her to do this, but then she settled into Kenton's embrace and knew it was where she should be.

The sales clerk helped Lettie cut the tags off what Lettie was wearing. "Want me to take them off all the clothes you're buying?"

"Yes, that would be nice," Lettie said, pleased.

When they were through, the sales clerk smiled pleasantly. "You've got some really great things here, and for a bargain, too." She stood back and studied her. "Have you ever thought of modeling? You'd be good at it."

Lettie frowned at her. "Me? With my hair all pinky and curly? I don't think so. My foster parents never liked what they called my wild looks."

The store clerk shook her head. "Crazy, their saying that. You're lovely."

"Thanks," said Lettie, not yet able to accept kind words like that.

CHAPTER EIGHT

The next ten days rolled out as sweet and wonderful as any piece of chocolate Lettie had ever tasted. Their days were filled with outside activities, sightseeing, walking the beach, swimming, and playing volleyball with a friendly group of kids. And nights? They were filled with even more satisfying activity. The best part of sharing so much time with Kenton, she decided, was the ability to relax and be herself, which she recognized would be unexciting to some. She and Kenton were content to read and talk and walk together like old married folks.

Kenton was full of surprises. His voice rang out from the shower each morning with a new song as good as the singers Lettie had heard on the radio. And to her chagrin, she discovered Kenton was a better cook than she was. When he offered to cook all their meals, she realized that cooking for a large foster family was a lot different from cooking the small, elegant meals Kenton liked.

They were eating grilled steak in the kitchen one night when Kenton said, "Lettie? Let's get married! We can do it right here in California, or we can fly to Las Vegas."

"Really? That's what you want?" Lettie laid her fork down.

"Sorry. Let me do this the right way." Kenton knelt in front of her. "Lettie Hawkins, will you marry me?"

The idea both excited and scared her.

"Well?" said Kenton, giving her a pleading look.

A bubble of laughter burst out of her. "Yes! I'll marry you!" Everything was happening quickly, but she knew it was a good decision. Their love came from their hearts.

Kenton let out a whoop of joy. He rose, swept her into his arms, and twirled her around. "I'll make arrangements. We'll fly to Vegas. That'll be the fastest way. I can show you the glitter of the town. A ring ... I've got to get you a ring."

"I've never flown before," she said, worried about the idea.

He gave her a look of consternation. "Then how did you get to San Francisco?"

Embarrassed, she gazed at the floor and then lifted her head. "I hitchhiked."

"No troubles along the way?" he said, his voice ringing with concern.

"I met only one creep, and I got out of that truck so fast it was still moving. The other drivers were nice."

"You do have a driver's license, don't you?"

"Yes, of course. Even though I never owned a car, I got my Ohio license as soon as I could, and I got an Oregon license about three weeks ago."

"Good. We'll fly from LAX right to Vegas. Okay?"

Another bubble of laughter burst out of her. "Okay? It's wonderful! I can't wait to be your wife!" She meant it too. He was the home she'd been looking for all along.

While Kenton made the phone call, Lettie went into their bedroom and over to the closet that now contained her new clothes. Kenton had insisted on buying her a dress. She took out the mint-green dress in a Diane von Furstenberg-style wrap and held it up to her before a mirror. Though it wasn't white, it would do quite nicely. She would, however, need new shoes. She certainly wasn't about to wear her new, sturdy, black tie shoes to her own wedding.

Kenton walked into the room. "Are you okay with this? We can celebrate with a fancy wedding later, maybe something for our first anniversary."

"I don't need a fancy wedding, Kenton. I just want you to be happy." She held up the dress. "This will be perfect for the wedding. 'Very classy' as you kept telling me." She looked down at her bare feet. "But I will need a new pair of shoes."

"Anything you want, my love," he said beaming at her. He tugged her into his embrace. "You'll never know how happy you've made me. Now, when I'm in 'Nam, I'll have someone to fight for, someone to come home to."

Lettie stepped away from him and stared up at him, horrified. "It's been such a wonderful holiday that I've pushed that terrible thought away."

Kenton gave her a sorrowful look. "There's nothing I can do about it. I have to go. But knowing you're my wife and waiting for me will get me through some bad times."

A shiver of fear crawled through Lettie and wrapped around her like a python ready to swallow them both.

"You okay?" Kenton said, caressing her cheek.

She nodded, but she knew she'd suffer every kind of worry when he was gone.

When they landed in Las Vegas at the McCarran International Airport, Lettie looked out the window at the desert scene with interest, glad to be back on solid ground. Flying had been anything but fun for her. Kenton had held her hand during the short flight, but she still hadn't liked the idea of being trapped in the air far above the ground. She'd worked hard not to act as frightened as she was. There were moments when the plane had dipped, that she'd clamped her lips tight to hold back her scream.

She caught a glimpse of palm trees outside. They disrupted the view of the flat, brown area. She tried to see the city in the distance, but the plane was positioned in such a way that made it impossible.

"C'mon, let's go," said Kenton, lifting down her new, small, brown-leather suitcase from the overhead bin. "We've got a lot to do."

She eagerly followed him out of the plane and hurried with him through the terminal to the outside.

A taxi pulled up to the curb. "Need a ride?" the cheerful cab driver asked.

"Yes! To the Flamingo Hotel," Kenton said, turning to her with a roguish grin.

After their luggage was stowed and they were settled in the backseat of the car, the driver studied the two of them with a knowing smile. "In a hurry?"

Kenton's face lit with an excitement that touched her heart. "Yes, sir. We're going to get married. I heard the Chapel of the Bells is a nice place."

"Yeah, a lot of people get married there," said the driver. "I guess you two don't care where it is as long as it happens, huh?"

Lettie and Kenton exchanged amused glances.

"Guess not," the driver said, chuckling.

In the distance, a tall, pink sign designed to look like the flared tail feathers of the flamingo for which it was named rose above the street like the long-legged, pink bird itself. The name Flamingo in white spread across the sign, inviting them in. Across the street, the sign for Caesar's Palace was every bit as impressive.

Wide-eyed, Lettie gazed at the front of the hotel as the driver pulled up to it. A wall of stacked stone offset a glass entryway. Glamorous people were entering and leaving the clean-lined building.

The driver stopped the car and said, "I'll get your bags."

"Hold on," Kenton said. "I've made an appointment at

Gabriel Jewelers. Will you take us there?"

The driver shrugged. "Sure. I'm at your disposal. All day, if you want."

"Great," said Kenton and turned to her. "Lettie, I want you to have a diamond ring."

"I don't need anything fancy, Kenton," she said gently, touched by how well he'd planned this unexpected trip.

"Trust me. I want it to be nice," said Kenton. "The best."

His excitement was contagious. "Okay. Whatever you want." She didn't have his sophistication and knew it.

"Ready?" said the driver. "The store is on 4th street. I'll get you there and back again as fast as I can."

Lettie was in a daze as they left Gabriel's. Kenton had insisted on buying her a large solitaire diamond in a yellow-gold setting. The simple design enhanced the size and quality of the diamond that now sparkled on her left hand. The wedding rings they'd chosen for the ceremony were simple gold bands that would match the ring perfectly.

"I wish we could get married right now," said Lettie, as she got settled in the cab again. She knew she wouldn't relax until the ceremony was over and she could simply enjoy being with Kenton.

The driver heard her and glanced at her through the rear-view mirror. "Do you want to head right over to the Chapel of the Bells? They're used to small, quickie ceremonies."

Kenton gave her a questioning look.

Still feeling a little overwhelmed by all that was happening so quickly, Lettie paused and then grinned. "We've got our suitcases with us. We can change there."

"Great. Then we can enjoy Las Vegas and ..." he wiggled his eyebrows playfully "... and each other."

Lettie laughed. *Perfect!*

When the driver, a man they now knew as Vinnie Borelli, pulled up to the chapel, she saw it was as garish, as eye-popping as she'd imagined. In front of the entrance to a blazing white, stucco-faced building, stood a tall white sign. Three bells were painted a sunny yellow and outlined with lights at the top of the sign's arch. Beneath the bells in an arc of blue, words in white announced "World-Famous Chapel of the Bells." Below that was the word "Weddings" in white against a background of the same blue as above. All the letters were strung with lights. Lettie couldn't help wondering what the sign would look like all lit up.

Vinnie carried their bags to the front door. "I'll wait for you outside. Take your time."

The first thing Lettie noticed when she stepped inside the chapel was the white grand piano. As flashy as the exterior was, the interior was tastefully done in neutral colors. She smiled at Kenton. This was more like it.

A gentleman greeted them. "Here for a wedding?"

"Yes. We want something quick and simple. Is there a place for us to change?"

The gentleman gave her a warm smile. "Yes, of course. Let's take care of paperwork, and then we can arrange a ceremony for you. The minister is non-denominational and is able to perform the ceremony you specify. We can also provide music, if you choose. And, if she wishes, we have flowers available for the bride."

Kenton turned to her. "Music? Flowers?"

The thought pleased her. "Yes, but please select both for me. For the flowers, anything but violets."

He chuckled. "I'll take care of it."

"And I'll get changed," she said, uncomfortable with hearing the financial arrangements.

After she was directed to a dressing area, Lettie set her suitcase on a white-velvet bench and opened it. Removing her dress, she was relieved to see that it hadn't wrinkled badly. And the high heels that she'd borrowed from the closet in Malibu were in good shape. Last night, when Kenton called his father's friend to ask about them, he was told that not only could Lettie borrow the shoes, she could keep them.

As Lettie stood at the sink to wash her face, she studied her image in the mirror. The years in Dayton, Ohio, seemed decades, not months ago. Her life had changed dramatically, and she owed it all to Kenton. Her fair skin, lightly tanned now, seemed to glow with the happiness she felt. Her hair, still curly and wild, looked suitable here in Vegas, at the beach, or walking the grounds of Chandler Hill. True, her nose still had a dusting of freckles, but even these had become acceptable because Kenton had whispered to her that he loved them.

She freshened her makeup, added the brown eyeliner and blue eye shadow that changed her blue-green eyes from interesting to extraordinary, and straightened. She'd done the best she could.

The green dress wrapped her body as if it was designed for her. Beneath it she wore the lacy bra and matching panties she'd bought with Kenton. She slipped large, gold-plated, loop earrings into her earlobes. Her foster mother would have considered them much too showy, but Lettie loved them.

At a knock at the door, Lettie hurried to answer it.

Kenton beamed at her. "Wow! You look beautiful!" He handed her a bouquet of pale pink roses. "I chose these for you because they remind me of you."

As she took them in her hands, he leaned over and kissed her cheek. "Ready to do this?"

Her heart filled with love for him. "Yes."

They walked into the chapel holding hands.

###

That evening, in the Golden Steer Restaurant, where Vinnie had insisted they go for their wedding dinner, Lettie sat in a red-leather booth gazing across the table at her groom. She could hardly believe she was a married woman. And, yet, it felt so good to "belong" to someone as wonderful as Kenton.

The ceremony had made her feel as if another woman, a woman so different from what she'd known on her own, had developed wings and was about to fly into the future. Kenton's eyes had filled with emotion when she'd said, "I do" in a ringing tone of affirmation.

The waiter brought two glasses of champagne to them. "While you're waiting for your dinner, one of the gentlemen across the room asked me to deliver this to you. How long have you been married?"

"About three hours," Kenton said, grinning.

Lettie turned around to see who Kenton was acknowledging. "Is that Elvis Presley?" she asked the waiter.

Giving her a smile, the waiter shrugged. "Can't say. He's here from time to time, along with a few other people like Sinatra."

After the waiter left, Kenton raised his glass. "Here's to us, Lettie. We're going to make a great life together!"

They clicked glasses.

Bubbles tickled Lettie's nose as she tipped the glass to her mouth. She giggled, took a breath, and then sipped the wine.

"I don't know what kind of champagne this is, but it's delicious," said Kenton. "No doubt it's from France."

"It's nice," said Lettie, taking another sip and looking around at all the well-dressed patrons.

When at last their steaks came, a contented silence descended on the table as they dug into the tender meat. Lettie had her first taste of Caesar salad with its crisp leaves of romaine, tart dressing, parmesan cheese shavings, and anchovies.

"Like it?" Kenton asked, leaning toward her eagerly.

Lettie swallowed and forked another leaf of the lettuce. "Delicious."

He laughed. "You may not know it yet, but you're a classy broad, as Sinatra would say."

"Oh, so now you're a member of the Rat Pack?" she teased.

He grinned. "I don't need to be in a pack. I've got you."

Later, after making love in their hotel room, Lettie lay on her back staring up at the ceiling, a small smile playing at her lips. Being married to Kenton made their lovemaking even more special because she knew she was the person with whom he had chosen to spend the rest of his life.

Sighing with contentment, she rolled over and nestled up against his strong body. Tomorrow, she decided, they'd relax around the pool and then take a more active part in this magical city that turned into a wonderland of colorful lights at night.

CHAPTER NINE

Lettie was lost in a dream of being in a field of flowers staring up at the sky when suddenly a giant bug flew at her. She moaned and slapped at the annoying creature.

"Hey!" cried Kenton, waking her up.

She opened her eyes and blinked sleepily at him.

"I'm just trying to kiss you," he said, holding a hand to his cheek.

She held out her arms to him. "Sorry, I was dreaming."

He nestled against her chest. "I'm going to call Dad. I can't wait to tell him we're married. He thinks you're very special, you know."

"I still don't know why."

He propped himself on one elbow and caressed her cheek. "You don't? He says you're one of the most genuine people he knows. He loves that you love Chandler Hill, and he wants you to be a part of its growth."

"I'd like that too."

He scrambled out of bed. "I'm going to call him now." He lifted the phone, got the hotel operator to give him an outside line, and dialed the Chandler Hill Inn's number.

He turned to Lettie. "I've put it on speaker."

The phone rang and rang, before a breathless voice said, "Hello?"

"Mrs. Morley?"

"Oh, my word! Is that you, Kenton? We've been trying to reach you. Where are you? Your father has had a stroke and is in the hospital in Portland. We need you to come home."

"A stroke? How bad is it? Is he going to be okay?"

"Oh, hon! We don't know for sure."

"When did it happen?"

"Sometime yesterday morning. I found him in his bedroom."

"Lettie and I are in Las Vegas. We just got married. Let me check the airlines, and I'll call you back. But, Mrs. Morley, tell him to hold on. We're coming home."

"Okay. Rafe will pick you up at the airport. He and Maria are engaged, and they'll be moving away after the holidays, but they won't leave until things are settled here. Goodbye. Hurry home."

Kenton disconnected the call and turned to her, his face drained of blood. "I can't believe it! Dad's never sick. And now this?" Tears filled the big, beautiful eyes that had always comforted her.

Now it was her turn to comfort him. She hugged him tight. "Rex is a strong man. He'll fight this."

He squeezed her hard and then said, "You'd better get dressed. We'll get out of here as soon as we can."

"Go ahead and make the arrangements. I'll take care of things here." Lettie raced into the bathroom for a quick shower.

Standing under a stream of hot water, she thought of Rex Chandler. A big, handsome, rugged-looking man, he'd always seemed so alive. The thought of him lying helpless brought tears to her eyes. After knowing him for even such a short time, she realized how miserable a situation like that would be for a strong man like him.

Anxious to get home to see him, she hurried through her morning routine. And then, while Kenton showered, she packed for both of them.

Placing her carefully folded dress into the suitcase, Lettie thought of the special day she'd shared with Kenton yesterday and felt guilty that, while they were having such a wonderful time, Rex lay suffering. She looked at the black bikini Kenton had bought her, pushing away disappointment at not being able to spend more time in Las Vegas. She was as anxious as Kenton to get home to Rex.

She folded Kenton's clothes and placed them into his suitcase, wondering if Rex's illness would mean a delay in Kenton's reporting for duty.

Kenton emerged from the bathroom, his hair still wet from the shower. "Ready?"

"I think so. I'll double-check the drawers and closet. Do you have all your things from the bathroom?"

"Yes." He snapped his suitcase closed. "Let's get the hell out of here."

They carried their luggage down to the lobby, where Kenton checked them out.

Outside, the hotel van was ready to take them to the airport. Kenton greeted the driver curtly. "We need to get to the airport right away. Family emergency."

"Yes, sir." The driver helped Lettie into the van, grabbed the luggage, and after settling the bags in the back, hurried to get behind the wheel.

As they traveled away from the strip, Lettie stared out the window. At night, the strip was alive with color. Now, in the daylight, the hotels seemed like old men lounging beside the road, sleeping off a hangover.

Kenton clasped her hand in his. "Sorry our honeymoon had to end like this. I'll make it up to you sometime."

"Oh, honey, I'm sorry too. I just hope your father is all right."

He clamped his lips together, unable to hold back his emotions.

###

Rafe was standing in the waiting area for arriving passengers after they had deplaned at the Portland International Airport. Seeing them, he hurried over and gave Kenton a quick, manly hug. "So sorry about your dad."

He turned to Lettie. "I hear congratulations are in order for the two of you."

"And for you and Maria. Congratulations," she responded.

"Where's Dad? The Providence Hospital?" said Kenton, gripping both suitcases tightly.

"Yes," said Rafe. "I'll drop you off there. So far, he's holding his own."

Lettie watched the lines of worry creasing Kenton's forehead visibly lessen, and she gave his arm an encouraging squeeze. "That's good. He's strong, Kenton."

He acknowledged her but didn't wait for her as he headed out the door of the terminal with Rafe. Lettie hurried to catch up.

As she approached, she saw Rafe clap Kenton on the back and heard him say, "Congratulations, Kenton. Lettie is someone special."

"Don't I know it," Kenton said. "The best decision of my life."

Lettie hurried to Kenton's side, but said nothing to indicate she'd overheard.

Rafe led them to Rex's black Cadillac. "Hop in. I'll drive."

Kenton helped Lettie into the black-leather backseat and, after loading the suitcases, climbed into the front seat next to Rafe.

They made their way through traffic to the front of a red-brick building. "Here we are," said Rafe, pulling to a stop.

Kenton opened the door and stepped out of the car.

"Thanks, Rafe. Please stay around until we know what our plans are. Okay?"

"Sure, that's what I was going to do all along."

Lettie got out of the car, and they walked through the entrance of the hospital to check in.

"We're here to see Rex Chandler," Kenton told the woman behind the reception desk.

"I'm sorry, but he's not to receive any visitors except immediate family," she said, eying Lettie.

"I'm his son and this is my wife," Kenton said with enough force behind his words that the receptionist blinked. "Okay, then. Mr. Chandler is on the fourth floor. The elevators are down the hall on your right."

"Thank you," said Kenton, and they hurried down the hall.

On the fourth floor, they found Rex in a private room lying on his back in a single bed. Cables hooked him up to some kind of monitor. An IV bag hung from a pole close by. His eyes were closed. Observing the way one side of his face had slid downward like melted wax and how his cheeks had sunk into his face, Lettie grew alarmed. This was not the vibrant man she knew.

"Dad?" Kenton said softly, leaning over the bed.

Rex opened his right eye. The other eye remained closed. From beneath the light blanket, his right leg stirred. His hands, resting atop the sheet covering his body remained in place.

"Hi, Dad," Kenton said, patting his father's hands. "We're here."

Rex's one-eyed gaze landed on him and turned to Lettie. For a moment, it almost looked as if he were attempting a smile.

"We got here as soon as we could. Dad, Lettie and I got married yesterday."

Rex's right eye brightened. "Ggggdd."

Lettie moved closer and clasped Rex's cold hands in hers. Then very carefully, she planted a kiss on the one cheek that wasn't drooping. Gazing into his eye, she spoke sincerely. "I'm so lucky, Rex. I love your son, and he loves me. Being part of this family is the best thing that's ever happened to me. I promise to be good to both of you."

Rex moved his head. "Ggggdd grl."

"Lettie is going to stay right here with you while I try to find the doctor," said Kenton. "I want to make sure they're doing all they can for you."

Rex let out a sigh of disgust.

"I'll be right back," said Kenton, exchanging a worried look with Lettie.

Lettie pulled a chair over to Rex's bed and sat down. She rubbed Rex's limp arm, willing it to move, but it was obvious that Rex's entire left side was immobile. Lettie didn't know that much about strokes, but it looked bad. Rex's speech was another indicator that it was no small matter.

When Kenton returned, the anguished look on his face told Lettie it wasn't good news. She turned to Rex but both eyes were closed now, and he was breathing shallowly.

Kenton waved Lettie toward the hall. She stepped outside the room and waited for him to speak.

Kenton's eyes welled with tears. "The doctor said the situation wasn't good, that because he wasn't found right away, there's little they can do to restore any functions to that part of the brain. He'll have to go to rehab to try and get some strength back into the affected parts of his body, but it will take time. Lots of time."

Lettie shook her head sadly. "You know Rex would hate for that to be his life. He's a man who likes to walk free and easy."

Kenton lowered his head into his hands, his shoulders

shaking. When he raised his face to her, it was wet with tears and creased with worry. “I can’t think of anything worse. What are we going to do? Having him here in Portland and us at Chandler Hill will be impossible.”

“Maybe we can hire someone to work with him at home. That would be a lot more comfortable for him.”

“Perhaps. Let’s say goodbye to Dad, go home, and see what arrangements we can make. We can turn your downstairs bedroom into his room. You’ll be with me upstairs now anyway.”

“Sounds like a plan. Let’s go see him.”

A sudden alarm came through the intercom system. “Emergency! Code blue! Code blue! Room 406.”

Lettie moved aside as doctors and nurses rushed into Rex’s room. Kenton started to follow them inside, but a nurse said, “Wait here. Let the team work on him.”

Kenton paused.

Lettie took hold of his hand and pulled him away. “We’re right here for him.”

The confusion and noise stopped suddenly.

Lettie’s heart sank. She stared at Kenton.

He slumped against the wall and covered his eyes.

As staff filed out of the room, Kenton and Lettie went inside.

A doctor was standing next to the bed.

“I’m sorry,” he said. “We did everything we could. It may not be of comfort to you now, but sometimes it’s best when this happens. The day will come when we can do much more for stroke victims, but right now, there wasn’t much that could be done to help him. Not when he didn’t get to us for so long.”

Kenton’s eyes filled. “Dad would’ve hated living like that. Thanks for all you did.”

They shook hands.

The doctor's expression was sad. "I understand from one of the nurses that you just got married. Too bad to have your time together start out like this. I'm so sorry. If there's anything we can do to help you make arrangements, please let us know. My nurse will be happy to assist."

He left, and Kenton and Lettie stared at one another wide-eyed. *What were they going to do now?*

A nurse came into the room. "Why don't I give you a few minutes alone with your loved one, and then I'll walk you down to the chapel. A counselor can meet you there."

Lettie nodded numbly, thinking of the strangeness of it all. Yesterday, she'd been in a chapel happily marrying Kenton. Today, they'd share the pain of his father's death in a hospital chapel.

"I'll say goodbye, then leave you with your father," Lettie suggested.

Looking as sad as she'd ever seen him, Kenton said, "Thanks."

Lettie went over to Rex's bed and stared down at the face whose waxy surface indicated that the spirit of the man was gone. She hadn't known him long, but the instant connection they'd made had given her a bigger gift than he could ever have imagined. Gently, she placed her lips on his cheek and then whispered, "Thank you, Rex Chandler, for everything. Rest in peace."

Fighting tears, she stepped away from the bed, hugged Kenton, and left the room.

CHAPTER TEN

After Kenton placed a phone call to Lew Barnes, Rex's lawyer, things moved fast. Rex had wanted his body cremated and his ashes spread or buried at Chandler Hill. With Lew's instructions, Kenton made those arrangements, signed necessary documents, and paid the hospital bills. Then Lettie and Kenton headed home. Lew would join them in the next few days.

Grim-faced, Rafe drove them home in the Fleetwood, his silence an indicator of how much he, too, had admired the man. Kenton rode in the backseat with Lettie, gripping her hand tightly.

Darkness was descending when Lettie saw the inn sitting at the top of the rolling hills she loved so much. Fresh tears blurred her vision. "I can't believe he's gone," she murmured.

Kenton continued to stare out the window. "It won't ever be the same without him."

Rafe pulled the Cadillac up to the front of the inn and waited while Kenton helped Lettie out of the car. "I'll bring your bags inside."

Before they were halfway up the front walk, Mrs. Morley burst out of the house. "Kenton! Kenton! I'm so sorry!" She held out her arms, and Kenton went into them.

In moments, Kenton straightened and, wet-faced, wrapped an arm around Lettie. "We were both able to see and talk to Dad and to tell him that we're married now. He seemed really happy about it. Right, Lettie?"

"Yes. He said 'good' and then later he called me ..." she

stopped to catch her breath. "He called me what sounded like 'good girl.'" The tears that had welled in Lettie's eyes slipped down her cheeks in hot streaks.

Mrs. Morley said, "Bless your heart. Come here." She wrapped her arms around Lettie, and the three of them held onto each other.

Rafe carried their suitcases past them into the house.

After a few moments, Mrs. Morley pulled away. "Let's go inside. Mr. Barnes called to say that he and Rex's accountant would arrive at the end of the week. I've got rooms ready for them. My understanding is that they will be with us for two nights."

As they neared the front door, Rafe headed out of the house. "I placed the suitcases in the front hall. I wasn't sure where you'd want them."

Mrs. Morley's eyes widened. "My word! That's right. Lettie, we'll have to move you into Kenton's room."

"Thanks for everything, Rafe. Talk to you tomorrow," Kenton said woodenly. Lettie took his hand and felt a tremor of grief roll through him.

"Sure thing," Rafe said. "You know my family and I are here to help any way we can." He went to the car. "I'll put the Fleetwood back into the garage and leave. See you tomorrow."

Kenton and Lettie followed Mrs. Morley inside.

"Guess I'd better take the suitcases up to my room," said Kenton, giving her a woeful look. "God! I can't believe that Dad is gone!"

"I'll help Lettie gather her things," said Mrs. Morley, bustling away and leaving them standing in the front hallway.

Kenton sighed and pulled her into his arms. "This isn't how I envisioned bringing you home." He lowered his lips to hers. "Sorry."

As they stepped apart, Lettie stared into his eyes, miserable with grief. "The important thing is we're home and together."

"You're right." He drew a deep breath and let it out slowly. "Meet you upstairs. I'll move things around in my closet for you."

Her eyes widened. "What are we going to do about our stuff at the beach? Your car?"

"We'll figure that out tomorrow."

After Lettie and Mrs. Morley had settled her few things in Kenton's room, she went downstairs. Kenton was in the library, sipping a glass of red wine.

"Come have a seat," he said, indicating the empty wingback chair opposite him.

She did as he asked and then quietly accepted a glass of wine from him. Her thoughts whirled inside her head. *What was going to happen next? Would the inn have to be sold?* With Kenton leaving soon, there was no way she could run both the inn and the vineyard.

"I've asked Mrs. Morley to make us something light for supper," Lettie said. "I don't know about you, but I'm bone tired. Still, I should probably help her." She started to rise.

Kenton waved her back into her chair. "No, Lettie, you don't work here anymore."

"But ..."

He held up a hand to stop her. "It'll all be resolved soon. Dad told me some of his plans. We'll see exactly what he set in motion after Lew Barnes and Dad's accountant get here."

Her emotions barely under control, Lettie managed to speak. "Okay. Whatever you say."

A short while later, Mrs. Morley came to the door to the library. "I have a hot meal ready for the two of you. I thought it might be cozier for you in the kitchen, but if you want me to set places for you in the dining room, I can do that."

Kenton looked at Lettie. "Okay?" At her nod, he said, "The kitchen would be great. Thanks, Mrs. Morley."

Lettie sat at the kitchen table reminding herself that it was okay for Mrs. Morley to wait on her, that it was only proper. But she knew it would take a long time for her to feel it was right. She'd always been the one to wait on others.

After they'd finished their meal, Mrs. Morley said, "I'd better get on home to Pat. He'll come pay his respects tomorrow, Kenton. I suspect a lot of others who've been working here as well as friends from town will want to do that too."

"Thanks. Guess we'll have to set up some sort of a reception, but we'll talk about it later, after we meet with Mr. Barnes."

"Of course," Mrs. Morley said kindly, placing a hand on his shoulder. "See you tomorrow. Someday, we'll have a little celebration for the two of you." She gazed at Lettie and turned to Kenton. "My blessings to you both."

After Mrs. Morley left, Kenton turned to her. "Ready for bed?"

She rose from the table, set her water glass in the sink, and followed him out of the room.

Upstairs, in the bedroom she'd once cleaned, she undressed.

Before sliding on the nightgown she'd bought for her wedding night, Kenton came up behind her. "Don't," he whispered. "I want to feel your skin next to mine."

After preparing for bed, they each eased beneath the warm, soft comforter on Kenton's bed and faced one another.

Kenton reached out and stroked her cheek, gazing into her

eyes with such sorrow her heart clenched at the sight.

"I'm so sorry, Kenton. I truly am," she said before kissing him.

Kenton's arms wrapped around her tightly. Their kiss extended for several moments, a wordless sharing of grief that was more intimate than anything they'd experienced.

When they finally pulled apart, Kenton said, "I just want to lie here with you, to feel alive."

Understanding his need, Lettie fit her body to his shape and cuddled against him. Within minutes, with his head on her chest, he fell asleep. It was a long time before Lettie joined him. In a matter of days, she'd experienced her happiest moments, and now her saddest. Both Rex and Kenton had welcomed her into their lives. She'd never stop loving them.

The next morning, Lettie awoke to an empty bed. Puzzled, she listened for sounds of Kenton, but all was quiet. She slipped out of bed and went to the window. He was sitting on a bench in the small garden between the main house and the wing where his bedroom was.

On this cool December day, his breath came out in puffs of steam as he talked to himself.

Curious, Lettie slipped on a pair of jeans and a sweater and went downstairs. She let herself out a side door and walked into the garden.

Kenton lifted his head and smiled at her.

"What are you doing, honey?" she asked.

His grin was sheepish. "Just talking to my Dad. There were so many things I wanted to tell him." He held out his hand to her. "I wanted to tell him how happy you've made me."

With fresh tears threatening, Lettie came over to him, took his hand, and lowered herself onto the concrete garden bench beside him. "You're the one who's made me happy."

"I love you, Lettie," he said. "Dad knew it even before you did."

"I love you too, more than you'll ever know. But it's too cold for me out here. Come inside. I'll fix us a quick breakfast. It's going to be a busy day."

"Okay." He stood, and still holding her hand, followed her into the house that seemed so empty with Rex gone.

CHAPTER ELEVEN

A few days later, Lewis Barnes arrived at the inn. Instead of the tall, commanding figure Lettie expected to see, he stood at about five-eight, was on the pudgy side, and had wispy, light-brown hair. But his intelligent, gray eyes made it clear he was no fool. He studied her with unabashed curiosity as she was introduced to him.

"So, you're Lettie, the woman who captured Kenton's heart and Rex's too," he said, surprising her.

"Yes, sir, Mr. Barnes," Lettie replied, unsure if that was the correct response.

He waved her formality away. "Call me Lew. I look forward to knowing more about you." He turned to the man beside him. "And this is Bernie Randolph, Rex's accountant."

Lettie smiled politely. "Nice to meet you, Bernie. Kenton will be right down. He's changing his clothes."

"Where would you like us?" Bernie said. "I need to spread some papers around."

Lettie studied him. About the same size and in similar physical shape as Lew, he lacked Lew's burgeoning self-confidence and spoke softly. He brushed a hand through his dark curls and gazed at her somewhat shyly with dark eyes.

"Why don't we use Rex's office in the north wing of the house? I think you'll be comfortable there." Lettie still felt uneasy about using the family's quarters, but she wanted them to have privacy from neighbors, friends, and vineyard workers who were stopping by with casseroles and other food.

Lettie led the men into the office. Its off-white walls, long windows overlooking the garden, and simple stone fireplace were all part of a bright, open space in stark contrast to the dark library that Rex had preferred in the main house. A blue Oriental carpet with red and gold accents was offset by chairs on either side of a couch. They were covered in a small-print, navy fabric, which went well with the white-and-blue-checked fabric covering the couch that appeared both masculine and welcoming. Two red-leather chairs faced a large, glass-topped, wooden desk that sat in the middle of one wall and faced the entrance.

"This is great," said Lew. "Give us a few minutes, and we'll be ready to talk."

"May we bring you some coffee, tea, water, wine, anything?" Lettie asked.

Lew checked his large gold watch. "It's after noon, and we had lunch a few hours ago. How about a glass of wine?"

"Sounds good," said Bernie.

Kenton arrived, and while introductions were being made, Lettie slipped out of the room to find Mrs. Morley. She was in the kitchen talking with Rita Lopez. Their conversation stopped when they noticed her.

"Yes, what is it?" Mrs. Morley said.

"The men are going to share a bottle of wine. I was thinking we should offer them some food." Lettie stopped talking. There was no way she was going to ask Mrs. Morley to serve it.

"Oh, yes," said Mrs. Morley. "Good idea. How about I put together a cheese, cracker, and fruit plate for them?"

"That would be lovely. I can come back to pick it up, if you'd like," Lettie said.

"No, no," said Mrs. Morley. "Kenton and I agreed that you're not to be working at your old job now that you're his wife."

Lettie blinked in surprise. "But it's an awful lot of work for you, Mrs. Morley. Of course, I'll help you."

"Thanks, hon, but I'm thinking we'd better hire Paloma on a regular basis."

Unwilling to argue in front of Rafe's mother, Lettie said, "Sure. We'll talk about it."

Back in the office, Lettie sat down beside Kenton on the couch. "Mrs. Morley will bring in the glasses and a snack for us."

Kenton stood. "I'll get one of Dad's better wines out of the wine cellar. Be right back."

After he left the room, Lew spoke up. "Well, Lettie, lots of changes for you. I understand you were in foster care in Dayton, Ohio. I bet you're wondering how in the world you ended up here in the Willamette Valley."

"It sometimes feels like a dream," she said. "But when I saw the inn and stood on the porch looking out over the hills, I knew I'd found the home I was supposed to have all along. Of course, I never thought I'd be anything but the maid, but I didn't care. The land spoke to me, you know? The vines are like soldiers lined up ..." Thinking of what lay ahead for Kenton, she stopped, closed her eyes, and gripped her hands together. When she opened her eyes, the men were staring at her with concern. "Sorry," she said. "I sometimes talk too much. At least, that's what I've always been told."

Lew said, "Rex liked the fact that you were open with him, that you loved the land. How would you feel if the land were sold?"

Lettie swallowed hard. "I ... I don't know. It's not my land, but I hoped I could stay and work here. This place, this land means so much to me."

Lew's gray-eyed gaze pierced her, and then he smiled.

Kenton and Mrs. Morley returned to the room together.

Lettie rose to help Mrs. Morley find a place for the food, but she waved Lettie away, set the plate down on the table, and left the room. After Kenton had opened the wine and poured some into each of the four glasses, he lifted his glass and said in a shaky voice. "Here's to Rex Chandler!"

"Hear! Hear!" said Lew.

Bernie and Lettie raised their glasses and joined in the chorus of sad notes.

Lew cleared his throat. "The official reading of Rex's will is scheduled to take place a little later. But, I want to go over some of the details with you two beforehand. It's important that we all have a clear understanding of it."

Kenton and Lettie exchanged worried glances.

"First of all, Kenton, your father told me he talked with you about the future of Chandler Hill before he met with me a few weeks ago. It was his understanding that you had every intention of seeing the inn grow and succeed along with the development of the winery. Is that correct?"

"Yes," said Kenton. "Dad really pushed me on it, to make sure I was on board."

"And you, Lettie, now that you're married to Kenton, which Rex foresaw by the way, how do you feel about those plans? Living in the valley and working the inn and vineyards is not a glamorous life. Are you going to be okay with it?"

Lettie clasped her hands together. "It would be a dream come true."

Lew leaned forward. "Okay, then. The next question. What if something happens to Kenton? Would you be willing to do as both he and Rex wanted and stay here, completing their plans?"

She turned to Kenton and took his hand in hers. "I pray nothing happens to him."

"But if it does?" Lew said, pressing the issue.

"I can't imagine leaving here," said Lettie honestly. "It's like I'm supposed to be here. And when Rex's ashes are scattered here like he requested, he'd want me to stay. I know he would. For several evenings last summer and fall, he and I sat on the back porch together talking about many things. He even sometimes read poems aloud to me to keep his vocal cords in shape."

Lew sat back in his chair. His eyes remained on her, making her wish she'd taken more care readying herself for their visit. She, like Kenton, had been so grief stricken that she hardly cared what she wore or how she looked. She let out a long sigh and gazed out the window. She'd been as honest as she could be. Lew and the others would have to believe her or not.

"What's this all about?" Kenton said. "The will is the will, isn't it?"

"Yes, but I needed to be sure in my own mind that after knowing Lettie for so little time, Rex was right in wanting to include her in his sizeable estate. He wanted me to be as convinced as he was about the two of you carrying on his plans for Chandler Hill."

"And now?" Kenton challenged.

"And now I know Rex was right. The two of you will remain with the land. Because Rex hasn't worked in some time, most of his funds were sunk into this venture. He grew to hate Hollywood and never liked the idea of leaving money behind to be spent in any crazy fashion. His one marriage taught him how greedy, how careless people can be with other people's money."

"Yeah," scoffed Kenton. "My mother." He straightened. "She's not going to make a grab for this place, is she?"

Lew shook his head. "She has no legal grounds to do so. Now, I'm going to turn the meeting over to Bernie."

Bernie lifted a three-ring binder out of his briefcase. "I have here a complete set of plans for the Chandler Hill Inn, including plans for two more expansions. Rex had hoped to show these to you himself. His aim was to go from six guest rooms to thirty, a nice manageable number for a small, upscale property. Also included are his ideas for the construction of a tasting barn for the time when guests could come for a fabulous experience at the winery here on the property. Rex was well acquainted with how Napa and Sonoma are growing and envisioned the same thing happening here in the Willamette Valley. We have invested his money in such a way that his plans should be able to be completed over several years."

Kenton and Lettie went over to the desk and stood by Bernie. He opened his notebook, and like Christmas unfolding before them, the drawings of what Rex had envisioned spread in front of them like a gift. Lettie's heart thudded with excitement as she realized what an enormous amount of work had gone into the planning stages, from both architectural and financial points of view. Chandler Hill Enterprises, as the company had been named, was a big deal.

The thought of her ever running it alone sent acid to her stomach.

Bernie laid a hand on her arm. "Don't worry. Lew and I have been hired to guide you and Kenton through the process, should it be necessary."

"Good idea," said Kenton, studying the sheets of paper. "I've always been interested in the winemaking aspect, but I'm not interested in running an inn." He turned to Lettie. "Do you think you could learn to do that in addition to learning how best to grow the grapes?"

Lettie bobbed her head with more confidence than she felt. If Rex trusted them to carry on, she'd make sure to do her part, no matter what it was.

"We can go into this in more detail later," said Bernie. "In fact, in the time before you leave for boot camp, Kenton, we will spend many hours on this. For now, this is enough."

"I agree," said Lew. "I've asked José Lopez and Mrs. Morley to join us shortly for the official reading of the will."

"I'd better get another bottle of wine," Kenton said.

"And I'd better refresh the tray of food," said Lettie, needing a quiet moment with her husband. Things were happening so fast she was feeling dizzy.

Outside the office, Lettie took hold of Kenton's hand. "Are you okay? I know how sad you are."

"Dad had all kinds of ideas. I just wish he were still here to share them with us." His brow creased with concern. "Are you all right with how things have been set up? It's a lot for anyone to handle—this place, all the plans, everything."

"As long as you're around to help me, we'll manage."

A look of sadness crossed Kenton's face, touching her heart. "And if I'm not?" he whispered.

She threw her arms around him and hugged him. Maybe if she held him tight enough, he'd never leave her. A sudden chill made her shiver. No woman wants her man to go to war.

Mrs. Morley and Joe Lopez walked down the hall toward them. "Ah, the newlyweds!" Joe exclaimed, beaming at them.

Lettie felt her cheeks grow warm, but she smiled gamely.

"Yes, we mustn't forget in all this grief that a happy event has taken place," said Mrs. Morley.

"A very happy one." Kenton wrapped an arm around Lettie and gave her a quick kiss. He turned to them with a smile. "I'll be right back. I'm getting another bottle of wine. I think we're going to want it."

"And I'll get two more wine glasses," Lettie said quickly.

###

Later, after the reading of the will, Kenton refreshed their glasses with the wine he'd brought in for the occasion.

Mrs. Morley sat dabbing at her eyes. "I can't believe Mr. Rex set up a retirement fund for me and Pat." She turned to Joe. "Or that he gave you the land and the house you've been renting for years. What a wonderful man he was."

"He had great faith in the two of you," said Lew. "He hoped you'd continue to work at Chandler Hill if anything ever happened to him."

A niggling thought crept through Lettie's mind. "Oh my God! Do you think he had any idea that something like this was going to happen? It seems like he had plans for all of us."

Lew shook his head sadly. "We'll never really know, but I can tell you he had a sense of urgency to get his will in order. It's not all that unusual."

At the idea, Lettie's stomach turned. She gazed at Kenton. As soon as she had a moment alone with Lew, she'd ask him if he could pull any strings to get Kenton out of serving in the war in Vietnam.

Mrs. Morley got to her feet. "I'm going to fix dinner. And I don't think Mr. Rex would mind if we made it a quiet celebration of Kenton and Lettie's marriage."

"Why don't you ask your husband and Rita Lopez to join us, and we'll eat all together?" Lettie said.

Mrs. Morley gave her a dubious look. "I don't know if that's quite proper."

"You're all Dad's friends, Mrs. Morley," said Kenton with enough authority for her to give him a relenting nod.

Mrs. Morley prepared a couple of roast chickens and put together a menu that would challenge any holiday spread. Whipped potatoes, gravy, and stuffing accompanied the chicken, along with a bacon-and-green-bean casserole, a fresh, green-leaf salad with dried cranberries and pistachio nuts, and her famous apple pie.

"Excellent," said Lew, sitting back in his chair and patting his round stomach. "Rex said you had a knack for cooking. If this is an example, he was absolutely right."

"Yes, thank you so much, Mrs. Morley," said Lettie, touched by the effort she'd put into the meal. She'd even rearranged some of the flowers that had been sent to the house into a more suitable, winter-wedding bouquet for the table.

After dinner, as people rose, Lettie stayed behind to help clear.

Mrs. Morley placed a hand on her arm. "No, Lettie, you don't work here anymore."

Drawing on a strength she didn't know she had, Lettie gave her a steady look. "Mrs. Morley, we're all going to have to work together to make this right for Rex. That includes me."

"Okay," Mrs. Morley said. "You're right. But I still want to ask Paloma to help on a more permanent basis."

"I agree. I've got a whole lot to learn and won't be able to do everything I did before."

They studied one another a moment. Then Mrs. Morley said, "You're a good girl, Lettie. Rex thought so too."

Fresh tears stung Lettie's eyes.

CHAPTER TWELVE

Christmas was as dismal as any Lettie had known. Outside, a cold rain pelted the windows of the house like the tears she held inside. Knowing that Kenton would be leaving her soon made it even harder to inject some cheer into the holidays. But he'd said he wanted it to be a nice beginning for them, and she was doing her best to make it a good memory.

The one celebration that had always been present in her foster home at the holidays was the baking of Christmas cookies. No wasteful presents nor popular holiday songs were allowed in the household, but working with one's hands for the good of others was not only allowed but encouraged.

While Kenton was still sleeping, Lettie packed a tin with the cookies she'd set aside for one of his gifts. In going through some of Rex's things, she and Kenton had found a photograph of Rex and Kenton laughing as they stood together. When Kenton wasn't looking, she'd hidden it away. Now, it was inside a brown-leather frame, wrapped and under the tiny tree they'd finally decorated, along with a new wallet and a pair of work gloves Kenton had told her he wanted.

Lettie sat in her robe in the kitchen, sipping her coffee, thinking of holidays and how they never seemed to turn out the way anyone wanted. For her, she'd learned long ago that the magic others felt for them just didn't happen for her. She had no bitterness about it; she simply knew it to be true.

Kenton came downstairs wearing jeans and a Christmas sweater they both had agreed was awful. But Mrs. Morley had given it to him, and he'd promised her that he'd wear it on

Christmas Day.

"I'm going to grab a cup of coffee and do a quick errand. I'll be right back." He gave her a sly smile.

"Want me to go with you?"

"Definitely not," he said, chuckling softly.

She could feel a smile spreading across her face. "Is this about Christmas?"

"Definitely," he said, laughing harder.

He took her in his arms. "Ah, my Christmas angel. I'm so happy you're here with me. I don't know what I would do without you. You make everything seem better."

Kenton's lips pressed down on hers in a sweet, tender kiss that was equal to the nicest holiday gift she could think of. When they parted, they simply smiled at one another, content to be together like that for the moment.

He broke away. "I'd better get going. I promised Joe Lopez I'd see him first thing this morning." He poured coffee into a mug, took a few sips of it, and set the mug on the counter. "I'll hurry back, I promise."

After Kenton took off, Lettie headed upstairs to shower. Stepping into the bedroom she now shared with him, she studied her surroundings. The large room was more like a suite, with a separate sitting area overlooking the back garden and the valley beyond.

Lettie hurried into the bathroom to shower and get ready for the day.

Later, she was stirring pancake batter when she heard a car making its way up the driveway. She set down her spoon and hurried to the front window. Staring through the glass, Lettie frowned at the unfamiliar yellow car. They weren't expecting guests.

Kenton got out of the car and hurried up the front walk, carrying something under his coat.

Lettie met him at the front door. “What’s going on?”

Kenton’s eyes glowed with excitement. He opened his coat and held out a black, wiggly puppy to her.

She took the puppy in her arms and laughed as its pink tongue swiped her cheeks with warm, moist kisses. “Oh, puppy! You’re the sweetest thing ever!” She glanced at Kenton. “She’s mine? Really?”

“Merry Christmas, honey!” he said, beaming at her.

She tried to hug him but stopped when the puppy got between them. She set the dog down and wrapped her arms around Kenton. “Thank you. It’s the nicest, best Christmas gift I’ve ever received.”

At the sound of a tiny growl, she looked down. The puppy had grabbed hold of Lettie’s shoelaces and was tugging on them.

“Oh my! What a busy little girl,” crooned Lettie, picking the dog up. “Maybe that’s what we’ll call you. Busy.”

Kenton laughed. “Sure. Why not? Or just plain Bee.”

“Oh, I like that.” Lettie knelt and clapped her hands. “Hi, Bee! Come here.”

The puppy’s pink tongue hung out of its mouth as she stared at Lettie and then trotted off down the hallway toward the kitchen, squatted, and peed.

“Guess I have a lot to learn about puppies,” said Lettie. “But, Kenton, thank you so much.”

“I thought it would be nice for you to have some protection when I’m gone,” he said quietly. “She’s a good lab, from a respected breeder. She’s just ten weeks old and will grow quite quickly and eventually weigh about 75 pounds, maybe more.”

Some of Lettie’s earlier excitement faded. She’d gladly do without a puppy if she could keep Kenton.

“Shall we go eat?” Lettie said.

“Don’t you want to see your new car?” Kenton asked.

Lettie stared at him with disbelief. "New car? Are you kidding?"

The puppy ran toward her, and Lettie picked her up.

"Come on," said Kenton. "I've picked out a VW Squareback for you. You do know how to drive a stick shift, don't you?"

"Yes," said Lettie, "but I haven't driven one in a while." She looked beyond him to the yellow vehicle sitting in the parking area. Emotions raced through her at such a speed she couldn't do anything but stare at the car.

"Are you all right?" Kenton said.

"You bought a car for me?" she said, clapping her hands, unable to hide her incredulity. She thought back to the Christmas mornings she'd wished for anything that seemed the least bit personal.

Kenton's lips curved happily. "I'd buy you the moon, if I could. The best I can do is this yellow car. It reminds me of you, all sunny and warm."

He opened the front door. "Let's go take a look."

Lettie handed him Bee. As soon as she stepped outside, she began to run, laughing and crying as her feet hit the cold surface. Since marrying Kenton, it felt as if her whole world had changed from a life that seemed gray and empty to a lush, colorful one filled with love and kindness.

"What do you think?" Kenton said, approaching her as she traced the lines of the outside of the car, wanting to feel the cold metal beneath her fingers as if to test whether it was real or an illusion. Things like this happened to others.

"Go ahead and get inside, and then let's take a spin in it." He handed her the keys.

Lettie grinned. "Okay. Climb in."

Lettie slid behind the wheel and waited for Kenton and Bee to get settled in the passenger seat.

She turned the key, and the engine started right up.

"Take it up to the barn and back," Kenton suggested.

Trying to coordinate her feet between the clutch and the gas pedal, she moved the car forward with a lurch, and then the engine stalled.

"Try again," said Kenton. "You'll get the hang of it."

The third try proved to be the charm. Lettie drove to the barn and back with a new sense of confidence.

After she parked the car, Lettie patted the steering wheel. "This car is amazing. I can't believe you're giving it to me." She turned to Kenton. "Thank you! I'll never be able to tell you how much this means to me. It's so much more than the car itself. It's the whole idea of all the wonderful things you do for me."

Kenton gave her a satisfied smile. "I knew you'd like it. Now, how about breakfast? I'm starving."

Lettie leaned over and kissed him. "Coming right up."

As they walked toward the house, Bee ran in circles around them. Lettie clasped Kenton's hand in her own, thinking life had never seemed so good.

The days leading up to New Year's Eve were full of laughter as Bee filled the house with her playfulness, even as she made a full night's sleep impossible. Though Bee was very determined to try to worm her way into bed with them, Kenton wouldn't allow Lettie to succumb. He'd been warned about starting the relationship off right by exerting authority over the dog in a kind but firm way.

Wanting to keep sadness and worry away for as long as possible, Lettie and Kenton decided to put off the task of sorting through Rex's clothes and personal items until after the New Year. Instead, Kenton invited Lettie to go into Portland with him.

"I think you need some better clothes," he explained, looking a bit uncomfortable. "Let's look for a jacket for you and other things you might need."

Well aware that her wardrobe was sparse, Lettie hid her embarrassment. Though Kenton hadn't said it, she realized if she was going to be one of the owners of the inn, she had to be more presentable to guests.

The next day, Lettie and Kenton left Bee with Mrs. Morley and headed into Portland.

"I've made a list of things, like you asked," Lettie said, almost shyly. She still couldn't get used to the idea that she could simply buy what she needed.

"Good," said Kenton, sitting behind the wheel of his car. They'd paid a driver to bring it and the rest of their belongings back to Chandler Hill from California. "After we go shopping, I want to take you to one of my favorite restaurants for lunch." His eyes changed, became full of sadness. "Dad and I used to eat there every chance we could get."

Lettie reached over and squeezed his hand. "I think he'd like to know we'll carry on the tradition."

"Yeah, that, and starting a few of our own," said Kenton. His smile couldn't hide the sadness in his voice.

"Bee is already changing things around the inn," Lettie said brightly. "Everyone adores her."

"We'll have to introduce her to our guests carefully. Not everyone will like having a big dog around."

Kenton parked in the center of Portland, and they headed out on foot. Meier & Frank was the first stop, where Lettie quickly found a brown-corduroy, belted, double-breasted jacket. With Kenton's encouragement, she purchased a simple black dress, a navy skirt, and gray slacks. As he guided her toward conservative choices, Lettie began to understand that fads would come and go, but conservative, classic clothing of high quality would last and always be in fashion.

She selected a number of sweaters and blouses that seemed suitable to the selections she'd already made, gaining more approval from Kenton.

"Let's go to lunch," he said, after she'd made the last of her purchases. "Huber's isn't far, and I'm hungry for their turkey pie."

They dropped off the bags of new clothes into the trunk of his car and then walked the few blocks to the restaurant. The sun that had beckoned to her that morning was now hidden behind clouds. The crisp air felt good to Lettie as she enjoyed the warmth of her new jacket.

Gold lettering on the window announced they were at Huber's, founded in 1879. They stepped beneath the dark awnings at the entrance and into the restaurant, which was alive with conversation from the crowded tables. Kenton asked the host to seat them in the bar, and as they were led to the room in back, Lettie studied every detail.

In the bar, wood paneling covered the walls more than half-way up from the floor. But it was the arched, stained-glass skylights that drew and captured her attention. She mentioned it to the host, and he smiled. "Ah yes, everyone is always curious about them. The yellow and amber skylights were made by the Povey Brothers Studio. Note the terrazzo floors. They go all the way back in time too. They're almost one hundred years old."

The waiter seated them at a table in the center of the room, giving Lettie a chance to look around. Seeing the way people here were conservatively dressed, Lettie was glad Kenton had helped her choose her new clothes. She realized now how sheltered she'd been, how unsophisticated she still was.

"Turkey is the specialty here. And Spanish coffee too. Though, you're too young to order that." Kenton gave her a devilish grin. "But if I order it, you could have a taste."

She laughed. "I'll be fine without it."

Later, leaving the restaurant, the thought of going back to Chandler Hill was enticing.

"Are you sure you don't want to stay in the city?" Kenton asked, throwing an arm around her shoulder.

She smiled up at him. "I'm ready to go home."

A grin split his face. He gave her a quick kiss on the cheek. "Who knew I'd fall for a homebody?"

"Do you mind? I don't want to take any fun away from you."

"Are you kidding? You're the fun for me. The truth is, I'm pretty much a quiet kind of guy. Mrs. Morley says I'm an old soul. Not one of the hippie types at all."

Lettie had liked that about him. Maybe she was an old soul too.

Back at the house, while they snuggled on the couch, Kenton proved to her that he wasn't old at all. And, apparently, neither was she.

CHAPTER THIRTEEN

The days following the holiday were quiet at the inn but filled with activity on the homefront. Rafe and Maria left for California, Lettie and Mrs. Morley packed up Rex's clothes and the personal belongings that Kenton wanted donated to charity, and Kenton and Bernie Randolph went through Rex's office, sorting through papers, setting up a filing system that both Kenton and Lettie could easily use, and shredding papers that were of no importance.

Then, Bernie, Kenton, and Lettie went over the plans Rex had left behind, coming up with a practical schedule they all agreed on. Adding a wing to the inn was the first thing on the list. They estimated that if the project were begun in the spring, it wouldn't be completed for at least six months, after which time they hoped to have a crop of grapes good enough to sell to one of the other wineries nearby.

With the income from the inn, they hoped in another year to build a small winery. Then they could begin winemaking on their own from next year's crop.

"There are many variables here," said Bernie, studying them thoughtfully. "It's good to make as many plans as is reasonable so you have options, and then take it one day at a time." His gaze rested on Kenton. "A lot will depend upon your survival."

Kenton stared at Bernie and then quickly averted his gaze to focus on something in the garden outside.

Lettie could feel her mouth go dry. She knew they were all thinking of Kenton's military service.

Bernie's departure two days after his post-New Year arrival brought a new quiet to the inn. The January weather, cold and rainy, added to the gloom inside. Kenton was due to report for his physical at a processing center in downtown Portland in two days. Lettie tried not to think about it, but neither she nor Kenton could help worrying.

Too soon, the time they were dreading arrived. As ordered, Kenton packed a bag in preparation for his visit to the induction center in Portland. There, he would have a physical and be sworn in. Then, he would, most likely, be sent to Fort Ord in California for Basic Training and then probably AIT—Advanced Infantry Training.

Though her nerves pulsed through her body in anxious rhythm, Lettie did her best to put on a brave front as she drove Kenton into Portland.

"Remember everything Bernie and I told you," Kenton said. "And if you need any legal help, Lew is ready to step in. The plans are carefully laid out. It's just a matter of following them." The tense tone in Kenton's voice sent worry racing through her like a frightened rabbit. He was usually so calm, so sure.

Outside the building where he was to report, Lettie put every bit of love she felt for him into the kiss they shared.

Kenton abruptly pulled away. His eyes glistened. "Guess I'd better get inside."

He got out, opened the door to the back, retrieved his bag, and headed into the building, his steps hitting the pavement with determination.

The tears Lettie had held back now blurred her vision as she pulled into traffic for the lonely ride home.

A part of her wished that Kenton had pulled every string he

could to get out of reporting for duty. But she'd learned he was a man who stuck to his principles of wanting to do the right thing. After two separate arguments about it, they'd resolved not to talk about it anymore.

Back at the inn, Bee greeted her with excited yips and wagged her tail so hard that her hind legs slipped out from under her. Laughing, Lettie hugged the dog and accepted warm licks on the cheeks from her.

"How'd it go?" asked Mrs. Morley when Lettie entered the house.

"He's there," Lettie said despondently.

"Well, if it's any comfort to you, there might be a chance he won't go to Vietnam if during his testing, they discover something special he can do. The Hartman boy ended up staying in California to teach at some military school there."

"Thanks for trying to cheer me up," said Lettie. "We'll see." She held no hope for such a thing. Kenton was the kind of guy who wanted to do as much as anyone else for his country.

That evening, alone in the house, Lettie was glad for Bee's company. The dog, young as she was, sensed Lettie's loneliness and stuck to her side.

When the phone rang, Lettie jumped with surprise, and then hurried to answer it.

"Lettie? It's Kenton. Can't talk long. Just wanted to let you know that I'm on my way to Fort Ord and might not be in touch for a while. God! I miss you already."

"Me too," said Lettie, trying to sound brave.

"Things are chaotic, but I'm told that after Basic Training, things should be a little clearer."

Lettie heard shouting in the background and then the phone went silent.

###

After six long, lonely weeks had gone by, Lettie got a call from Lew Barnes. She and her lawyer exchanged pleasantries, and then Lew said, "I've found someone who can do some consulting with you. She's a young woman, a graduate from the College of Hotel Administration at the University of Nevada, Las Vegas, and the daughter of an associate of mine. While the inn is empty, it might be a good time for her to come and stay for a while and coach you on running an inn or a small hotel. What do you say?"

"I like the idea. If we're going to do a good job for Rex and Kenton, we're going to need all the help we can get. And this is a good time with little activity in the vineyard."

"Good," said Lew. "I'm glad you see it that way. Her family has been in the hotel business for some time, and she wants to break into the business herself. In the meantime, she has a lot of information she can share."

"Who is this person?" Lettie asked.

"Her name is Abigail Wilkins."

Lettie could feel her eyes widen. "Is she related to Adelaide Wilkins?" In San Francisco, Lettie had watched a television special about the successful owner of the Bradley Wilkins hotel chain. Dubbed the Leona Helmsley of the West, she was the woman everyone hated.

"I understand she's a niece by marriage and born to an estranged brother of Adelaide's husband. So, there's not a lot of affection or interaction between them."

"Oh, that's good," said Lettie, her mind racing. "With the inn empty, why doesn't Abigail come here for a few days?"

"Great. I'll get in touch with her and let you know. Everything else okay?"

"Kenton is still at boot camp, so it's been very quiet here. But, he's coming home on leave in another two weeks and then he'll have to return to Fort Ord for Advanced Infantry

Training. Mrs. Morley is thinking of retiring. I'll be looking for someone to take her place. Right now, we don't need anyone like her because the inn isn't booked."

"Okay, keep in touch. Talk to you later."

After Lettie hung up the phone, she walked onto the back porch and stared out at the scenery below. The rolling hills were dusted with a coating of snow, like sugar on cakes. Some of the older people in the area were declaring this an unusually cold and snowy winter. Though there was a dampness to the cold air, it didn't seem as bad to Lettie as winters in Ohio. Or perhaps she felt that way because the inn was her cozy and warm home.

When Lettie went back inside, she walked into what was once Rex's office and took a seat behind the desk, thinking of the responsibility on her shoulders. The phone rang.

Lettie picked it up. "Hello?"

"Is this Lettie Chandler?" asked a husky female voice.

"Yes?"

"This is Abby Wilkins. I understand from Mr. Barnes that you're interested in hiring me to consult with you about the inn you own. Is that right?"

"Yes," said Lettie, intrigued by the voice, the confident way she conducted herself.

"I'm free. I'm wondering if this is a good time for me to look at the place?"

"Yes. At this time of year, we're not busy. The weather isn't good, and there's not much going on with the grapes."

"Perfect. I'm meeting with someone in Portland tomorrow. After that, I'll drive on down to your place. You're right outside McMinnville, right?"

"Yes. If you ask almost anyone in town, they can direct you to Chandler Hill."

###

The next afternoon, Lettie paced back and forth in the inn's living room where she could watch through the front windows for anyone approaching. After spending nights alone in the big house, the idea of having someone like Abigail Wilkins staying at the inn was pleasing.

At last, Lettie saw a small, black car making its way up the road.

"Here she comes, Bee!" Lettie said to the dog, who wagged her tail and barked.

As the car pulled to a stop in the parking area, Lettie hurried outside to greet her guest.

She approached and then waited for Abigail to get out of the car. Moments later, Lettie stared up at the tall figure who rose to stand before her.

"Hi! Welcome to Chandler Hill," Lettie said, studying the tall, dark-haired beauty. Her facial features were defined by high cheekbones, startling, tawny-colored eyes, and a wide mouth that easily curved into a smile.

"I'm Abby Wilkins. You must be Lettie." Abby held out a hand and Lettie shook it, wincing a little at Abby's tight squeeze.

"Oh, sorry," said Abby. "I'm used to meeting with men who put a lot of energy into their handshakes. Apparently, it's important to them." She stood next to her car and gazed at the façade of the inn.

"Beautiful," she murmured.

"Let me take your bags," said Lettie, keeping Bee at bay. "This pesky puppy is Bee. She's just over five months old and is still being trained."

"Aw, very cute," Abby said, giving Bee a pat on the head that made her entire body wiggle.

As they walked to the front door of the inn, Lettie studied Abby's flared trousers and double-breasted suit jacket. Made of a tweed fabric, the outfit looked anything but masculine on her, yet gave her a business presence she admired.

Inside, Lettie led Abby upstairs to one of her favorite guest rooms, one that overlooked the rolling hills and valley below.

Abby looked around the room. "Very nice. I hadn't expected anything quite so upscale."

"Rex wanted to make our guests feel pampered."

"Good," said Abby, nodding with satisfaction. "That's something we can use in our advertising campaign. Lew Barnes said we were going to work on a long-term plan for building business."

"Yes, that's what we're hoping to do," said Lettie. "Any help you can give us will be appreciated."

Abby stood back and studied Lettie. "I'm so glad Mr. Barnes called me. I don't know him very well, but he and my father sometimes play golf together."

"I'll leave you to get comfortable," said Lettie. "We're very casual around here. No need to get dressed up." Her cheeks grew warm at the shy admission. "But I love the pantsuit you're wearing."

Abby grinned. "It's my power suit."

Downstairs, Lettie set out a plate of cheese and crackers and pulled a bottle of wine from the rack in the wine closet.

Abby came into the kitchen. "Anything I can do for you?"

Lettie shook her head. "I'm not much of a cook. Mrs. Morley made a casserole for us."

"Sounds good. Don't worry about cooking while I'm here. My mother's maiden name is Agnolli, and both she and Grandma Agnolli made sure I can cook. They told me I'd never get a man if I didn't know how to fill his stomach with good, Italian food. Gloria Steinem would roll her eyes at that, I'm sure." She laughed, and Lettie joined in.

Lettie lit the fireplace in the library, and the two of them basked in its glow. Bee slept at Lettie's feet.

Abby was easy company, answering Lettie's questions about her life with fun-filled stories.

Hearing her speak in such a knowledgeable way, Lettie vowed to listen carefully to everything Abby said. She'd never met anyone so comfortable in her own skin or so adept at dealing with men in business.

As they sat down to dinner, Lettie was impressed by Abby's ease in the kitchen as she added salt and pepper to her meal and talked about the chicken piccata she prepared at home in L.A.

"How long have you known Kenton?" Abby asked her. "A friend of mine used to date him a couple of years ago. It didn't work out, but she said he's a nice guy."

"I met him in June. He made me a sandwich then offered me a job here at Chandler Hill."

"Wow! You guys moved fast!" Abby gave her an appraising look. "But I can see why he was so attracted to you. After the way the girls can be in L.A., you must have seemed like a breath of fresh air to him."

"I sometimes can't believe we're married. It happened so quickly." The memory of their wedding in the Las Vegas chapel brought a smile to her face. "I'm glad, though."

"So, tell me a little about your background." Abby wiped her mouth with her napkin and sat back in her chair.

Lettie told her about the family who'd raised her, her wishes to get away from Ohio, and how she'd reacted to her first sight of the inn and the rolling hills around it.

"Running an inn takes a lot of hard work, but it sounds as if you're already used to that," said Abby. "That's good. How are you with math and numbers?"

Lettie shrugged. "Okay, I guess."

"Well then, tomorrow we'll start with the basics of running

an inn, then we'll move on to running the numbers. I understand Bernie Randolph will be your accountant, but you need to understand the numbers yourself. Sound good?"

"Sounds a little scary," Lettie admitted. She knew she and Kenton were lucky to have inherited the inn and vineyards, but it meant she'd be tied to them for the rest of her life—a thought that sometimes worried her. Yet, she didn't want to let Rex or Kenton down.

CHAPTER FOURTEEN

For the next ten days, Lettie felt as if she was in school again. Abby was full of energy and liked to move at a fast pace. Once or twice, Lettie announced she needed to take a break, and the two of them would go outside and walk the hills. Then it was Lettie's turn to show Abby what she'd learned from Rex, Joe, and others about growing grapes.

At this time of year, Joe and his nephew Rico were sometimes in the fields checking the vines for damage and, where needed, building up soil at the base of the plants to protect them against freezing.

When it came time for Abby to leave, Lettie was both sad and relieved. Sad because she'd miss the young woman who knew so much and gladly shared her knowledge and friendship. But she was feeling overwhelmed, exhausted, and sometimes nauseous over the responsibility of the inn and vineyards in addition to worrying about Kenton.

After Abby left, Lettie cleaned her guest room and then went through the inn and house putting it back in order. As Abby had told her, the inn had to be ready to receive guests at any time.

More importantly, Kenton would be coming home on leave! It would only be for a short time. The administration in Washington, D.C. had requested a two-year extension of the draft, making Kenton's chances of avoiding going to Vietnam next to none. More men were needed.

Lettie crossed off each of the following days on the kitchen calendar with growing excitement. She could hardly wait until

Kenton would hold her in his arms again.

On the day Kenton was to be released from boot camp, he called her from California. "Hi, sweetie! I'm on my way! I caught a ride with a buddy I met here who lives outside Seattle. I'm helping him drive so we'll get there as fast as we can."

"Be careful," Lettie said. "Can't wait to see you!"

"See you soon. Love you!"

"Love you too!" Smiling, Lettie hung up the phone and went back to work, her heart singing with excitement.

She'd just finished cleaning when Mrs. Morley called. "Are you going to be all right? Pat and I are going to visit our daughter in Seattle for a few days. Pat heard there was a winter storm on the way. You'd better stock up on food."

"Thanks, I'm going to the store today to get ready for Kenton's visit. Have fun with your family."

"You too. Enjoy having that handsome husband of yours home for a while."

Lettie hung up the phone and pulled out a pen and paper from the desk drawer. She went through the items in the cupboards and the refrigerator, adding what she needed to her growing grocery list. Then she went upstairs to check on the status of things in the bathroom.

It wasn't until she searched the cupboard beneath the bathroom sink that she realized she hadn't needed any sanitary napkins or tampons for quite some time.

Gasping with dismay, she sat on the edge of the bathtub and started counting back. Almost three months had come and gone. *Oh my God!*

She closed her eyes and let out a shaky breath. How stupid of her not to realize what was happening. She'd thought her sore nipples were because of the lovemaking that she and Kenton had enjoyed, and she'd attributed her infrequent bouts of nausea to worry over him. She crossed her arms over her stomach and fought tears. She didn't want a baby. Not now. Maybe later when life was a little more settled.

As if responding to such unwelcoming thoughts, her stomach turned, and she threw up in the toilet. Later, sitting back on her heels, patting her mouth, Lettie couldn't stop the flow of tears from streaking down her face. At the moment, the thought of having the care of a baby on top of handling the inn and vineyard was overwhelming. And what if Kenton wasn't ready to be a father?

Later, as she was putting away the groceries, her phone rang. Warily, she picked it up.

"Hello?"

"Hi, Lettie. This is Rico. Joe wanted me to tell you that I'll be staying in the cabin for the next couple of nights. A winter storm advisory is out, and he's asked me to take care of the animals for him. We just wanted to give you fair warning."

"Thank you so much," Lettie said with feeling. With Kenton finally coming home, the last things she wanted to worry about were the animals. The chickens she could handle, but the thought of being responsible for feeding and milking the cows was intimidating.

Eating alone in the kitchen that night, Lettie reviewed much of what Abby had told her about supply and demand, financial forecasting, standing out in a crowd. Her mind was still spinning when she heard the sound of a car coming up the driveway.

She ran to the window. An unfamiliar car was pulling to a stop in front of the inn.

It wasn't until she went to the door and looked out that she saw the dome on top of the car. She stared at it with a growing sense of shock. Why would a trooper be coming to the inn? But when the state trooper headed her way with purpose, she gripped the molding around the door with numb fingers.

"Mrs. Lettie Chandler?" the trooper said.

"Yes. What do you want?" she managed to say in a mouth gone dry.

The trooper took hold of her arm. "Here, let me help you out of the cold." He led her inside to one of the couches in the living room.

"Is this about Kenton?" Lettie asked, already feeling a knot inside her stomach.

"I'm so sorry, Mrs. Chandler. There's been an accident south of here and the car he was riding in went off the road. Neither he nor the driver survived."

Lettie collapsed on the couch and began sobbing. "No! No! Kenton was coming home to me." She lifted her tear-streaked face to him. "We were going to be together. I was going to tell him about our baby."

The trooper took a seat at the far end of the couch and studied her with sympathy. "Is there someone I can call for you?"

Lettie shook her head. She couldn't bear to see anyone else. Then she'd be forced to explain it to them and the truth of what had happened to Kenton would be all too real.

"I really don't think I should leave you alone at a time like this," said the trooper, who appeared to be not much older than she.

"A hired hand is staying in the cabin on the property. If I need anything, he'll come. Right now, I need to be alone."

The trooper stood. "Again, my sincere condolences. Someone from my headquarters will check on you tomorrow. She'll help with any arrangements you may want to make."

Staggering, feeling as if she were in a nightmare, Lettie

walked him to the door and watched in a daze as he walked away. Whimpering softly, she closed and locked the door behind him, wishing she could just as easily shut out the truth he'd dared to bring her.

She stumbled back to the couch and threw herself down on it, crying so hard to could hardly catch her breath.

Sitting at her feet, Bee lifted her dark, furry head and yowled. Lettie didn't realize at first that the little puppy was simply echoing her own howls of anguish.

Sometime later, eyes heavy and swollen from endless tears, she rose from the couch and numbly headed upstairs to the bedroom she and Kenton had joyfully shared.

She took Kenton's bathrobe out of the closet, and without changing her clothes, she slid beneath the covers on the bed. Turning on her side, she brought Kenton's robe to her nose and inhaled the lingering scent that was his alone.

No-o-o-o! her mind screamed. *It can't be true! He wouldn't leave me. He promised to love and protect me all my days.*

"Why? Why? Why?" she wailed, sending Bee under the bed in terror.

Painful silence surrounded her.

She pounded the pillow, furious that Kenton hadn't come home to her. Then she began to cry again at the thought of him suffering.

Exhausted, she lay back among the pillows. The wind had picked up and sleet was tapping against the windows like the long-nailed finger of a monster wanting to get inside.

Too tired even to close the drapes, she turned her back to the window and pulled the quilt above her head. *Maybe*, she thought in desperation, *I'll die in bed and won't have to face the future without Kenton.*

CHAPTER FIFTEEN

The next morning, Lettie heard the sound of knocking at the door but couldn't make herself move out of bed to answer it.

Next, she heard the sound of someone in the kitchen. *Paloma!*

Lettie forced herself to her feet and went to the doorway. She opened her mouth to call out to her, but Paloma was already running up the stairs to reach her.

"Lettie! Lettie! I heard the news! It's all over town. I'm so sorry!" Paloma's arms wrapped around her.

Giving in to the sorrow that made her heart want to stop, Lettie settled in her embrace and let more tears come.

Over the next couple of days, Paloma remained a constant companion, listening to Lettie rail against the army, fate, and whatever else she could blame. It was she who stood by her side as she went through the agonizing moments of receiving condolences from staff and townspeople.

Mrs. Morley hovered nearby, ready to step in at any moment.

And later, when it was warm enough, Lettie took a shovel to the earth in the grove of trees where they'd buried Rex's ashes and buried the container of ashes that was all she had left of Kenton.

"There," she told Paloma and Mrs. Morley. "Kenton can rest beside his father." It seemed only right that the two of them remain part of the land they loved.

As the baby grew inside her, Lettie often made the trip to

the grove of trees to talk to Kenton and Rex about the mantle of responsibility she'd taken on as she'd promised them.

In June, the ground was broken for the addition of the wing to the inn right on schedule. But as exciting as it was to others, Lettie saw it as another burden.

And when, in August, it came time for her to give birth to the baby Kenton would never see, Lettie had to draw on an inner strength to see it through.

Paloma stood at her side when she struggled to bear down as the nurse suggested. "You can do this, Lettie."

"I can't," she protested. "Kenton should be here."

"Mrs. Chandler, one more big push," commanded the nurse.

Suddenly there was a cry and within moments a baby was placed atop Lettie.

"A beautiful baby girl" cried Paloma. "A friend for Isabel."

The joy that should have been there was missing as the nurse held up the baby so Lettie could better see her. Warring emotions filled Lettie. This was Kenton's child. She couldn't get past the idea that in the past few months life had taken away those she loved. Maybe it would be best not to get too close to this little one. Maybe it would be better that way.

Later, as Lettie fingered her daughter's dark, straight hair and checked all ten toes, she wondered how she could carry on with the growth of the inn while trying to become a good mother. She was only a young, inexperienced nineteen-year-old with way too much to handle.

One August day, Lettie held her baby in her arms and wished she knew how to make her more comfortable. Autumn Ann Chandler seemed to know she was part of an unhappy circumstance. She fisted her tiny hands and screamed even as

Lettie tried to comfort her. Lettie had named the baby Autumn because autumn had been the happiest time of her life. But this fussy little girl chose not to honor the choice of her name.

"There, there," said Paloma, taking Autumn from Lettie's arms. With two children of her own, Paloma seemed to know exactly what to do with the screaming baby because, in seconds, Autumn stopped crying and lay in Paloma's arms, looking up at her with interest.

Lettie let out a frustrated sigh. "I'm not very good at being a mother. I think Autumn knows I wasn't ready to be a mom, especially with Kenton gone." She sighed again. "I just feel so lost, so tired, so helpless. I'm afraid I'll never be able to do a good job with this baby of ours." Lettie's lips quivered.

"You'll be just fine." Paloma gave Lettie a sympathetic smile. "You have a lot going on at the moment. Maybe later, when things are more settled, it'll be easier on both of you."

"I've got a bottle warming in the kitchen," said Lettie with resignation. Nursing the baby was not working that well. "Could you feed her? I've got to meet with the construction crew to go over today's progress."

"Okay, I understand." Paloma took the baby and rocked her in her arms, quietly shushing her as they left the room.

Left alone in the bedroom she'd moved into following Kenton's death, Lettie got to her feet and stared out the window at the rows of grapes lining the hills in even stripes. Breathing easier now, Lettie thought back to the months of despair she'd barely survived. Mrs. Morley, Paloma, and Lew Barnes had worked together to pull her out of her depression by forcing her to follow Rex's plans for expanding Chandler Hill.

Now, Mrs. Morley had retired, Paloma had taken over for her, and Lew had taken to calling on a regular basis to check on the construction of the new wing of the house.

Never having had many friends growing up, Lettie treasured her friendship with Paloma. She was the mother, the sister, the friend she'd always wanted. In return, Paloma was grateful for the chance to be the capable, creative person she was, not simply the mother and wife everyone expected her to be.

Lettie held a hand to a glass window pane, as if she could reach beyond it to the grove of trees in the distance. "I have a confession to make to you, Kenton. I'm not a very good mother. I'm a lot more comfortable with the inn and vineyard than I am trying to parent a baby. I try. Honest. But it doesn't seem to be working." She drew a breath and let it out. "But the vineyards did well. We sold a crop of grapes to a winery down the valley. And at the inn we're moving forward with twenty-four new guest rooms, as you wanted. I think you're both going to like it."

"Who's going to like what?" Paloma said, coming into the room. The baby was asleep in her arms.

Lettie felt her cheeks grow hot. "I think Kenton and Rex will be pleased with the new addition. It's coming along nicely."

Paloma smiled. "I think so too."

It was one thing for everyone associated with the inn to believe she was in charge. It was quite another to convince the construction crew. Lettie had had more than one face-off with the construction boss, a tall man named Bert Hillman, who insisted upon looking down at her short stature with something between a sneer and a leer.

On this particular day, Lettie discovered that Bert had gone ahead with a change to the layout of the walls which meant that a small alcove designated for shelving in each room was covered instead of being exposed.

"You know this needs to be done according to the specs, Bert," said Lettie. "These areas will need to be redone so we can install the shelving intended to be there."

Bert hefted his pants and shook finger at her. "Listen, I've been building houses in these parts for many years, and I'm telling you it's a waste of space."

"A space that we'll put to good use," Lettie countered, forcing herself to stand up to him. "It's part of the plan that was approved. I did not approve your changes, so please go back and rebuild according to the specs."

She felt a familiar tug in her breast and realized her milk was coming in. Rather than stay and face the humiliation of any leakage, she said sharply, "Just do it."

As she left, she heard one of the workers say, "Guess the little lady told ya, Bert."

It was those kinds of comments that made things more difficult. But each time she thought of backing away from an argument, she remembered Kenton's and Rex's faith in her, and she stood her ground.

Weeks later, when the wing was finally finished, she was glad she'd worked hard to be strong with the crew. It was every bit as wonderful as Rex had envisioned.

The rooms were light and airy, every space put to good use. Best of all, the rooms had beautiful views over the back hills, or if they faced the front, had a view of the long, winding road and fields that led to the inn.

Lettie stood at the front door of the inn greeting the first of her special guests staying in the new wing to celebrate the inn's first Thanksgiving weekend.

"Lew, so glad you and Emily could make it," Lettie said graciously. "This celebration wouldn't be the same without you." Her relationship with the lawyer was one she treasured. He'd always supported and encouraged her.

"Thanks. Bernie and his wife, Debbie, are on their way," said Lew. "And I heard Abby Wilkins is coming too."

"Yes." Bernie continued to serve as her accountant, and when she'd talked to his wife on the phone, she'd seemed pleasant. And Abby? She couldn't wait to see her.

"Abby's been a big support for me working on the advertising campaign. Without her help, I'm not sure we'd get anyone here."

"She's very capable," Lew said. "I'm glad her consulting is working out nicely for you."

"Mrs. Chandler?'

Lettie turned And faced an unfamiliar woman.

"I'm Susan Connell from *The Oregonian.*" An older woman with gray hair, Susan's blue eyes snapped with intelligence as she held out her hand. "I'm happy to be here. Such a lovely idea to include someone from the media like me to spread the word about your new operation in the valley. The growth here is quite exciting. You must be pleased to be a part of it."

"Yes. My father-in-law felt Chandler Hill was going to be the beginning of many such places."

"It's amazing that this is all in your hands now. As Abby Wilkins reminded me, that's a story unto itself. One I'd like to do. We don't see many women taking the helm of businesses."

"I have a lot of support, believe me." Lettie wasn't about to tell Susan or anyone else that sometimes she wished she could walk away from overseeing the inn, that it was the grapes that interested her. She'd hardly been available during the picking season and overseeing the harvest. And the guilt she felt about not spending time with her baby was another issue.

Just then, Abby arrived with a friend. “Excuse me, we’ll talk later,” she said to the reporter.

Smiling, Lettie hurried over to her. “Hi, Abby! I’m so glad you’re here. So far, everyone who reserved a room has shown up. It’s going to be a very busy holiday.”

“That’s why I brought Terri.” Abby returned Lettie’s hug and turned to her friend with a smile. “Lettie Chandler, meet Terri Hadley. A *special* friend of mine.”

Lettie studied the young woman standing close to Abby. Of average height and thin, Terri was striking with her short, brown hair, fine features and dark eyes that sparkled with a sense of fun. Abby and Terri smiled at one another.

Ah, is that how it is? Lettie thought, giving Terri a welcoming hug.

“I’ve put you in the room in the main house where you stayed last time,” Lettie told Abby. “I hope you don’t mind.”

“Perfect. I’ve told Terri all about the Chandler Hill Inn, and I’m anxious for her to love it as much as I do. In fact, she’s going to help me in the kitchen, like I promised.”

“Are you sure you don’t mind? Paloma was concerned about handling this crowd, and when I told her that you offered to help, she was relieved.”

“I’m sure, all right. And if things go well, I have some other ideas for the inn.” Abby gave her a teasing grin that brought a laugh out of Lettie.

“Great.”

“Where’s the sweet little baby of yours?” Abby asked. “I’ve told Terri about her too.”

“She’s with her nanny, but I’m sure you’ll see a lot of her over the weekend. Bee, too. The dog stays right with Autumn. It’s cute.”

After showing Abby and Terri to their room, Lettie headed downstairs to the kitchen.

"How are things going?" Lettie asked Paloma.

"I've set out cookies, cheese and crackers, and fresh fruit in the dining room and in the reception area in the new building. Guests can help themselves anytime."

"Good. Abby is here with her friend. They seem excited about working with you to prepare the Thanksgiving meal."

"I'm so glad," said Paloma. "Elisa is doing fine with the cleaning, but she's no help in the kitchen."

Lettie and Paloma exchanged smiles. Friends from grade school, Elisa and Paloma were as different as they could be. Paloma was organized and a steady worker. Elisa tended to be flighty and worked in bursts of energy.

Thanksgiving morning, Lettie rose and quietly dressed, eager to have a few moments alone before the demands of the day and her guests took over.

Stepping outside into the cool air, she drew in its freshness and studied the sky. A beautiful shade of blue, its color would deepen as the day unfolded. As she headed toward the grove of trees where Rex's and Kenton's ashes were buried, Bee raced ahead of her and then circled back to make sure she was following. By now, the dog was well acquainted with Lettie's routine morning visits to the grove, some of which included Lettie bringing little Autumn with her. Others might consider her foolish, but Lettie enjoyed her "talks" with Rex and Kenton. She swore those talks gave her a better sense of what she needed to do to make the inn and vineyards the successful operation they'd envisioned.

When she got back to the house, several of the guests were already in the dining room eating breakfast. She greeted each one and then went into the kitchen for a cup of coffee before checking on the baby. Paloma's mother, Dolores, had taken on the duty of full-time nanny.

"How are things here?" Lettie asked, observing Paloma, Abby, and Terri working together on the breakfast meal.

"You're going to need a bigger kitchen," said Abby, carefully moving around Paloma who stood at the sink.

"I've already talked to Bernie and Lew about it," Lettie said. "We're thinking of converting the back bedroom and bath to additional kitchen space."

"Good idea. The quiet months are coming up. That would be a good time to do a lot of the work," said Abby.

"Yes, I know." Lettie liked the fact that Abby was so invested in making the inn work. "But we're not going to expand the dining room. We'll have separate seating times or put in additional tables for meals when necessary. Like today."

"It's exciting to see so many people here," said Paloma.

"It's a lovely place," Terri said. "From a distance one would think the addition had always been part of the house. It's that well designed."

"Thanks," said Lettie. "It's pretty much the way Rex wanted it. In time, more additions will be made to the property."

"What about the cabin?" Abby asked her, turning to them.

"We're still thinking about how to best use it."

"I have an idea. Let's talk later," said Abby.

"Okay," Lettie quickly agreed. "Now, if you'll excuse me, I want to make sure everyone has enough to eat."

"More eggs and bacon coming up." Terri followed Lettie out of the room with a platter of food.

As Lettie went about talking to guests, refilling coffee cups, and making sure Elisa and her new cleaning crew were set to begin working, she realized how much extra work was involved with the additional rooms. Going from six guest rooms to thirty changed everything. She and Paloma would have to sit down together and address the issue. And while Abby was at the inn, Lettie intended to talk to her about a number of things, including staffing. She drew in a long breath. At times like this, Lettie felt as if she'd been thrown into a fast-rushing river, leaving her survival up to chance as much as to her own determination.

That afternoon, Lettie stood at the doorway to the dining room and surveyed the happy, assembled group of guests.

"Thank you so much for being here at our first annual Thanksgiving at Chandler Hill. It's a tradition that I hope will last for many, many years. Happy Thanksgiving to each and every one of you." Lettie smiled bravely. One year ago, she'd been a single, naïve girl who had yet to fall in love with the husband she still mourned. Now, she had a baby and was struggling to carry out the plans that had been left to her to complete, along with the role of mother.

Later, in her private living quarters, Lettie placed Autumn on a blanket atop the carpet and watched as the baby kicked her feet. At three months, Autumn was less fussy than she'd been earlier. Still, Lettie struggled to form a steady, easy bond with her. Dolores said it was because Lettie was worried about being a good mother, but Lettie knew it was based in part on the guilt she felt because she hadn't wanted this baby and partly because she was afraid of forming an attachment to someone she loved and might lose. Or maybe, at nineteen, she was still overwhelmed by all that had happened to her in a matter of months.

At a knock on the door, Lettie went to answer it.

Abby and Terri stood there. "Hi, can we come in?

"Sure," Lettie replied to Abby. "I'm just trying to get Autumn settled down for the night."

Autumn began to cry.

"Aw," Terri rushed to the baby's side. "May I pick her up?

I'm pretty good with babies."

At Lettie's nod, Terri picked Autumn up and rubbed her back.

When a huge burp echoed in the room, they all laughed.

"Please sit down." Lettie indicated the small couch and two chairs in the living area beside the bedroom.

After they were all seated, Abby cleared her throat. "You know how much I love the inn. And now that it's grown into a small hotel, I think I can be of great help to you." She indicated Terri with a nod of her head. "Both of us can."

Lettie looked from one to the other. They'd been a wonderful addition to the special staff for the holiday.

"What would you think of hiring us on a full-time basis? Me, to help with the business end and Terri to help in the kitchen. As you already know, she's a wonderful cook. In fact, that's how we met."

"At an Italian restaurant." Terri smiled at Abby.

"I'm not sure how much I can pay you." Lettie was intrigued by the idea.

"Well, I can continue to work at my consulting business as well as helping you out from time to time."

"And I'll help Paloma with the cooking," said Terri. "She told me she's not used to cooking for large groups. But I am."

"I think you can build a nice restaurant business here," Abby commented. "There aren't that many unique restaurants around, and the population is growing. Having good food will help put heads in beds." She grinned. "If you allow us to live in the cabin, that will go a long way toward compensation for our work. We've been looking for a way to get out of San Francisco. Living and working here will give us the kind of life, the kind of privacy we want."

Lettie's mind spun happily at the idea of having Abby and Terri on the property helping her. Paloma could then take over more of the daily management of the inn, overseeing Elisa and the rest of the staff. That would leave her more time to fulfill Rex's plan for Lettie to learn about growing grapes and making wine.

"I love the idea!" said Lettie. "Let's talk to Paloma tomorrow morning and work things out. We'll need to see what upgrades the cabin needs and go from there."

"Great!" Abby jumped to her feet and gave Lettie a quick hug.

Terri rose and handed the baby to her. "I can't tell you how happy you've made us. I promise you won't regret it."

Lettie grinned. She was pretty sure it was a good move.

CHAPTER SIXTEEN

The arrival of Abby and Terri in addition to the publicity that followed Susan Connell's article in *The Oregonian* about the wonderful new inn and the young, brave woman who owned and ran it ushered in a new era to the inn. Seeing her picture in the paper and reading about herself, Lettie had been embarrassed. But Abby was thrilled with the publicity and told her so. As the valley filled with more people wanting to try their hand at winemaking, the demand grew for quality dining and nice places to stay. Instead of being just a spot to spend the night, the Chandler Hill Inn became a destination. Known for its excellent kitchen, the inn evolved into a retreat for those who wanted to escape busy work lives and spend several days unwinding in the beautiful countryside.

For the next several years, Lettie worked hard at the inn, oversaw the establishment of the winery, and did her best with a daughter who never seemed satisfied with the attention Lettie could give her. On those nights when Lettie was free to spend time with Autumn, she loved seeing how bright, how determined, how much fun her daughter could be. The most pleasurable times were when Lettie curled up on the bed with Autumn and read stories to her. Lettie had always used books as a means to escape, but now she used them as a means for Autumn to make memories of home.

She laughed when one evening, Autumn stared at her wide-eyed. "Do we live in a castle?"

"Nooo. We live in an inn, which is like living in a very big house."

"But everyone calls me 'Princess,'" Autumn protested.

Lettie wrapped an arm around her daughter. "That's because they love you."

"Okay. You can call me 'Princess' too."

Lettie laughed. Autumn could never get enough attention.

At the inn, things continued to change and grow as Lettie tweaked the plans for it. In the main house, she added a separate breakfast room to the expanded kitchen, and opened the library to the living room, where wine, beer, soft drinks, and appetizers were offered to guests in the evening. She had a special events center built away from the main house, where private functions, including weddings, could be held. Attractive groupings of plantings with arbors, a gazebo and interesting benches created locations where wedding parties could have settings for wedding photos.

And then in 1979, when Autumn was eight years old, David Lett's '75 Eyrie South Block Reserve Pinot Noir took second place behind famed Burgundy producer Joseph Drouhin's 1959 Chambolle-Musigny in a blind tasting of American Pinot Noir versus French Burgundy. Everything went crazy in the valley. People looking for a piece of the grape-growing action bought up every naked piece of Willamette Valley loam. Turkey farms disappeared, and grapes were planted. Hazelnut groves became more prominent. And a man named Rod Mitchell bought 50 acres of land next to Chandler Hill.

Two years later, with blessings from both Lew and Bernie, Lettie began construction of the tasting barn Rex had envisioned.

Abby, restless with the requirement to travel for her

consulting business, agreed to take charge of the barn after it opened. They envisioned making it much more than a place for simply tasting wine. They intended to make it a retail store for selling anything related to wine, including glassware, wine-serving and storage equipment, artwork, and clothing and gift items of every kind.

On the morning the pouring of the foundation was to take place, Lettie stood with Abby, Terri, Paloma, and Autumn watching the cement truck spin out its load.

"I want to help Aunt Abby in the store," Autumn announced. "I know how."

"I'm sure you do." Terri laughed. "I don't think there's anything you don't know how to do."

"Except clean up her room," said Lettie, cocking an eyebrow at her daughter.

"Aw, Mom. We have maids to do that," said Autumn.

Lettie shook her head at her daughter. At ten years of age, she herself was already cooking and cleaning in her foster home.

Abby ruffled Autumn's auburn hair. "We expect you to help. Understand?"

Autumn's frown disappeared. "Okay."

They turned as a gray-haired man approached. "Guess we're going to have us a tasting barn, huh?"

Lettie smiled at Ben Kurey, the man Rex had coaxed from Napa on a consulting basis to help him start the vineyard. Later, when things became more and more active in Oregon, Ben left California to help several other people get started. But, he'd always remained loyal to Lettie. Now, Lettie and Scott, Ben's nephew, were the winemakers for Chandler Hill.

Lettie caught sight of Rod Mitchell heading their way in jeans and a flannel shirt. Her pulse quickened at the sight of him. Tall and good-looking, his features were rugged yet refined with blue eyes, a strong nose and a bold chin. He had a way of making her feel beautiful by simply smiling at her.

"Hi, Rod!" Autumn cried, running over to him. "Come see. It's going to be my barn. I'm helping Aunt Abby run it."

"That's nice," Rod said, the corner of his eyes crinkling with amusement.

"It's Mr. Mitchell to you, Autumn, and we'll see about the rest." Lettie wrapped an arm around Autumn's shoulder and gave him an apologetic look.

He waved away her concern. "It's good for a kid to have ambition," he said easily. "Speaking of that, I'm hoping I can entice you away from here for dinner. It's been a while."

"Me too?" asked Autumn hopefully.

Rod shook his head. "Maybe another time." He turned to Lettie. "How about it?"

"Dinner would be nice," said Lettie. "Things are pretty slow at the inn for the next day or two." Even though she calmly spoke the words, her pulse raced with anticipation. She knew that this time when Rod asked her to his house for a late-night drink, she'd finally say yes. They'd been dating for a while now.

The grin that spread across Rod's features lit his blue eyes. In his late forties, he was a successful entrepreneur who'd made his money in the electronics industry and was used to getting his way. But, Lettie didn't mind his persistence. Rod reminded her of Rex in his appearance and Kenton in his determination to win her over. It was, Lettie thought, flattering to be sought after.

After Rod left, Terri elbowed Lettie. "Going out with Mr. Wonderful, huh?"

Lettie laughed. "We'll see how wonderful he is. But it'll be good to get out of my usual routine."

"Your usual routine being working twenty-four hours a day

and ignoring any guy who dares to make a pass at you," Terri teased.

"Aw, you know I've been too busy getting this operation up and running and trying to perfect our winemaking to worry about dating some guy." Or to spend much time with my child, she thought, feeling a surge of guilt.

"Yes, but you're too young to give up on having a love life. It's been ten years since Kenton died. Abby and I are happy to see you take an interest in getting out more. It'll be good for Autumn too. She's surrounded by women and needs a male figure in her life."

"We'll see," said Lettie.

Later that morning, Lettie thought about the situation at the inn. Abby, Terri, Paloma, and she had become a tight group overseeing the inn and all other operations at Chandler Hill. She knew people in the area called them "The Sisterhood" and made nasty jokes about them, and she didn't care. But maybe, like Terri said, it would be healthy to bring a man into the picture. Then again, what kind of man would want to work with them?

By the time evening arrived, Lettie was determined to relax and have a good time with Rod. It would be a healthy turn of events for both her and her daughter.

As she was dressing, Autumn came into the room and threw herself across Lettie's bed. "Why do you have to go out tonight? I want you to stay home."

"Mothers need to get out now and then, do something on their own," Lettie responded, pushing away the guilt about to drain her excitement. Were all mothers in such demand or was it because Lettie gave her daughter too little time?

"Mr. Mitchell likes you, Mom. I wish he liked me too."

Lettie faced her daughter, unsure how to answer her. Giving Autumn a reassuring smile, she said, "Mr. Mitchell has always been glad to see you."

"I guess. But then he should take me out to dinner too."

"Someday, you'll have lots of men asking you out to dinner," said Lettie, slipping earrings into her earlobes. "Now, how about homework? Is yours done?"

"Humph, you're never any fun," Autumn announced before flouncing out of the room.

Lettie watched her daughter leave and wondered why the two of them couldn't seem to get along for any length of time. She'd heard about mothers and daughters having troubles. Maybe it was normal.

She turned to the mirror and studied the simple beige dress she'd selected for the evening. It would do, she thought, smoothing the fabric over the appealing curves of her hips. She fluffed her hair. The fashion was for big hair, and her strawberry-blond curls were more than happy to oblige. Lettie leaned closer to the mirror to check her eye makeup. Eyeliner accented the round shape of her eyes; green eye shadow brought out their turquoise color. Satisfied she'd done the best she could, Lettie straightened.

Rod beamed at her when she walked into the front room of the inn. "You look ravishing."

"Thank you." Lettie felt her cheeks grow warm. He was looking at her as if he wanted to take a bite.

"I thought we'd go to Nick's for dinner and then back to my house," Rod said as he helped her on with her coat.

"Sounds good," said Lettie, telling herself it was time to see where this relationship might be going.

In McMinnville, the streets were not crowded. The midweek days were usually quiet. Rod parked the car, and they walked into the Italian restaurant that was still a favorite of Lettie's. Inside, savory aromas greeted them. There was something about the smell of garlic, bread, and tomatoes that always excited Lettie's appetite.

Rod took a seat facing the entrance, and as she knew he would, he greeted most of the people who came inside by name. He'd been in town for only two years but already knew more people than she did. Another reason, she supposed, that she should get out more.

After their meal, Rod helped her into his car, a silver Ford Thunderbird, and they took off for his home.

As she stared out the window at the countryside masked in darkness, a worrisome shiver shook her shoulders. She hadn't shared intimacy with a man in over ten years, and even though she was still young, she felt old and worn. And more than a little shy.

Seeming to sense her nervousness, Rod reached over and gave her hand a squeeze. "We'll relax by the fire, have another a glass of wine, and simply enjoy one another."

Lettie remained quiet. Didn't someone once say that sex was like riding a bicycle—once you learned how you never forgot it?

Rod's house was a modern version of a Victorian farmhouse with a sweeping front porch that overlooked the rolling hills of the valley. The exterior consisted of clapboards painted a pleasing light gray, offset by a bright-red front door. Soft-white trim edged bay windows and the double French doors that led to the screened-in porch. A round tower rose from the far corner of the house, a welcoming beacon to visitors.

Inside, the openness to both the outside and to all the interior gave one a sense of space that was appealing to Lettie. Observing it again, Lettie remembered why she'd been uncomfortable with Rod's earlier advances. As much as she loved the idea of open space, she knew she needed a sense of privacy for any initial lovemaking.

She followed Rod into the kitchen and stood by while he opened a bottle of wine and poured the rich, red liquid into two stemmed glasses.

"Take off your coat and stay awhile," he joked when he noticed her huddled into its warmth.

Feeling foolish, she laughed. "Don't mind if I do." She took off her outer wrap and placed it on a chair.

In the living room, Rod lit the fire he'd previously built in the fireplace and then took a seat next to her on the long, gray couch that faced the burning wood. Lights recessed in the ceiling were set on low, adding to the romantic atmosphere.

"How about some music?" Rod said.

Lettie returned his smile. "Okay."

He got up, and after a moment of fussing with his stereo, music from speakers in bookcases on either side of the fireplace exuded the soft sound of jazz.

"There," he said, rejoining her on the couch. "That's better."

Lettie let out a long, satisfied breath. After constantly being with people, seeing to their wants and needs, it felt good to be able to sit and relax. She hadn't realized how much she missed having time to herself or sharing it with someone like him.

He turned to face her. "Anyone told you lately how beautiful you are?" He brushed a curl away from her cheek. His steady gaze sent a frisson of excitement through her. She knew he wanted to kiss her. Resisting the urge to turn away, she leaned forward.

His warm lips caressed hers with a tender kiss that grew more demanding. She opened to his tongue and felt new sensations rolling through her. His hands moved to capture her breasts.

When she moaned softly, he lifted her onto his lap and cuddled her close.

Lettie leaned her head against his broad chest, loving the feel of such strength.

"Shall we go upstairs?" Rod's voice came out in a sexy rasp that sent shivers dancing up her spine. "Ready?"

"Yes," she whispered. She'd run away from her emotions with others for far too long.

He helped her off the couch, took her hand, and led her up the stairs to the master bedroom.

She took a moment to look around. Through a skylight, she could see stars sparkling in the dark sky like wishes waiting to be answered.

"Nice, huh?" Rod said, coming up behind her and wrapping his arms around her. "Many times, I've thought about making love to you under these stars."

She turned to him.

He kissed her until they both needed more.

Wordlessly, he swept her up in his arms and carried her over to the king-sized bed and set her down beside it.

"Let's take that dress off," he whispered huskily.

Lettie shimmied the dress off and watched as it fell onto the floor, exposing her body. She was happy she'd worn the lacy pink panties and matching bra that she'd whimsically bought one day.

Rod slipped off his shirt and pants, and then took off his undershorts, making it very clear how ready he was.

"You're overdressed," he said, giving her a teasing grin. He helped her remove her bra and slid her panties off her legs.

Lettie took a breath, pushing away the idea that her subtle stretch marks would be an issue. By the looks of the smile that was spreading across Rod's face, he didn't care at all.

"Ah, Lettie, you're as beautiful as I thought you'd be," he murmured, wrapping her in his embrace. She had a few flashbacks to making love with Kenton and forced herself to concentrate on Rod.

"Come," said Rod. He held out his hand, and she took it.

Atop the bed, they lay together, getting used to one another with touch and taste.

"Ready?" Rod whispered in her ear.

At her nod, he entered her, and they moved together in a dance as old as time.

Later, as Rod slept beside her, Lettie stared up at the stars. Making love with Rod had been satisfying, but she was overwhelmed by feelings of guilt. She hadn't been with any man since Kenton. Thinking of him, she wondered what her life would have been like if he hadn't been killed. His death at such a young age seemed as senseless now as it had then.

Quietly, she rose from the bed and went into the bathroom to freshen up.

Rod stirred, and when he realized she was dressing, he said, "Can't you stay?"

She shook her head. No matter how much she would have liked to spend the night, she wouldn't ... couldn't. Autumn was an impressionable child, and Lettie didn't want her to get the idea that her mother was someone who slept around.

If the relationship between Rod and her grew into something more permanent, it would be something she wanted her daughter to respect.

CHAPTER SEVENTEEN

Lettie's days became fuller, happier now that she'd allowed Rod into her life. She'd dated before but had never let it go beyond a casual dinner or two. With Rod, she was experiencing a new sense of freedom. Their lovemaking didn't have the raw passion of her time with Rafe or the sweet, tenderness with Kenton, but it was satisfying. She had no idea where it would lead and was content for the first time in her life to take things as they came instead of following a plan laid out for her.

With Rod being so social, she met a lot of new people in the valley. Many were from California, hoping to start up wineries with the pinot noir grape that was finding an audience. Lettie knew from experience how temperamental, how sensitive the grape was. But after working with Scott for several years, they were starting to produce an exceptional pinot noir—fruity, smooth, and with body.

Lettie was flattered by Rod's interest in Chandler Hill's winemaking. He even suggested having her introduce some of his young grapes into the mix—something she politely declined. She didn't want anyone to intrude on her process.

Her vineyard was now in four sections or blocks, each providing its own unique qualities. The Chandler Hill Reserve was still the workhorse of the group, but the Chandler Hill Kenton series was especially sought after.

Lettie loved the process of winemaking and was becoming known for her palate. Just as she'd been able to identify the different components of the wine when she'd first tasted it with Rafe and Kenton, she was able to distinguish when and how different grapes in her vineyard would react favorably to crushing. No one could match her for determining when the sugar content of the grapes was perfect for picking.

As good as her winemaking was doing, the inn was doing even better. They'd added a pool and small spa to the property, making it even more of a destination. Paloma continued to help oversee the inn. Lettie suspected her many hours on the job were an escape from her husband who'd returned from Vietnam an angry, scarred man. Lettie, Abby, and Terri had tried talking to Paloma about the bruises they sometimes saw on her, but Paloma pushed away any suggestion of help, declaring that it wasn't that bad.

Following the bud break in April, they carefully watched the growing shoots. In June when the buds bloomed, more intense work began on the canopy of green leaves making sure there were open spaces and no leaves were hiding another.

One day, Paloma arrived at the inn earlier than usual, both her children in tow. Lettie took one look at Paloma's battered face and quickly called Terri from the kitchen into the front room.

Speaking as calmly as she could, Lettie said to Terri, "Will you take Mikey and Isabel into the kitchen for some breakfast? Paloma and I will be back shortly. Perhaps you can see that the children get to school?"

Wide-eyed, Terri looked from Paloma to Lettie. "Of course. Come on, kids, let's make you something special for breakfast."

With the kids out of the room, Paloma sank down into the couch and began sobbing. "I can't do this anymore. I thought Manny was going to kill me. He wanted to. He thought I was some guy in the jungle who was out to kill him. I love Manny, but the guy I knew is long gone. The man I'm living with is a monster."

"He needs help, and so do you," said Lettie, sitting beside her and wrapping an arm around her shoulder. "I'm taking you to Salem to the hospital there. You need someone to look at your face. Are you hurt anywhere else?"

Paloma rolled up the sleeves of her shirt. The bruises that marred her arm were beginning to swell. "I tried to protect myself. Mikey even tried to stop him, but Manny was lost in one of those dreams he gets."

"Okay, let's go. You head out to my car; I'll speak to Terri and the kids."

"My mother can take them," Paloma said. "She's done it before."

Feeling sick to her stomach, Lettie headed to the kitchen. Mikey was thirteen and Isabel eleven—old enough to have seen and heard upsetting things.

At the kitchen doorway, she waved Terri over to her and quietly told her what Paloma had said. She then turned to the kids. "I'm taking your mother to see a doctor in Salem. I'll call as soon as we know anything. Your grandmother will come here and will take you home with her."

Isabel's eyes overflowed with tears. "Dad hurt Mom."

"Yes, I know," said Lettie. "We'll make sure she gets better and that your Dad gets help."

Mikey stood, his hands fisted at his side, a look of anguish on his face. "I tried to stop him."

Lettie place a hand on his shoulder and looked him in the eye. "You couldn't. Nobody could. It's not your fault. We'll get help for you and him."

###

At the hospital, the police were called in to talk to Paloma. Photos were taken of her face, her arms, and her torso. These would be used as evidence to force her husband into a rehabilitation program. Post-traumatic stress disorder was something many soldiers fought after arriving home. It was, in its own way, as difficult as the battles they'd fought in the jungles of Southeast Asia.

Paloma's nose was broken and a tooth knocked out, but she hadn't suffered a broken jaw. Still, it would be several weeks before signs of the abuse would be gone. Lettie studied her friend sitting in the car beside her, and knew she had to do something.

"Would you consider moving into the inn with your children? I've been thinking of building a small house on the property for Autumn and me. I'll be happy to give up my private rooms to you when it's done. In the meantime, you can use one of the large end-suites. You and they can have privacy there. I'm sure Autumn would love the company."

Tears welled in Paloma's eyes and then rolled down her bruised cheeks. "You'd do that for me?"

"Of course," said Lettie with feeling. "Paloma, you're the best friend I have. You and Abby and Terri mean the world to me."

Paloma lowered her head and quietly sobbed. "We've already received an eviction notice from the house we were renting. With Manny unable to work, we couldn't keep up the payments."

"Why didn't you tell me?" Lettie reached for her hand. "We might have worked something out."

"I couldn't." Paloma's lips quivered. "I just couldn't let anyone know how awful things were at home. How threatened I was, how frightened. I had to keep up a brave front for the kids."

"They know how bad it is," Lettie said quietly. "I thought that might be another reason to stay with me at the inn. School will be out soon, and they can keep busy."

"Do you remember your first Thanksgiving here? When I met you, you were a sweet young girl. But, Lettie, you've grown into a wonderful woman. I wish Rex and Kenton could see how you've grown, what you've done for the inn, everything."

"A lot has happened since then," Lettie said. "I liked you right away, you know."

Paloma gave her a crooked smile which caused her to wince. "Me too."

The end of spring jumped into summer like a child leaping for joy. The inn was busy as ever, with guests arriving to see what all the buzz was about in the valley. With Paloma and the kids on site, things settled into a smoother routine. Isabel and Autumn became good friends, Mikey took to following Scott around checking the canopies, and Paloma's presence gave Lettie time to begin planning for her house.

As she often did when big decisions were made, she spent time in the grove of trees. Sitting on a stone bench she'd moved there under the umbrella of leafy tree branches and among the pines, she could express her thoughts and reasoning behind her decisions. It was a way for her to clear her mind and to plot the future as carefully as they would, if they could.

Lettie decided she wanted to build something fairly small and hidden away from the inn, with a contemporary feel. Spending time in Rod's house had convinced her to go with open spaces and clean lines. And skylights.

Working with the architect who'd designed many of the

inn's projects, they quickly arrived at a plan that suited Lettie. For someone who'd grown up in an unstable environment, building the house grew in importance.

Lettie spent a portion of every day overseeing progress on the house she'd already come to love. It was the first time that a project at the inn was not carried out by Rex's ideas. He hadn't conceived a private home for her, but she thought he'd like what she was doing.

Rod often met her at the building site. When he began commenting on a feature he didn't like, Lettie did her best to ignore it. This was her project, not his.

But one afternoon, when he suggested extending her driveway onto his property so their properties could be merged, her heart fell to her feet. She had the creepy feeling that the land was what he'd been after all along.

"What are you saying, Rod?" she said in a deceptively calm voice.

"I figured that when I can convince you to marry me, we'll join the two operations," he said, winking at her.

"And who would run those two properties?" she asked, each word frosted with dismay.

"Well, I've been a very successful businessman. There's no reason I can think of for my not handling both properties."

Her stomach clenched. "Was this your plan all along? Is that why you wanted to start dating me? For Chandler Hill?"

While she waited for his answer, Lettie wrapped her arms around herself in a vain effort to hold in the hurt.

Rod's cheeks flushed. He looked away and turned back to her. "Knowing you owned Chandler Hill may have been a reason I was interested in a relationship at first, but you know how much I care about you. What's wrong with a man wanting to take care of his woman?"

Fury rose in Lettie like a lion ready to pounce. She

straightened to her full height of five-three. "First of all, I don't consider myself 'your woman.' We've never even talked marriage, for God's sake. Probably because you know what my answer would be to that. I could never leave Chandler Hill or let anyone else run it. I owe it to both Rex and Kenton to do as they wanted with the property."

"Come now, Lettie," Rod said with a nasty edge to his voice. "They're both long gone, and up until now, you've done what they've asked. Isn't it time for you to have a normal life with a live husband and family?"

Lettie fisted her hands on her hips and glared at him. "And what about you? I'd be your third wife in a string of them? No, thanks. As far as family, I've got my own."

"Your own? You mean all those women living together doing God knows what?"

His words slapped at her with a venom she didn't know he had. She raised a hand to her cheek and stepped away from him. "Get off my property right now. I never want to see you again."

"You'll be sorry. You and I together could make something really big happen with this place."

"It's just the way we all want it," said Lettie. "Now go!"

Rod narrowed his eyes at her. "I thought you were smarter than this. I thought you'd know a good thing when you saw it. Someday, you'll see I was right."

"Today, I know I'm right," said Lettie. "I'm just sorry it took me so long to see you for who you are."

Muttering about women who think they're smarter than they are, Rod stomped to his truck, got in, and roared away.

Lettie watched him go and then went inside the house. Sitting on a stack of two-by-fours, Lettie covered her face. She felt so ... so ... stupid! Why hadn't she seen past Rod's flattery, his interest in her work, to the man he really was?

She decided she'd talk to Joe Lopez tomorrow and ask him to oversee putting in a fence along the line where Rod's property met hers. She had a feeling her troubles with him weren't over.

She rose with a new sense of determination to carry on.

As she crossed the hill toward the inn, she took a moment to study the scene before her. The inn was even more imposing, more beautiful than it had been the moment she'd first seen it. Now, the house was just the hub of the inn, which extended on either side of it. Behind the house, the pool, patio, and functions building had been added. Off to one side, the new tasting barn greeted arrivals with the promise of good things inside. The barn for the animals that served a major purpose in keeping the vineyards organic now had a garage added to it to house the tractor and cars for her and the staff. The remodeled cabin where Abby and Terri lived remained among the trees.

Lettie knew very well what an accomplishment this was, due, in part, to Rex's planning and her willingness to follow through. No one was going to take that away from her.

CHAPTER EIGHTEEN

Lettie continued to put her energy into the inn's growth and success. Having her own house as a retreat from the daily grind was a blessing for her. There were times when she desperately needed to get away from the activity at the inn. And there were other times when sitting alone in her house after Autumn had gone to bed, she thought she'd die of loneliness. Then, and only then, did she admit to herself how much she wished she had someone with whom to share her life.

As the years flew by, Lettie's biggest worry was her daughter, Autumn. She'd always been an outspoken, willful child. As a teenager, she was impossible to control. Lettie blamed herself for much of it. She'd never been able to give Autumn the attention she'd demanded. And though the thought filled her with guilt and made her feel inadequate, Lettie believed she'd tried to do her best she could under the circumstances. But it didn't make the present situation any better.

The year Autumn was due to turn sixteen, she was suspended from school for doing drugs.

When Lettie sat Autumn down in the living room and tried to talk to her about it, Autumn was defiant. "It wasn't anything like heroin. It was just some grass. You've been on my back for weeks, finding fault with everything I do. I think you're just jealous because Rod Mitchell thinks I'm hot. He even told me so."

Lettie felt the blood drain from her face. "When were you

talking to Rod? And why would he say such a thing? You're just a young girl."

"No, Mother, Look at me. I'm a young woman. Ask any boy at school. You've been too busy with this godforsaken inn to even notice."

Lettie stared at her daughter. Dressed in denim jeans and a knit top that emphasized her ample breasts, Autumn was no longer a girl, but someone on the cusp of womanhood. One, apparently, who didn't mind displaying her curves. Lettie wondered how she'd failed to notice, like Autumn was accusing her of doing.

"Autumn, please ... You know how demanding my job is ... how hard I work for you."

"You work for yourself, not me!" Autumn jumped to her feet. "I'm going to stay with Abby and Terri. They understand what it's like for me to be your daughter."

Furious, Lettie drew herself up out of her seat. "We need to discuss this. You cannot disregard all the rules. You need to be responsible. Someday, Chandler Hill will be yours and you'll need to be ready."

"I don't give a damn about Chandler Hill. I never did, and I never will."

"But ..."

"I'm outta here."

Stunned, Lettie watched her daughter storm out of the house. As she calmed, Lettie wondered if Autumn was right, and she was someone stuck in the past, doing her duty to men who'd long been dead. Rod had all but accused her of that. She'd turned thirty-five, but for the last sixteen years she'd grown up fast as she assumed the responsibility of being left in charge of Chandler Hill at such a young age. She sometimes felt trapped by the idea that she'd never be able to leave, but, how could she? She'd promised Rex and Kenton that she'd honor their wishes. She, a nobody from Dayton, Ohio, had been given their acceptance, their love, and their generous gifts. She'd never do anything to break her promise to them, even when she sometimes wanted to leave it all behind her.

After several attempts to reason with Autumn through the spring term, Lettie finally turned to her friends for help. Both Abby and Terri suggested that a private school with strict rules might be an answer. They knew of a friend who taught at a small school in California and thought they might be able to help Lettie get her daughter accepted.

At the end of the summer, and with arrangements made for her to start the fall term at the school, the three of them sat down with Autumn to convince her to give it a try. They hadn't brought it up earlier for fear that she'd turn it down, but the summer had mellowed her a bit.

"What have you got to lose?" Abby asked Autumn, who sat on the couch facing them with her arms crossed.

"My friend who teaches there is really cool. You'll like her, and she says the kids are great," added Terri, smiling.

"I think you'll be happier," said Lettie quietly. Though Autumn acted as though things were fine, Lettie knew they weren't. Her old friends, like Isabel, wanted nothing to do with the wild girl she'd become, and it was becoming harder for Autumn to hide the hurt.

"Okay, I'll try it," said Autumn. "I hate living here."

Lettie stopped herself from rolling her eyes and prayed it would be a good move for all of them. Trying to keep an eye on her daughter and fighting with her daily had become exhausting.

###

With Autumn's departure, life at Chandler Hill settled down into a quieter routine. Lettie was able to sleep through the night without worrying about her meeting a curfew or arriving at the house drunk or stoned. But the freedom from worry emphasized how alone Lettie was.

Abby and Terri still lived and worked on the property, but they needed time together. Paloma, a widow now, was busy with her own children and a new beau. The rest of the staff was either younger or tied up with families of their own.

In desperation, she accepted an offer of dinner with Scott Kurey. But while she enjoyed working with him, they both realized there was no real romantic spark between them. A few other dates followed, but Lettie grew weary of trying to make herself feel something that wasn't there.

When Autumn returned home for the winter holidays, Lettie swept her daughter into her embrace with genuine joy. "I'm so glad to have you home, Autumn! I can't wait to show you how we've decorated for Christmas! It'll be fun to have you be a part of the holidays. I've missed you so much!"

Autumn stepped away and looked at her with chagrin. "Mom, I hope you don't mind, but I promised Tiffany, my roommate, that I'd go skiing with her at Vail right after Christmas. I know I should have asked you first, but I knew you'd be busy with the inn. Her father will be calling you to confirm."

"Oh?" Lettie struggled to hide her disappointment. "That was nice of her to invite you. Sounds like fun."

"Yeah, well the kids my age around here are boring. Most of the girls at school have been to Europe several times and have lives these kids would never even dream of."

"Because someone hasn't the money to travel doesn't make them boring," said Lettie. She bit her tongue at the eyeroll Autumn gave her. In time, she hoped her daughter would be kinder, more willing to let go of the wall of superiority she'd recently built around herself. For now, Lettie wanted to try to make the holidays as pleasant as possible. Autumn was her daughter and even if at times Lettie didn't like her attitude, she loved her.

On Christmas morning, Lettie rose early. Christmas Day was the one day of the year the inn was closed, and it had become a tradition for Lettie to fix breakfast for Abby and Terri. She normally served mimosas along with eggs benedict and the hazelnut muffins for which the inn had become famous. Lettie could hardly wait for Abby and Terri to arrive with the packages she and they had bought for Autumn.

At the noise of their arrival, her sleepy daughter padded into the kitchen in her pajamas.

"Merry Christmas!" Abby threw her arms around Autumn.

Terri embraced the two of them. "Merry Christmas!

Standing aside, Lettie felt left out until Terri signaled her to join the group.

The four of them huddled together until, laughing, Autumn said, "Stop it! I can't breathe!"

But, for a moment, a serene peace had settled around them—a moment Lettie knew she'd always treasure. And later, when Autumn opened her gifts and saw the ski pants, sweater, hat, and gloves for her trip to Vail, tears of gratitude filled Autumn's eyes.

"Thank you so much," she said with feeling. "I'm so excited to make this trip, and these gifts are perfect."

"Your mother arranged everything," said Terri.

Autumn turned to Lettie. "Thanks, Mom."

"You're welcome, sweetie," Lettie said, accepting her quick hug with pleasure.

###

With the inn filling with people who wanted to spend New Year's Eve in wine country, Lettie didn't have much time to think about Autumn's trip except to hope she was having a good time. Her roommate's father was in the movie industry, and he'd promised both girls a fun time.

On New Year's Eve, Lettie was dressing for dinner when her phone rang. Seeing the out-of-town number, she tensed. Only a handful of people had her home number. Her heart pounded as she picked up the phone. "H-hello?" Her voice cracked with worry.

"Is this Lettie Chandler? Autumn Chandler's mother?"

"Yes," she answered, feeling her heart stop and then lurch onward. Was this another instance of losing someone she loved?

"I'm sorry to inform you that your daughter has had a skiing accident. She's here at the Vail Valley Medical Center."

"Oh my God! Is she going to be all right?" gasped Lettie.

"She's broken her left leg. We'll need your permission to go ahead with surgery to set it properly as soon as the swelling is under control. Dr. Johnstone is a very capable orthopedic surgeon and doesn't expect any complications."

"Yes, of course, do whatever is necessary. Is it possible for me to speak to Autumn?"

"She's pretty drugged at the moment, but we'll have her call home as soon as possible. And, of course, you can call Dr. Johnstone's office to speak to them. Mr. Bellinger and his daughter are with her now."

"Thank you." Lettie's mind spun as she hung up the phone. There was no way she'd let Autumn go through surgery without her. She thought of her past fear of flying and grew sick at the thought of getting on a plane. She called Abby, told her what the situation was, and accepted Abby's offer to call the airlines for her.

At the airport, Lettie swallowed the pill Abby handed her.

"This will help settle your nerves. It might make you a little sleepy so be careful. Are you sure you don't want me to come with you?"

"You're needed at the inn. I wish we could trade places, but Autumn would never forgive me if I didn't come."

"Maybe the flight will be easier than you think," Abby said, rubbing her arm.

Lettie smiled agreeably but knew nothing would make any flight easy for her. The good thing was, she wouldn't be in the air for long periods of time. That, she knew, she could never do.

In a daze from the medication, Lettie stifled a scream and gripped the armrests of her seat as the small plane dipped down and onto the tarmac at the Eagle County Regional Airport. Seeing the land outside, her eyes filled with tears of gratitude. She felt as if she'd crossed several continents to get there when, in fact, she'd flown only from Portland to Denver and to this small airport.

The flight attendant gave her a smile as Lettie prepared to leave the plane. "You okay now, hon?" the stewardess said to her. "It helps to breathe into the paper bag we supply."

"Thanks, but the only thing that'll help me is feeling my feet on the ground again," said Lettie.

The hotel's transportation service delivered her to the

Bavarian-style hotel where she was staying. It and the quaint ski village in which the hotel sat were stark reminders of how isolated she'd become at Chandler Hill. At home, a trip by automobile to Portland was a big deal.

Feeling better now, she checked into the hotel and got her bags settled in her room. Then after washing up from the trip, she headed downstairs to find a ride to see her daughter.

The Medical Center, though small, was a busy place. Apparently, winter sports accidents kept a lot of people like Dr. Johnstone busy, Lettie thought as she made her way to the check-in desk.

After receiving directions to Autumn's room, Lettie hurried to her.

When Autumn saw her, she burst into tears. "I told everyone you wouldn't come."

"Aw, honey, why would you say that?" Lettie asked, genuinely hurt.

Autumn's tawny eyes remained shiny with tears. "Because it's New Year's Eve, and the inn is open. I told them you'd never leave it at a busy time like that. Not for me."

"Oh, my dear one," sighed Lettie. "You judge me so harshly. You're my daughter, and I love you. Of course, I'm going to be here for you. I came as quickly as I could. Abby helped me."

Autumn sniffed. "They have to operate on my leg. I feel like such a dope. Everyone else was going on the big runs while I was on the bunny hill. Even then I screwed up."

"It's not screwing up. These things can happen when you're learning something new."

"Yeah? I bet it would never happen to you."

Lettie wrapped her arms around Autumn. "You have no idea how clumsy I can be."

"So, you think I'm clumsy?" she wailed.

Lettie drew a deep breath and told herself to remain calm.

"I didn't say it, nor do I think it." She put a hand to Autumn's forehead. "When did you last eat?"

"I can't eat. Not until after the surgery."

Lettie turned as a distinguished-looking, gray-haired man entered the room. "Hello. You must be Lettie. I'm Tiffany's father, Lyle Bellinger."

Smiling, Lettie shook his hand. "I'm glad to meet you. It was nice of you and your wife to invite Autumn on this trip."

Lyle looked uncomfortable and then said, "My wife and I are divorced, though she did agree to the trip."

"When we spoke on the phone before Christmas, you made it clear that you would be present for the girls both on the slopes and in the evenings."

"Yes, they're still at an age where that's important. And until today, everything was going really well." He indicated Autumn with a tilt of his head. "Such a shame this happened. She was on her way to becoming a very good skier."

"I can't imagine ever skiing again," said Autumn woefully.

A tall blonde walked into the room wearing jeans and a thick, white ski sweater. She smiled at Lettie and held out her hand. "Hi, Mrs. Chandler? I'm Tiffany. I'm so sorry about Autumn's accident."

"Thank you. I am too. But I'm happy to meet you. It means so much to me that she has such a nice roommate."

"She's the best," said Tiffany, smiling at Autumn.

A man in a white coat entered the room and introduced himself as Dr. Johnstone. Short, a little overweight, and with a baby face, he looked more like a boy than the well-known doctor he was. But when he began to talk about how the surgery would be done to secure the reduction of the tibia with screws, Lettie realized he wasn't the boy she thought he was.

"Don't worry." His voice was pleasant. "We'll have your daughter good as new."

"How long will it take for her leg to heal?"

"I'm guessing anywhere from three to six months." He gave an encouraging smile to Autumn. "With a healthy, young girl like this, she should do well."

He handed Lettie a clipboard. "If we can get your signature, we'll get this show on the road. Right, Autumn?"

"Yes, if it means I can have something to eat afterwards." Autumn gave him a sweet smile.

Everyone, including Lettie, laughed.

A nurse came in and administered medication into the IV hooked up to Autumn's arm.

"Well, we'd better go and give the two of you some privacy. We'll be in the surgical waiting area," said Lyle heading out the door.

Lettie was grateful for the time alone with her daughter.

Autumn's eyes began to close.

Lettie leaned over the bed and whispered in her ear, "I'll be here waiting for you. I love you."

Autumn mumbled something that sounded like "me, too, Mom", and then Lettie stepped back so the nurse and an aide could lift Autumn on a gurney and roll it out of the room.

Left alone, Lettie walked over to the window and looked out at the snow-covered mountains. Then, on impulse, she checked Autumn's chart which had mistakenly been left on a bedside table when the nurse had helped place Autumn onto a gurney. Looking through data like weight, height, blood pressure, her eyes came to rest on blood type. Type O positive. Lettie frowned. She was Type A positive, and Kenton's army medical records had indicated he was Type AB.

Lettie thought back to her high school biology class and felt her legs go weak. She'd done a paper on blood types. A positive and AB positive could not produce an O positive child. She tried to recall if she'd seen Autumn's blood type before but couldn't remember any such times or any reason for doing so. Autumn had always been a healthy child.

Her heart pounding, Lettie picked up the chart again. There it was. O positive.

The room spun around her.

Oh my God!

In their two encounters, had she and Rafe produced a baby? If Kenton was not Autumn's father, it had to be Rafe.

Lettie raced into the bathroom, feeling as if her whole world was spinning out of control in nauseating circles.

CHAPTER NINETEEN

Lettie felt as if she was moving in slow-motion as she went through the next several days of overseeing her daughter's recovery, waiting for her to be ready for the flights home. Lettie wondered if it would be easier to drive, but Dr. Johnstone suggested Autumn would be more comfortable in the long run by getting her home as quickly as possible.

Once more, with the help of the medicine Abby had given her, Lettie managed to make herself board the flights for home. The airline aided them with Autumn's care.

But back inside the Portland airport, the fear that had frozen Lettie's insides erupted in a queasiness she could no longer control. She made a running dash to the ladies' room, where she rid herself of everything she'd eaten.

When she returned to Autumn's side, she gave her mother a worried look. "Are you okay?"

Lettie shook her head. "I won't be until I'm home again."

As Abby drove them up the hill to the inn, the sight of it made Lettie's stomach relax. Then she thought of the grove of trees and Kenton and felt sick again. She turned to Autumn, checking as she had so many times for characteristics that might have come from Rafe. Her eyes were a tawny brown, not blue like hers or Kenton's. Lettie had never been concerned about it before because she had no idea what her parents looked like and how it might affect her child. Autumn's hair was dark brown with streaks of natural red making her a genuine auburn beauty. Now, Lettie noticed that her facial features had a bit of Rafe in them—his straight nose, the broad brow, the cleft in his chin were shared with his daughter. Lettie gazed out the window wondering how she could have missed all the signs when it seemed so obvious now. Holding in a sob, she blinked back the tears that stung her eyes. She needed time to sort out her feelings before talking to anyone else about it.

They moved Autumn into a ground-floor room at the inn, so she could receive all the attention she needed and wanted. With Lettie gone from the house all day, it made the most sense. And truthfully, Lettie was glad to have moments alone while she wrestled with what she should do about the new information she had discovered about Autumn's real father.

Lettie managed to hold herself together until it was time for Autumn to return to school.

Standing in the driveway while Abby helped Autumn into the car, Lettie clutched her hands. She hadn't mentioned anything to her about Rafe being her father. The idea was still so new, so shocking that she couldn't bring herself to do it.

"You don't mind that Abby and Terri will accompany you?" Lettie asked her. "They're anxious to see their old friend still teaching at the school."

Autumn shrugged. "It doesn't really matter. I just want to leave the inn. I don't know how you can stand it here. There's nothing to do."

"I'm hoping someday you'll run the inn," said Lettie, and stopped as a sharp pain went through her. Would it be right for her to inherit the inn?

Autumn gave her a worried look. "Are you all right?"

Lettie knew she wasn't all right at all and might not feel that way ever again. She gave Autumn one last embrace. "'Bye, sweetie. Talk to you soon. Say hi to Tiffany for me."

As the car moved away, Lettie stood in the driveway for a

long time watching Abby's station wagon until it was little more than a speck of blue traveling through the valley. She couldn't hold back her tears. Autumn, who was so precious to her, seemed a symbol of how foolish, how naïve she'd been at an age not much older than her daughter now. She'd never been given the time to tell Kenton that she was pregnant—something that had bothered her in the past, but now seemed a gift of sorts because she hadn't deceived him in any way.

Paloma came out of the inn and stood beside her. "Sad to see her go, huh?"

Lettie nodded, struggling to hold in her emotions.

Paloma put an arm around her shoulder. "Are you going to tell me what's wrong? I've watched you suffer ever since you returned from Vail. You know I'm here to help you any way I can."

As Lettie turned to her, tears blurred her vision. "You're my best friend, and I need to talk to you."

"Okay, let me tell one of the staff inside, and we'll go to your house where we can have privacy."

Paloma returned and handed Lettie her jacket. "Let's walk. I know how much you like to do that."

"Yes, it helps me," said Lettie.

As they walked away toward the house, Lettie glanced at the grove of trees that represented the love she had for the Chandler men. She hadn't gone to visit it since her return from Vail because she didn't know what to say when she got there.

At the house, Lettie fixed fresh coffee and motioned Paloma to a chair at the kitchen table. Somehow a kitchen was the best place for woman-to-woman talks, and this was going to be a difficult one.

After handing Paloma her mug of coffee fixed the way she liked it, Lettie sat in a chair opposite her.

"What I have to say can go no further," she said. "But I need your help in trying to decide how best to handle it."

"You have my word." Paloma reached over and gave Lettie's hand a comforting squeeze. "You and I go back to when you first came here to the valley."

"That's another reason I didn't want to talk to anyone else but you," said Lettie. "You knew how unsophisticated I was, how naïve."

"Yes," Paloma said simply.

"I have uncovered some disturbing information, and I don't know what to do with it. When I was in Vail, I learned that Autumn's blood type is O positive."

"And?" Paloma gave her a quizzical look.

Tears spilled from Lettie's eyes. She hid her face in her hands and let them come.

Paloma rose from her chair and came over to her. Hugging her close, Paloma let her cry until she had no more tears.

When Paloma finally took a seat again, they looked at one another in silence.

"I think I know where this is going," Paloma finally said quietly. "Want to tell me about it?"

Lettie drew a deep breath. "Okay. Kenton's blood type was AB positive and I'm A positive. Together, we would not have an O positive child. There's only one other person who could be the father."

"Rafe," said Paloma. "I saw how you were with one another. His parents were afraid for you two to be together. That's why he got engaged to Maria so quickly. It's what all the families wanted."

"But I loved Kenton. I truly did," said Lettie with such feeling her voice broke.

"Nobody doubts that. The two of you together were precious," said Paloma. She gave Lettie a wry smile. "I used to be jealous of you for that."

"What am I going to do? Do I tell Rafe? Does that mean that Autumn can't inherit the inn? What do I say to my daughter?"

Paloma took a sip of her coffee and set the mug down. "Why don't you let things take a natural course? Rafe and Maria are still married, but it's not a happy one. Rafe bought land here and wants to begin farming grapes in the valley, but Maria won't leave California."

"Do they have children?" Lettie now realized how odd it was that nobody talked about Rafe or Maria anymore. Did they know their marriage was a mistake?

"No, they don't have children. My guess is they will end up here in the valley sooner rather than later. As far as the inn goes, both Rex and Kenton gave it to you. You've worked hard to do everything they imagined with it and much, much more. It's yours to give to Autumn no matter who her father is."

Lettie shook her head sadly. "They never knew I was pregnant."

"For the time being, I'd say nothing to anyone about this situation. When the time is right, you'll know it. Both Autumn and Rafe deserve to know the truth."

"Paloma, you are indeed my best friend," sighed Lettie. "Thank you for not judging me. I know I won't get the same treatment from my daughter."

"Give her a chance. She's starting to grow up."

"I'm hopeful she'll stay out of trouble and be ready to settle down," said Lettie. "Isabel still doesn't have much to do with her."

"I'm sorry ..." Paloma began.

"No, no!" said Lettie. "I know how changed Autumn is. And she still doesn't want anything to do with the inn."

"She should remember everything you've done for all of us in the valley by making the inn a success. Without your help I don't know what I would have done. And now I have my own house, thanks to you."

"You deserve it, Paloma. You're more like a sister to me."

Lettie and Paloma stood and hugged.

"Guess I'd better get back to work. Guests are arriving this week—a group of women from Idaho, here for a spa weekend." Paloma got to her feet.

"Maybe Sonya at the spa can fit me into her schedule after they leave."

"She's so talented." Paloma grinned. "I'll put in a good word for you."

Lettie laughed, feeling much better.

A couple of years later, Autumn was a healthy, happy, young high school graduate about to embark on a college career. She'd been accepted at University of California, Berkeley and was excited about the future. As the summer progressed, Lettie gazed upon her daughter with a sense of pride. Except for her physical appearance, Autumn reminded her of herself with her curiosity, her desire to see and know more. Better even, she was at last exhibiting a kinder, less-selfish attitude. For the first time, Lettie could imagine her daughter taking over the inn.

As she had so many times, Lettie almost broached the subject of Autumn's father. But at the last minute, she wasn't ready to deal with the fallout of confessing the truth, disrupting this precious, congenial time together. When Autumn left for college in her own car with Lettie's full blessing, Lettie was sorry to see her go, but Autumn promised to come home for both Thanksgiving and Christmas. Lettie thought perhaps then she'd be able to tell Autumn the truth about her heritage.

Before leaving school for the Thanksgiving homecoming, Autumn called Lettie to say she was staying in California, that she and her boyfriend were going to entertain friends who had nowhere else to go. Lettie reluctantly accepted the news, hiding her hurt, pleased Autumn was thinking of others.

But, when Autumn called to say she wasn't coming home for the Christmas holidays, Lettie pressured her into agreeing to appear for at least Christmas Day. "Besides me, Abby, Terri, Paloma, and the rest of the inn family want to see you," she pleaded.

"All right," said Autumn, "but I'm not staying. Richard doesn't believe in Christmas and refuses to come home with me. So, I'll come back to California early to spend New Year's Eve with him."

"Richard? You haven't mentioned his name before. Tell me more about him." Lettie felt as if a rock had landed in her stomach. A man who didn't believe in Christmas and who had such great influence over her daughter were signs of danger.

"Richard is the smartest man I've ever met. He has a view of the world that totally makes sense. Getting rid of the old hacks in the school, defying outdated rules, letting the small people speak is what it's going to take for us young soldiers to set the world right. That, and getting rid of the rich guys who run everything, just so they can fill their pockets."

"And you believe that?" Lettie said, unable to hide her disbelief. Autumn, of all people, should know how much hard work it took to get ahead.

"Just because you've been successful with the inn doesn't make it right that you think you have all the answers for everyone who works for you. Why not give Paloma the inn? She's worked hard for you all these years. Abby and Terri, too."

"But, Autumn, it's so much more than that. It's the land.

We can use it to make things grow. And it's so beautiful. I remember ..."

"Look, I've got to go. Richard is waiting for me downstairs. We're off to a rally."

"But, Autumn —"

"Goodbye, Mother."

Lettie stood with the buzzing phone in her hand, then slumped down in a chair, feeling weak kneed. She was only thirty-seven, but she felt as if she were ninety. Was all her work at Chandler Hill going to be for nothing? She'd fought against the idea of selling it or turning it over to a professional manager, as some people had suggested. There was no way she'd give up the idea of carrying on the business that had been left to her. This was, and always had been, the one place on earth where she truly felt at home. She'd hoped to have Autumn take it over, maybe have Autumn raise children of her own there. Now, that seemed an impossible dream.

Life was full of more disappointment. Before Christmas, Terri discovered a lump in one of her breasts. After a biopsy proved it to be cancer, Terri scheduled surgery to be done right after the first of the year. In her fifties now, Terri was a sweet woman who managed the kitchen for the inn with a sense of fun that made both staff and guests love her. Abby, Terri's long-time partner, was distraught at the news.

Autumn arrived home for the holidays to a gloomy group. Everyone tried their best to follow their old routines, but no one's heart was in it. Richard Nance had refused to come to Chandler Hill for Christmas, but he might as well have made the trip because his stamp of disapproval emanated from Autumn like a poisonous gas.

When Lettie tried to talk to her about it, Autumn lashed out at her with words that Lettie knew were not her own. All this from a man who was no longer a student at the university and who was known as a troublemaker, if newspaper articles about him were true.

Lettie's voice quavered. "Someday, Autumn, you'll appreciate all that you have here—our family, the inn, the vineyard, the land itself."

"You don't understand. I don't want any of it. I'm going to Africa with Richard. He's paying for my airline ticket, and through his connections, I've already got a job there. I can be a big help there instead of being pampered here."

"Africa? Isn't that a little far to go to prove your point?" Lettie tried in vain to rein in her frustration.

Autumn shook her head. "I knew you wouldn't get it. That's why I haven't told you I'm leaving for Africa in two weeks."

"What about school?" Lettie felt sick.

"I'm taking a leave of absence. I've already made the arrangements. So, you don't have to worry about me and my school grades anymore."

"Getting an education is important. Especially now when things are just beginning to open up to women."

Autumn snorted. "I'll be old and gray before that happens. I want to make a difference, go where it won't matter whether I'm a woman or not."

"But ..."

Autumn held up a hand to stop her. "There's nothing you can say to make me change my mind. Someday, you'll understand. Right now, you're so stuck here that you can't see the big picture."

Over the next two days, Abby, Terri, and Paloma each tried in her own way to dissuade Autumn. But one morning, Lettie woke to find a note on the kitchen table and her daughter gone.

> "I can't stay here. I'll be in touch. Until then, you can send mail to my old address at school. Someone will get it to me. Love, Autumn."

Lettie sank into a kitchen chair. She might be a successful businesswoman, but she'd failed as a parent.

CHAPTER TWENTY

Over the next couple of months, change continued at Chandler Hill. Terri went through surgery and followed up with chemo. But the cancer had already spread to other parts of her body and became a hungry creature ready to devour her.

Lettie and Paloma helped Abby keep watch over Terri as she struggled to hold on. But it was a race, and all knew the winner. When Terri finally succumbed, Lettie was both sad to lose her and relieved that one of her dearest friends didn't have to suffer anymore.

Terri's death was hardest on Abby, who went into a downward spiral of depression. She announced she had to get away for a while and said that when she came back she wanted to live anywhere except in the cabin she'd shared with Terri.

Lettie spoke to Paloma about taking over the cabin. Still single following her husband's death from a drug overdose, Paloma readily agreed. Her daughter Isabel was getting married, and Paloma loved the idea of offering the young couple her house for a low but acceptable rental fee.

When a letter finally came from Autumn, Paloma and Lettie met at Lettie's house, so they could read it together. Lettie opened the envelope and read it aloud.

> "Dear Mom, I'm so sorry to learn that Terri did not make it. After being in Africa for less than a year, it seems ironic that with so little medicine, like vaccines, we can save so many lives, while cancer is

> still such a killer. Please give my love to Abby. Hope all is well with you, Paloma, and the others. Much love."

Lettie and Paloma studied one another.

"She sounds good," said Paloma.

"Yes, she does. More grown up." Lettie folded the letter. "I wonder if Richard is still with her."

"It doesn't sound as if he is."

"I'm going to write her another long letter tonight." Lettie laid the letter on the table. "Maybe that's how we'll form a stronger bond."

Paloma patted her back. "Sounds like a good idea."

Lettie was surprised to learn in 1992 that the land next to her on the opposite side from Rod Mitchell's property had been sold. The couple who owned it hadn't done well. Word was that they wouldn't listen to advice from anyone, even when everyone in the valley knew how delicate the pinot noir grape was.

Even though land on both sides of Chandler Hill was owned by others, there was enough acreage at Chandler Hill to allow Lettie the privacy she wanted for herself and her guests. With more and more people recognizing the facilities at the inn, weddings and small group events were becoming a stronger segment of business.

Paloma came into Lettie's office and sat down. "Did you hear the news? The Taunton property next to you, the one that sold recently, has been bought by Rafe Lopez." Paloma's gaze remained on Lettie.

Lettie tried to hide the fluttering in her belly. She was anxious to see him again, but the thought of the secret she'd withheld from him sent a streak of panic through her.

"Seems he traded some land he bought years ago to help pay for it. Joe and Rita are ecstatic, because Joe, as you know, is slowing down. Joe hopes that he and Rafe can work together to get his land in shape and keep working here. You know Joe. He's never going to leave Chandler Hill after all Rex did for him, giving him the house and the land with it."

"Is Maria coming with Rafe?" Lettie asked.

"Yes, though she's not happy about it. I'm not sure why she agreed to move here. I've heard rumors that she's not well, but I don't know if what people are saying is true."

Lettie rose, went over to the window, and looked out at the pool. A couple of guests were lying in deck chairs soaking up the sun. In the distance, she saw Joe driving the tractor, making sure the soil between the rows of vines was free of weeds.

The summer day, which had started off nicely, seemed even brighter, even warmer. But, Lettie noticed that gray clouds were gathering at the horizon. Considering the mixed emotions that were roiling through her, it seemed appropriate.

Lettie lived in suspense as she waited for the moment she'd run into Rafe. The few times he'd been home for holidays or family visits, she hadn't seen him. But with his living here and owning the property next to hers, it was inevitable that they'd meet.

One summer morning, she stepped outside of her house, and seeing how beautiful it was, decided to walk to the inn instead of driving. She was crossing one of the sections of the vineyard when she noticed Rafe in the distance, standing at the barn next to the tractor.

He lifted his head and gave her a steady gaze as she made her way toward him.

Heart pounding so fast she thought she might faint, Lettie kept walking. It was past time for them to meet.

She was overcome with shyness as she approached him. She took a moment and then said in a friendly voice, “Hello, Rafe. I understand you’re my new neighbor. Welcome home!”

A smile lit his face. Seeing him up close like this, Lettie realized how much Autumn looked like him. True, her coloring and her build were different, but that cleft in her chin was the same as his.

She didn’t realize she’d been staring until he turned away from her and then back again.

“You haven’t aged a day, Lettie,” he said softly.

She shook her head. “As much as I’d like to think I haven’t changed, I know I have. And a whole lot has happened to me since I first came to Chandler Hill.”

Rafe raked his fingers through his dark hair and sighed. “I haven’t forgotten what you were like back then. If you don’t mind my saying so, you’re even more beautiful now.”

“It’s good to see you, too,” said Lettie, as attracted to him as she’d always been. But she wouldn’t act on it. He was a married man.

“Say, who is this Rod Mitchell?” Rafe frowned. “He warned me to stay away from his property and yours.”

“What?” Lettie could feel her eyes round with surprise. “Why would he say that?”

“I thought maybe you and he had something going.” Rafe’s brown gaze bored into her.

She shook her head. “He had big ambitions about joining properties and taking over the inn. I ended anything with him a long time ago.”

“Good. I know how Rex and Kenton felt about your

handling things at Chandler Hill, and I admire the way you've overseen the development of the inn and the vineyards. I hope my pinot noir is equal to yours. You've built a reputation for a very nice wine. Through the years, Dad has saved several of your special bottles for me. I understand Scott Kurey is working with you on making the wines."

"Yes, he and I make a good team," said Lettie, flattered to think Rafe had followed Chandler Hill Winery so closely.

"Here comes Dad," said Rafe.

"I'll leave you two to your work. I understand your father is working with you on your land. What are you going to call it now that the Tauntons have moved on?"

"I'm going to stick with the name Taunton Estates Winery but breathe fresh life into it. They never took the time to know the grape, the land, the process. I can't wait to prove to everyone that I can change the reputation of the name by producing a wonderful, upscale wine."

Joe Lopez joined them. "Hello, Lettie. Looks like it's going to be a nice day."

"I think so." Though Joe hadn't wanted Rafe to have anything to do with her, Rafe's marriage and time had changed things. Now, they'd be working together to keep Chandler Hill productive and to help Rafe with his own wines.

"I've got to go. We've got a big party arriving today." As she started to walk away, she realized she'd never mentioned Rafe's wife. She turned back. "Welcome Maria to the area. I hope she'll enjoy being back home."

A sad expression crossed his face, turning down his mouth. "You haven't heard? Maria is fighting cancer. That's why we're here."

Lettie felt the blood leave her head. "Oh, Rafe! I'm so sorry. If there's anything I or any of my staff can do for either of you, just let me know."

"Thanks."

Joe placed a comforting hand on Rafe's shoulder. "We're all very sad about it."

"Of course," said Lettie. "We're still trying to get over Terri's death. Someday, we'll be able to eliminate cancer, but I'm afraid it won't happen for a long time. Please give my best to Maria."

As Lettie walked away from the two men, she felt their eyes on her.

Later, as she sat talking to Paloma, Lettie told her about the conversation Rafe had with Rod Mitchell. "If he thinks he's still got a chance of taking over Chandler Hill, he's crazy. I'm never going to sell this place. And if Rafe and I are friends, it's nobody's business. He's married, for heaven's sake!"

"Being married doesn't stop some people." Paloma shook her head. "Look at poor Elisa. She's forced to put up with a lot."

"I don't understand why she doesn't divorce Ricardo."

"She can't afford to live on her own. We pay her a decent salary, but it's not enough to take care of her and their five children. He has a good job. She needs the money he brings in."

"Do you ever miss being married?" Lettie asked Paloma. "I know you've dated."

"I love going out with a man, having dinner, even making love with him. But after seeing Manny through his return from Vietnam, his recovery, and finally his suicide, I don't want to marry again. I like my freedom. Somebody else can cook and clean and take care of a guy, but that's not for me."

"I understand," Lettie said. Though she was still shaken by her reaction to Rafe, she'd do nothing about it. Look what had happened with Rod. For the short time she'd been married to Kenton, their marriage had been so perfect no other could compare. Plus, in so many ways she was already married—to the land and the inn.

Lettie turned to Paloma. "Let's do something really nice for Maria. Think of how we can help, and we'll do it. The few times I met her, I liked her."

Chandler Hill had a bountiful harvest that summer. They were, Lettie decided, some of the sweetest, most perfect grapes they'd ever grown.

Heralded as the vintage of the century, 1992 was different in that there were long, hot days, warm nights, and very little rain during the growing season. Local winemakers described the vintage as a California one. Lettie found it necessary to harvest early, and by mid-September, picking was in full swing.

They'd just put the wine in barrels when Lettie got a letter from Autumn telling her that she wouldn't make it home for the holidays.

Disappointed, Lettie kept busy.

CHAPTER TWENTY-ONE

Another two years went by before Lettie finally heard the news she'd been waiting for. Autumn was coming home for the holidays.

Inside the Portland International Airport, Lettie paced back and forth, unable to keep still. It had been over four years since Autumn had gone to Africa, and though Lettie had missed her terribly, she had persisted in building a relationship between them through letters. But any mother knows letters are not enough, and Lettie couldn't wait to wrap her arms around her daughter.

As passengers deplaned and made their way through the terminal, Lettie's eyes remained glued on the arrivals. She noticed a tall, auburn-haired woman walking toward her holding onto a baby in a carrier. She took another look. Was that Autumn? But in all their communications she'd never mentioned a baby of her own.

"Mom?" Autumn smiled and shifted the baby carrier in her arms.

"Autumn, is it really you? And who is this?" Lettie's gaze settled on the little girl whose red hair and brown eyes were part of a cherub-like, chubby-cheeked face.

"This is Camilla," Autumn said. "But I call her Cami. Cami Chandler."

Lettie clasped a hand to her chest. "I'm a grandmother? How fabulous! Where is her father?"

"Off to India. I'm here for just a short visit. We'll talk later. Right now, I know a little girl who needs her diaper changed.

Want to help?"

She handed Lettie the baby carrier and searched through the diaper bag she was carrying. Lifting out a diaper, she grinned. "Success."

As they walked through the terminal to a rest room, Lettie gazed at the baby. "How old is she?"

"Six months," said Autumn.

"Is her father Richard?" Lettie asked, thinking with dismay of Autumn's old boyfriend.

"No, no. Richard and I broke up some time ago. It's someone I knew briefly. He doesn't even know about the baby, and I don't plan to tell him."

"Oh, but ..." Thinking of her own situation, Lettie stopped. How could she even dare to counsel her daughter about such a thing?

They changed the baby's diaper and then went to baggage claim to pick up the two suitcases Autumn had brought with her.

"Why don't you hold the baby? I'll get the luggage," Autumn suggested.

The baby looked at Lettie and smiled, exposing two little teeth. The awkwardness Lettie had felt disappeared in a rush of love. This precious, beautiful child was her granddaughter.

Cami reached up and tweaked Lettie's nose.

Lettie laughed and poked Cami in the stomach, eliciting a giggle from her. Then, they laughed together.

Once the luggage was stowed in the Volvo station wagon Lettie had bought several years earlier to replace the VW Squareback Kenton had given her, Lettie got behind the wheel and took off.

"It's going to be so different being home," said Autumn. "I've grown to love Africa—its people, its beauty."

"You're continuing to help in Zaire?"

Autumn's expression became serious. "Yes. There's still so much to be done there. Their leader is corrupt, leaving most of the people in such poverty it's unimaginable. And now Hutu refugees are being hunted down. Drinking water for everyone, medical care, education—all the things we take for granted are not available to most. My work has become an important part of a village, and I need to go back. I'm sorry, but it's going to be a shorter visit than I'd imagined."

"What about the baby? Is it safe for her there?"

"Not as much as I'd like." Autumn gazed out the window, ending their conversation.

Lettie continued driving, casting glances at her and the baby buckled in her car seat in the back.

"Do you want to talk about it?" Lettie asked tentatively. At the mention of the plight of the people, sadness had crossed her daughter's face and lingered.

"Not yet," she said.

By the time Lettie drove the car up the driveway to the inn and on to her house, both Autumn and Cami had fallen asleep. Lettie pulled into the driveway, turned off the engine, and sat a moment, hating to disturb them.

Gently, she shook Autumn's shoulder.

Alarmed, Autumn came wide awake, sat up, and studied the area around her. "Ah, we're home."

Tears came to Lettie's eyes unexpectedly. She'd waited a long time to hear those words. "I'll take the baby, if you wish, and then you and I can get the luggage inside."

"Okay. I suppose we can get a crib from the inn," Autumn quickly agreed.

"Oh, yes. Good idea," Lettie said, thinking of other things they might need. "I'll call and ask one of the staff to bring one here, along with sheets and blankets. Tomorrow, we can go to town for anything we don't have."

"I brought what I could with me. Cami has a couple favorite toys and a favorite blanket, though I suspect she'll need warmer clothes."

Still shocked by all the changes, Lettie stared at her daughter. "I can't believe you're a mother, but you seem to be a natural, doing such a good job of it."

"Thanks," said Autumn giving her a misty-eyed smile that reminded Lettie of the little girl Autumn used to be.

Cami began to cry, shattering the tender moment.

"Hush, baby," crooned Lettie, picking Cami up and rocking her as she carried her inside.

In the kitchen, Autumn opened the diaper bag and brought out an empty baby bottle and a container of Similac. "I think she's hungry. I'll get a bottle heated up, and you can give it to her."

Lettie watched Autumn quickly put together a bottle of milk for the baby and then hand it to her.

Once settled in a rocking chair in the guest room, Lettie held Cami close as the baby gobbled down the milk.

Autumn handed her a dishtowel. "Before burping her, you might want to put this over your shoulder. Cami can be a spitter."

Lettie lifted the baby to her shoulder and rubbed her back.

"A little harder," Autumn coached.

Lettie patted Cami's back, and this time, Cami burped and then spit up on a part of her sweater Lettie hadn't covered with the towel.

Autumn gave her a sympathetic look. "Sorry. I tried to tell you. Here, I'll take Cami while you clean up."

"Thanks. It'll take me just a minute, and then I'll pour us some wine. The last few years have been good for grapes in the valley."

"That sounds wonderful."

"I've ordered dinner to be delivered here around eight o'clock. Is that okay? Our new cook at the inn is fabulous. She's an older woman from California, and though she isn't as much fun as Terri was, the staff likes her."

"Sure, that will be fine. My time table is so messed up, I guess it doesn't really matter."

"In the meantime," said Lettie. "I'll call for the crib."

As she changed her sweater, Lettie wondered at all the changes in Autumn. She was a different person—a mother no less! She'd thought communication between them had improved but, obviously, there was a whole lot that hadn't been shared. Lettie glanced at herself in the mirror and a slow smile of satisfaction crossed her face. If she wasn't mistaken, Cami looked a lot like her.

After leaving her room, Lettie answered the doorbell and then helped one of the housekeepers set up the crib in one of the two guest rooms. After feeling alone for so long, she was pleased to see the house with guests.

In the living room, Cami lay on a blanket kicking her feet happily.

Lettie walked the housekeeper to the door and thanked him. After he left, she turned to Autumn. "How about that wine now?"

"Yes, that would be nice," said Autumn, letting out a long sigh.

Lettie returned to the living room with an open bottle of pinot noir and two red-wine glasses. "I'm really proud of this one. It has such a smooth finish I think you'll like it."

Autumn accepted the glass of wine Lettie offered her and waited for her to pour some wine into her own glass.

Lettie sat down beside Autumn and lifted her glass. "Here's to the Chandler women—all three generations!"

"I'll drink to that." Autumn took a sip of wine and gave her a warm look. "Nice. Very nice."

"Thanks. Now let's hear what's going on with you." Lettie set her glass down on the coffee table and leaned forward.

"I was going to wait before telling you, but I want to put it out there now," said Autumn. "I'd like to leave Cami with you while I return to Africa. The political situation can be iffy, and I think Cami will be much safer, much happier here."

Lettie felt her jaw drop. "You want me to raise Cami?"

"No, no, it's not like that. She's my daughter, and I love her, but I can't keep her safe with me." Tears filled Autumn's eyes. "I don't know how long I'll be gone, but of course, I'll come for her as soon as I feel it's safe."

Wonder entered Lettie's voice. "You'd trust me to do this? But you always thought ..."

Autumn took hold of Lettie's hands and looked into her eyes. "Mom, that was a long time ago, and I've grown up. Will you take care of Cami for me? Keep her safe and happy?"

Lettie glanced at the baby and swallowed hard. "Of course, I will. She's my granddaughter."

The frown that had lined Autumn's brow was replaced by a bright smile. "Thank you! That means so much to me. I see how comfortable she is with you already."

Lettie clasped her hands. It seemed like such an insane idea because it was obvious that Autumn loved her daughter. But a nagging question kept popping up in her mind. *Then, why hadn't Autumn told her about the baby?*

Cami started to fuss.

Lettie and Autumn looked at each other.

"Why don't you take care of her." Autumn's voice filled with quiet anxiety. "It will be hard enough for me to leave her, and I want to be sure she's accustomed to you."

Lettie picked up the baby, checked her diaper, and carried her to the rocking chair in the guest room next to the crib.

She held the baby close, rocking her until she fell asleep. Carefully, Lettie placed her in the crib on her back as Autumn had instructed and covered her with a blanket.

Autumn looked on. “Tomorrow, I’ll purchase some more suitable things for her.”

When they returned to the living room, Lettie once again took a seat on the couch with Autumn. “When are you going back to Africa?”

“The day after tomorrow. Like I said, I can’t be gone long, I’m working with people in government to get permission to dig a well. I’ve received some threats, which is why I want Cami here with you.”

“What about staying here until things calm down?” Lettie’s voice was hopeful, hiding the deep worry inside her.

Autumn shook her head firmly. “I can’t do that to the people of my village.”

“I admire what you’re doing, but I’m concerned you won’t be happy with my having Cami here.”

“Who better to ask? And Abby and Paloma are around. They can help you.” Autumn’s face flushed with emotion. “I wish the situation were different, but I can’t take a chance on anything happening to Cami.” Her voice wobbled. “I love her so much.”

Lettie sat back against the cushions of the couch feeling as if a hundred-pound weight had been dropped into her lap. If she was totally honest with herself, she’d admit she hadn’t enjoyed raising Autumn. In her forties now, would she be better at mothering? She’d always felt she’d become a mother too soon. Would she feel the same way about being a grandmother?

Autumn reached over and patted her hand. “It’s a lot to request of you, but I wouldn’t ask you to do this if it weren’t necessary.”

"I know," Lettie said, feeling more at ease about this predicament. She'd do as her daughter wanted and become the best grandmother around.

The next afternoon Lettie joined Autumn on the swing on the back deck. Several times she'd attempted to have a conversation with her about the baby's father and birth. But each time, she'd been shut down. Now, she decided to give it one more try. "As your mother, I want to know why you didn't even let me know you were going to have a baby. I wish you'd talk to me now about Cami's birth and her father."

Autumn let out a long sigh. "I can't say anything about him. I wish I could, but people would only get hurt. I thought long and hard about not going through with the pregnancy, and then it was too late. I didn't want to make that choice anyway." Her dark eyes shone with unshed tears. "My friends in Africa stayed with me for the delivery. They said it was an easy one. Once Cami was born, I was going to tell you about her, but I kept thinking I was coming home and I'd show you instead. When I got those death threats, I knew I had to bring her to you right away."

"I wish I had known about your pregnancy. I would have helped," Lettie said with regret.

Autumn looked away and then turned back to her with a sad smile. "At first I thought you'd just criticize me. But then I realized I couldn't ask you to come and be part of the bad scene going on around me. Rebel soldiers would have loved to get their hands on you and that strawberry-blond hair. Besides, I knew with your fear of flying, you could never make the trip."

Lettie's breath left her in a rush. She felt sick to her stomach. What kind of mother wouldn't help her child when she needed it?

Autumn rose and clasped her hand. "Mom? I understand. I really do. Let's leave things as they are. It's all behind us now."

Tears blurred Lettie's vision as she hugged her daughter. "I'm so sorry. I know you haven't always felt that I loved you, but I do, and I always will."

Autumn patted her back. "I know. I know."

Watching Autumn say goodbye to Cami, Lettie held back tears. As unsure, as without patience as she'd been as a mother, she would never have wanted to send Autumn away. Except maybe as a teenager.

"Okay, I'm ready. Let's go to the airport," said Autumn in a shaky voice. She left the house and went to Lettie's car, her steps stiff-legged with determination. Tears rolled down her cheeks.

"I should be back in a couple of hours or so," Lettie told Paloma. "Autumn doesn't want me to wait with her at the airport."

"We'll be here," said Paloma, jiggling Cami on her hip.

It was quiet in the car as Lettie headed north.

Autumn stared out the window at the passing scenery.

Lettie knew there was so much she could say, should say, even talk about Autumn's father. But she held back. Now was not the time to add complications to the unsteady circumstances between the two of them.

CHAPTER TWENTY-TWO

With Cami's presence in her life, Lettie's days became fuller than ever. But she didn't mind. Tired of centering her life around the inn, she handed more responsibility over to the staff so she could spend time with Cami and continue overseeing the growing of the grapes.

Lettie hadn't remembered that having a baby in the house took up so much room, but then, as a new grandmother, she was overwhelmed by all the pieces of equipment that were now available. Enjoying her granddaughter in a way she hadn't her own child, Lettie took to placing Cami in a baby carrier on her back as she wandered through the vineyards. She talked to Cami about the grapes and anything else she could think of. The baby couldn't answer, of course, but Lettie told herself that Cami's beautiful, brown eyes brightened at the information she was receiving.

Lettie also became more social in town as people responded to Cami with her. She loved hearing how much the little girl resembled her and realized how much fun it was to be this child's grandmother.

At the inn, Cami was a hit with everyone and took all the attention given her in stride.

One morning, Lettie walked into the inn's kitchen and found Rafe sitting at the table with a cup of coffee. Startled to see him, she paused a moment, holding Cami in her arms. Gray strands appeared in his dark hair at the temples now, and the lines around his eyes had deepened. But he was more handsome than ever.

He looked up at her and smiled. "'Morning. Heard you had a baby in the house."

"Yes, Cami's my granddaughter." Lettie's heart pounded with dismay. Cami was his granddaughter too, but he didn't know that. And with his wife dying of cancer, this was definitely not the time to tell him. Autumn didn't even know about him yet.

"She's a cutie. Looks a lot like you," Rafe said, getting to his feet.

Cami reached out to him.

Without missing a beat, Rafe took Cami in his arms.

"Wow! You're good!" said Lettie.

He grinned at her. "Uncle Rafe knows a thing or two about babies. I've got fourteen nieces and nephews."

Lettie laughed. "Guess that will do it." She held out her hands. "I'd better take her, though. It's time for a snack. By the way, how are your grapes doing? I heard the old Taunton place looks terrific."

"All it really needed was a lot of tender care," said Rafe, "but, thanks. You'll have to come over and see it for yourself one day."

"I'd like that. And, Rafe, I appreciate all the help you've given your father on my place. It's going to be a great growing season." She started to leave and then turned back. "How are you? Paloma keeps me up to date on the situation with Maria, and I got a sweet thank you note from her for the basket I sent her, but I wonder how you're doing with her long illness; it can't be easy."

"No," Rafe said, giving her a sad look. "I don't like to see Maria suffering. She's hoping it will soon be over. Can't say that I blame her. Cancer is a bad disease."

"Yes, I'm so sorry. For both of you. If there's anything I or anyone at the inn can do for you, please let me know."

"Thanks." His dark eyes studied her a moment with a touch of tenderness, and then he turned away. He quickly walked out of the room, leaving Lettie to wonder about that look.

With April came the bud break of the grape vines and Cami's first, hesitant steps. Autumn, too, had walked at an early age, but Lettie still thought her granddaughter was remarkable for her strength and determination. More than that, Cami was a sweet child who seemed to know which battles she could win. Though she had a temper when the occasion called for it, she didn't overuse it.

The whole valley mourned when Maria finally succumbed to the disease that had ravaged her body. It seemed so unfair for such a beautiful woman to have suffered the indignities of such an ending. Lettie joined others to pay their respects to Rafe and his family. His mother, Rita, had long since given up working at the inn. Lettie easily gave her a hug.

"I'm so sorry," Lettie said sincerely.

Rita's gaze swung to her son. "Rafe has had so many disappointments. I hope after things settle down, he can find a nice woman in our community who will be happy with him living and working in the valley. It's all he's ever wanted to do. He tried to be happy for Maria's sake, but he never really liked California."

"There's something special about the Willamette Valley. I knew it the first day I saw it."

"Yes, I remember that well," said Rita. "You and Rex hit it off right away because you loved this land as much as he did. Funny, how things turn out. Who would've thought Chandler Hill would be the great success it is. It was a turkey farm back in the day."

"I think the whole valley was one turkey farm at one point.

Look at it now! It's amazing to see all the vineyards and orchards."

From across the room, Rafe glanced at them and smiled.

Rita looked from him to Lettie and frowned, no doubt recalling how they'd always been drawn to one another.

"I'll talk to you later," Lettie told Rita, stung by her reaction. Rafe's parents had never wanted him to be with her. Did they think something was going on between them now?

Lettie moved away from Rita and went to find Maria's mother. She couldn't imagine how painful it must be to lose a daughter.

After extending her sympathy to both of Maria's parents, Lettie headed for the door.

"Hey! Where are you going?" said Paloma, rushing up to her. "There's lots of food and wine for everybody. Maria's parents will feel you're disrespecting them if you leave now."

"I thought Rita might feel more comfortable if I left. I don't know what she thinks is happening between Rafe and me, but I hardly ever see him, and then it's only out in the fields."

Paloma pulled Lettie aside and spoke quietly. "She and everyone else here know that Rafe has never gotten over you."

Lettie felt her eyes widen. "But he ... I mean we ..." Her voice trailed off in confusion.

"I know. But when the two of you are together, there's a certain undeniable chemistry between you. Surely, you feel it."

Lettie sighed and looked away.

"Okay, then, you'd better stay and do your duty by pretending he isn't even here. Understand?"

"Okay." Lettie couldn't let Rafe or any other person dictate where she could go or with whom. She did, however, stick to Paloma's side as they returned to the kitchen, where a mound of food had been displayed on a long, wooden table sitting in the middle of the room.

As soon as she could go graciously, Lettie headed toward the front door. Cami would be getting up from her nap, and Lettie wanted to be there for her.

"Leaving?" Rafe's deep voice came from behind her.

She turned. "Yes. I'm so sorry for your loss, Rafe. Maria was a beautiful woman."

"Thanks. And thanks for coming. Guess you'll be seeing more of me as the vines come alive with blooms, and I help my father. You've probably noticed how much he's slowing down."

"Yes, but don't worry. I'm not about to replace him."

"Good. See you around."

On the drive to the inn, Lettie's thoughts spun. Did everyone in the valley think something was going on between Rafe and her? The idea was both unnerving and unsettling. Her thoughts went back to the brief encounters she'd had with him when she'd first come to Chandler Hill. She'd been rocked to the core by his lovemaking and then hurt beyond belief when it was made clear that his family didn't want him to have anything to do with her. Those feelings had been pushed aside when Kenton began to court her in earnest. Then, when she'd discovered the magic of deep love between Kenton and her, all thoughts of Rafe had disappeared.

She caught a glimpse of herself in the rearview mirror. Sometimes, she had to remind herself that though responsibilities had weighed heavily on her for years, she wasn't that old. In her forties, she looked young for her age. Maybe it was the strawberry-blond hair that she'd allowed to go free in a mass of ringlets or the alertness of her green eyes in her smooth face.

Lettie let out a sigh, remembering how satisfying it had felt to make love with Rod Mitchell. In truth, he was just an okay lover, but she'd still enjoyed the feel of his hands on her. Aware of his ultimate intention to take over the inn, she wondered how many other men had shown interest in her over the years only because of the property under her control.

What they didn't know is that she would never turn the land over to anyone who wasn't in the family.

With the buds in bloom on the vines, Lettie worked with Joe and Rafe to manage the canopy, making sure there were open spaces and all leaves were exposed. Even on days when Joe and Rafe were working on Rafe's property, Lettie kept an eye on the vines. She knew how important it was for each grape to have the chance to grow well.

Now that Cami was walking and running, her times to do this kind of work were often in the afternoons when the little girl was sleeping in the care of a babysitter..

One afternoon, as she was kneeling on the ground, checking on a shoot, she heard a voice behind her. "Your cuttings have developed into nice shoots."

Silently urging her heart to slow down, Lettie got to her feet and faced Rafe. "Thanks. How are you doing?"

Rafe shrugged. "Okay, I guess. It gets lonely in that big house of mine."

"I know what you mean. Of course, now I have the baby and all her toys and equipment to make it less lonely, but being alone isn't easy."

Rafe studied her. "Do you remember when I told you that after being with you I never wanted to be with anyone else?"

"I remember," she said quietly and looked beyond him to the rows of vines.

"I meant it," said Rafe. "After the harvest and winemaking, I'm going to knock on your door."

"But, Rafe, your mother and father—"

He cut her off. "Listen to me. I gave you up once. I'm not going to do it again. I should never have married Maria. She knew it. I knew it. I took good care of her, did as she asked, but I didn't love her the way she wanted me to. I couldn't. I've always loved you, Lettie."

"We can't ... you can't ... it's only been a few months since Maria died." Longing battled with the need to do the right thing by respecting Maria.

"I know. I'm just giving you fair warning. I'm not going to let you go this time." He lowered his lips to hers.

Awash in sensations, her body felt as if all the bones and muscles had suddenly melted. She clung to him.

When he finally stepped away from her, he gave her a crooked smile she thought she'd forgotten. "Yeah, that's how I remembered it."

Her eyes filled as they studied each other. "Me, too," she whispered. Battling her desire to kiss him again, she turned and hurried toward the inn.

Later, all she could think of was Rafe's kiss. It was everything she remembered and more. Next time Rafe wanted to kiss her, she wouldn't run away.

As the holidays approached, Lettie waited to hear from Rafe. But after the harvest, he left the valley. Paloma said it was to see to the house he still had in California. But Lettie wondered if there was more to the story. Perhaps it was his way of saying he'd changed his mind about seeing her.

She sent a message to Autumn asking her when she would arrive for the holidays. When she hadn't heard for a while, Lettie finally received a phone call from her.

"Mom, I'm sorry, but I'm not coming home for Christmas.

I can't leave at this time. I'm needed here. I figure at her young age, Cami won't miss me. Besides, it would be especially hard on both of us if I were to appear for a few days and then leave. I'll come when I know I can stay longer than that."

"Your daughter needs you too." Lettie knew she sounded harsh, but she couldn't help herself. Cami was one of the sweetest babies ever and deserved to know her mother.

"Now, Mom," Autumn said quietly. "I know Cami's in good hands and getting all the love and attention that she deserves. If I didn't believe that, I wouldn't let her stay with you. I love her and want the best for her. And right now, it isn't being with me."

Chastised, Lettie drew a deep breath. She knew from earlier emails how busy Autumn was, how important her work was.

"All right, I won't keep at you about it. But the day will come, I hope, when you place your daughter first."

"Like you did for me?" The sarcasm in Autumn's voice was unmistakable.

"What do you mean?" Lettie was taken aback.

"That inn meant more to you than I did," said Autumn. "You can't deny it."

"Wait a minute," said Lettie, fighting to keep a steady voice. "I had to keep that inn from failing. For you and your future as much as anything else. Remember, I was an overwhelmed nineteen-year-old. I know I wasn't perfect. Far from it. But it was the best I could do."

Autumn's voice softened. "Oh, Mom, I'm sorry. Let's not fight. I love you and thank you from the bottom of my heart for taking care of Cami. As soon as I'm sure my people are safe and protected, and Cami will be safe with me, I'll come for her."

"All right. I'll take you at your word. Cami's asleep, but I can wake her, if you want."

"No, let's allow her to sleep. It's such a blessing that she's not hungry, but safe and dry and warm with you. I wish all children were so lucky."

"Yes," said Lettie. "I'm proud of the work you're doing. Too many children need your kind of help with medicine, education, clean water, and all you're doing for them."

"Thanks, Mom. I've got to go, but I'll keep in touch. I promise."

"Okay. Love you, Autumn," said Lettie.

"Love you too. Kiss my sweet baby for me."

With a click, their phone call ended.

Instead of staying at the inn for Christmas, Abby opted to go to San Francisco to spend the holidays with a new girlfriend. Lettie understood, but felt abandoned, even with Cami present to brighten the day.

Still, she went through the motions of making a mimosa for herself and whipping up a small batch of hollandaise sauce for the eggs benedict she usually served every Christmas morning. While Cami happily played with her new toys, Lettie sat in the living room watching her, sipping her drink of orange juice and champagne.

At the sound of a knock at the front door, Lettie set down her glass and stood, still in her pajamas. Automatically, she fingered her hair, fluffing her curls.

Opening the door and seeing Rafe, she clasped a hand to her chest. "Hello."

"Hi. I just stopped by to wish you a Merry Christmas. My parents are out of town visiting one of my sisters, and I was sitting alone in my house ..." His voice trailed off.

"Won't you come in? I'll make a mimosa for you. It's been pretty lonely for me, too. Of course, I've got Cami, but our conversations are a little one-sided."

Rafe chuckled.

Lettie waved him inside, wishing she'd taken the time to get dressed. At least she was wearing her red-plaid flannel pajamas, not her sexy, silky ones.

Rafe stepped inside her house and paused to look around. "Nice. I like all the artwork."

"Thanks." Seeing the scene through his eyes, she thought the house wasn't that large, but the openness, the sliding-glass doors, and many windows made it seem bigger than it was. The pale gray walls served as a subtle background for the contemporary paintings exhibited there. The wooden floors were offset by colorful Oriental rugs that were suited to the colors in the paintings on the walls.

Rafe went over to Cami and knelt beside her. "What do you have there, Cami?"

Cami held up her favorite new toy.

"Ah, Tickle Me Elmo," said Rafe. "Several of those are appearing in my family."

"Who can resist that laugh, huh?" said Lettie, knowing she'd soon tire of it. Cami loved to make Elmo laugh.

Lettie left Rafe with Cami, went into the kitchen, and returned to the living room with his drink.

He took the glass from her and raised it in a salute. "Merry Christmas, Lettie. And a Happy New Year!"

She smiled and clicked her glass against his. "And to you. Hopefully, it will be a happier new year than the last one."

He set down his glass and let out a long breath. "I'm thinking of hiring a live-in housekeeper. The place is bigger than I need and could use some care. Besides, I hate coming home to an empty house."

"I'm thinking of getting a dog," said Lettie. "It's been several years since Bee died. It would make me feel safer alone here in the house, and I think Cami would like it."

"Of course, we could scrap all those plans and move in together," said Rafe, his dark eyes twinkling with mirth.

She laughed, secretly thrilled with the idea.

"Seriously, I think you already know how attracted I am to you. I want to get to know the woman you've become." Rafe's gaze was steady.

"Yes, I know," She quietly studied him. "Why is your family so opposed to the idea of you and me together? Your mother …"

Rafe took hold of her hand. "We're middle-aged people. We don't need anyone to tell us what we can or cannot do."

"But …"

"My parents have this crazy idea that it would be disrespectful on both our parts to be together."

Lettie heard the bitterness in Rafe's voice and realized he'd already had a similar conversation with his parents. It might be different if his family weren't so old-fashioned, so close.

Cami fussed and toddled toward them.

Lettie rose from the couch and went to pick her up.

Sitting back down with Cami in her arms, she murmured to Cami. "This is Rafe. Remember him?"

"'Afe," said Cami, smiling shyly at him.

He smiled and shook her hand. "Nice to meet you, Cami." He gazed at Lettie. "With that hair and those eyes, she's going to break a man's heart one day."

"I hope not," said Lettie. She kissed Cami's cheek and squeezed her tight. "I can't believe how much I love this little girl. When Autumn was a baby, I was so busy with the inn I didn't take time off for her. Autumn recently accused me of neglecting her, and she was right."

"You're such a good grandmother I can't believe you weren't a good mother too. Everyone sees the two of you together all the time."

Her heart warmed. His praise meant so much to her.

"It's time for Cami's morning nap. Want to stay for a late breakfast? I'm fixing some eggs benedict, a tradition for me."

"Sure," he said eagerly.

"Make yourself comfortable. I'll put Cami down for her nap, change my clothes, and be right back."

"Okay. I'll be here," he said giving her a bright smile.

Lettie quickly got Cami settled in her crib and hurried into her bedroom to change. The day seemed so much better, so much brighter sharing it with Rafe. She dressed in gray slacks and a soft-pink cashmere sweater that went nicely with her hair. Standing in front of the bathroom mirror, she spritzed perfume behind her ears, slid the diamond earrings she'd bought herself into her ear lobes, and took the time to add eye shadow and mascara.

She returned to her living room to find Rafe standing in front of one of the paintings. He turned to her and let out a low whistle. "Wow! You look good."

Feeling suddenly shy, her cheeks grew warm. "Thanks. I'm not always in jeans and heavy boots, walking the land."

He grinned and then indicated the painting. "I didn't know you collected art."

"That's one of my favorites. I started picking up a few things at various arts and crafts fairs and then really got into it when I took a class from one of the art galleries in Portland. I'm no expert. I simply know what I like. Sometimes the artwork is expensive, but most of the time it's not, depending on the artist."

"You have a beautiful home, and with your flair, it's spectacular." He studied her. "Would you ever consider helping me with my house? With Maria so sick, she was unable to add any finishing touches to it."

They continued to stare at one another, sending silent messages. "Sure. I'd like to do that for you. With you."

Eyes shiny with emotion, Rafe leaned forward.

Lettie knew he wanted to kiss her, and though she told herself to be careful, she eagerly met his lips. And then, when he drew her closer, she wrapped her arms around him, unable to control the desire that pulsed through her.

His kiss deepened, telling her in his own way how much he'd missed her.

When they finally pulled apart, they stood facing one another, breathing deeply.

"Oh, Rafe," she managed to say. "What are we going to do about us?"

His gaze was steady. "We're going to enjoy being with one another. In every way."

Lettie's breath came out in a sigh of relief. She wanted him. It was that simple. That wonderful.

He held out his hand, and she took it.

CHAPTER TWENTY-THREE

Lying beside Rafe, Lettie traced his broad chest with her finger, letting her touch trail over the planes and curves of his body. For a man close to fifty, he was in terrific shape. He'd just proved it to her.

He rolled over to face her. "I've waited a long time for this—being with you, making love to you. You're every bit as wonderful as I'd remembered. And even more beautiful."

His lips met hers.

Lettie knew her body was aging. There were the stretch marks she could never get to disappear, the roundness to her stomach, the way her breasts had softened. But if Rafe didn't mind, why should she? For the first time in a long time, she felt cherished for being exactly who she was. She knew tomorrow might be different, but she intended to enjoy this day. Tomorrow, after giving staff members time off until the New Year's Eve rush, she'd be busy at the inn. And Rafe would have to face his family. While she was not flaunting their relationship, she wouldn't hide it either.

At the sound of Cami's voice through the baby monitor, Lettie got out of bed. "Guess I'd better go get her. Breakfast is still an option. Still hungry?"

"Oh, yeah," he said, winking at her.

She placed her hands on her hips and laughed. "You know what I mean."

He grinned. "Guess I'll have some of those eggs you were talking about." He got out of bed and headed into the bathroom.

Lettie grabbed a robe and went to get Cami. Lifting Cami from the crib, Lettie nuzzled the folds of the baby's warm neck, and hugged her close. It had become a ritual between them.

After changing her, Lettie carried Cami into the kitchen and placed her in her highchair.

Content for the moment, Cami carefully picked up Cheerios from the tray in front of her and popped them, one by one, into her mouth.

Rafe entered the room, his hair still damp from the shower. "Ah, the princess has arisen."

"Can you watch her for a minute while I get dressed?" Lettie asked.

"Sure. Cami and I can get to know each other better. Right Cami?"

Cami smiled at them. "'Afe."

Rafe grinned. "She sure is smart."

Lettie couldn't hide her pride. "She really is. Have fun, you two. I'll be right back."

After hurrying to freshen and change, Lettie returned to the kitchen to find Rafe playing a clapping game with Cami. The sight of the two of them together brought tears to her eyes. She wondered if this was the right time to tell him about his connection to the baby.

"I'm hungry," Rafe growled playfully.

Chuckling, Lettie let that thought go and set to work putting together breakfast.

Over the next few days and weeks, Lettie and Rafe settled into a comfortable routine. After seeing that things were situated at the inn with dinner in full swing for guests, Lettie would call Rafe and then meet him at her house.

Once she realized what a good cook Rafe was, she gave him free rein in the kitchen. Sitting with a glass of wine, watching him create a meal became a treasured time for her. Cami was usually content to play in the eating area, or if she was fussy, Lettie often used this time to read to her. Cami was already pointing to letters and animals when prompted, encouraging them both to keep going.

One evening as Lettie was reading to Cami, Rafe said, "This is such a peaceful scene. I wonder if this is what it might have been like if Maria and I had ever had kids. We tried, you know."

"I'm sorry. After seeing how you are with Cami, I'm sure it must have been a disappointment to you." Lettie felt bad that he'd never had the chance to know Autumn as his child.

"Yes, but then who knows if our children would have turned out to be as easy as Cami. Maria was a very discontented person." He stared into the distance.

"I can't believe it was your fault she was unhappy. As I remember, she had dreams of acting or modeling in California. That doesn't work out for most."

"Guess you're right. Enough talk. Get ready for a delicious meal. Chef Rafael thinks you're going to be happy with this."

"It smells delicious. What are you cooking?"

Grinning, he rubbed his hands together. "A roasted chicken with root vegetables cooked in a blend of lemon juice, olive oil, and garlic." He winked at her. "There are some secret herbs involved, too."

Lettie set Cami down on the floor with her book and came over to Rafe. "I'm happy you're here." Neither one of them had used the L-word, but Lettie knew she couldn't hold back any longer. "I love you. I did back then too."

He wrapped his arms around her and brought her close. "Yeah, me too. It's all happening so fast, but like Paloma says, it's meant to be."

Lettie cocked an eyebrow playfully at him. "So, you're talking behind my back, are you?"

"More like Paloma catching hold of me and telling me how happy you are. Guess that's what best friends do for one another."

Lettie felt a smile spread across her face. It felt good to have Paloma's blessing.

After a delicious meal accompanied by a lovely pinot noir from a neighboring vineyard, Lettie left Rafe in the kitchen and hurried to bathe Cami and get her ready for bed.

Later, clean baby in arms, Lettie entered the living room to find Rafe sitting in front of the fireplace, soft jazz playing in the background.

"Thought you might want to say goodnight to her," said Lettie, placing Cami in his arms.

He grinned and bounced Cami in his lap. "Can you say 'night, night?'"

"Night." She pointed to him. "'Afe."

Lettie exchanged looks of surprise with Rafe and burst out laughing.

"She's going to be a talker, like one of my nieces," said Rafe. He ruffled Cami's hair. "Good night."

Her mind and heart swirling with emotions, Lettie took Cami from his arms and carried her into the bedroom to put her down for the night.

Lettie returned to the living room intent on telling Rafe about his true relationship with Autumn and Cami. But Fate had other ideas.

Rafe was sound asleep on the couch.

The rest of January and all of February were quickly

consumed by working in the field, pruning the vines. Lettie kept to the annual schedule of having the shoots or canes of the grapevine completely cut off. She knew the numbers, and the weight of the cane was a good gauge of the work needed for pruning and canopy management in the coming months.

The bud break at the end of March was as exciting as usual. Lettie never got tired of seeing the vines emerge from a quiet winter. This year she identified with the feeling more than usual, because after spending time with Rafe, she felt as if she was emerging from a long, deep sleep. He made her feel so alive, so loved.

Others did not accept their happiness. Maria's family was furious that Rafe wasn't showing the proper amount of respect for her by waiting at least a year before dating another woman. And though his parents interacted with her, she sensed their disapproval.

Lettie, who'd always worked hard to be accepted, to be successful, tried to overcome her hurt. What she felt for Rafe was so deep she couldn't and wouldn't deny it. And Rafe made it easy for her to keep her resolve. His delight in their time together was obvious, whether it was a romantic dinner at home or simply being with Cami.

Many times, Lettie started to tell Rafe about Cami being his granddaughter, and something always came up to stop her. But Lettie knew she couldn't wait any longer. Autumn was coming home for Cami's second birthday in June.

On a warm evening in late May with the vines in bloom, Lettie arranged for Rafe and her to have a pleasant meal on the back deck of her house. One of her favorite spots, the deck overlooked the hills that rolled and dipped into the landscape that always seemed to her to be part of a painting.

As Lettie left the inn, her heart pounded with dread. She didn't know how Rafe would react to the news that he'd fathered Autumn, and she'd kept it from him. In just a short time, their relationship had grown and deepened into something she'd never experienced, not even with Kenton. But then, Kenton and she hadn't had much time together.

Before Rafe's arrival, Lettie hurried home to make sure all was well with Cami. Paloma's niece was acting as nanny for Cami and was doing a great job with her. Still, Lettie liked to know each little tidbit of how their day had gone. And then, left alone with Cami, Lettie would, for some precious moments, have the little girl all to herself.

Lettie was outside on the front lawn, rolling a big rubber ball to Cami, when Rafe arrived in his silver truck. Cami's eyes lit at the sight of him. "'Afe!" she cried, hurrying to him on toddler legs. Watching Rafe swing the little girl up into his arms, some of Lettie's nervousness ebbed away. Rafe and Cami had formed a sweet relationship.

With Cami still in his arms, Rafe strode over to Lettie. "Hi there, beautiful!"

He kissed her, and then Cami said, "Me!"

Laughing, Lettie kissed Cami and took her from Rafe.

"I've got a nice meal planned. Grilled steaks, tossed salad and some of your favorite garlic rolls from the inn. I thought we could fix it together after Cami goes to bed. In the meantime, let's enjoy a glass of wine on the deck. I've got a play area set up there for Cami."

"Sounds good. It's a great night to cook out. We're supposed to have a spectacular sunset. Seems impossible that not long ago most of the valley was suffering from the floods that hurt so many people."

"I know. Makes me appreciate my land up in the hills even more," said Lettie.

She set Cami down in the play area on the deck and went to the kitchen. When she returned with an open bottle of wine and two red-wine glasses, Rafe was standing at the deck's railing, gazing out over the valley.

From behind, she admired his tall, slim body, wide shoulders, and cute butt. Having had a non-existent sex life over the years, she now found herself thinking about it a lot. She and Rafe were no youngsters, but sex was very much a part of their relationship, and she loved it.

He turned around and smiled at her.

She set down the glasses and the bottle of wine on the table and went into the arms he offered her. Snuggled up against his chest, she hoped she'd always be able to be like this with him.

"Isn't Cami ready for bed?" he teased. Amusement filled his words.

She stepped back. "Not yet. But after she's settled for the night, you and I need to talk."

"Oh? Something serious?" His brow lined with worry.

"It's something I've wanted to tell you for some time." She squeezed his hand. "I love you, you know? I hope you'll hear me out. In the meantime, why don't you pour the wine while I get the cheese and crackers."

"Okay, but you know I don't like secrets, right?"

Her heart bumped in her chest. "I know." Sick with apprehension, she left to go into the kitchen.

After Lettie got Cami settled for the night, she returned to the deck. The sun was nearing the horizon, sending shards of pinks, reds, and oranges into the sky. She gasped at the beauty of it. Someone had once told her it was God's way of painting. She could almost believe it. Colors like this were hard to reproduce with ordinary paints.

"I poured us another glass of wine," said Rafe, giving her a crooked, impish smile that she'd grown to love.

"That's good. I'm going to need it."

Rafe drew his eyebrows together. "Is this about the talk you wanted to have?"

Feeling the strength leave her legs, Lettie took a seat in one of the chairs. She took a sip of the wine and set down the glass with determination.

Sitting in a chair opposite her, Rafe faced her with a look of concern. She took a moment to study the features of the man she loved, searching in her mind to see if any of them could be found in Cami. Aside from the little cleft in Cami's chin, there were none. It was different with Autumn. Besides the chin, her dark eyes and the shape of her nose were Rafe's. And she tanned easily for someone with red tones in her dark hair.

"Go ahead, tell me," Rafe urged.

Lettie emitted a long breath. "We've often talked about the time when we first met. I've told you how I felt about you then and how much I loved Kenton."

"Yes."

"A few years ago, Autumn had a skiing accident," Lettie continued, "When I was with her in the hospital in Vail, I was shocked to learn she had O positive blood."

"It's pretty common," said Rafe, "but go on."

"Kenton's blood type was AB positive and mine is A positive, which means Kenton isn't her father ..."

She rose and knelt by Rafe's chair. Taking hold of his hands, she said, "Autumn is your child, and Cami is your granddaughter."

Shock registered on his face. And then a look of wonder coated Rafe's handsome, tan features. "What! How? I mean, when?" He let out a laugh that held a note of hysteria. "I know how, of course." His eyes filled with tears. "You're talking about us making a baby all those years ago?"

She nodded, feeling miserable about not telling him earlier. "Yes. Our love produced her."

"My God! Do you mean it?" His look of shock morphed into anger. "We've been together almost six months, and you never said a word about it. You should have told me."

"I know," Lettie said quietly. "I wanted to tell you about Autumn all along. I've been holding back, thinking I should tell Autumn first. But I realize that's not being fair to you. I decided to go ahead and tell you now before Autumn comes home. I can't keep it from her any longer, and I want you to be prepared."

"What is she going to think?" Rafe rubbed the back of his neck.

Lettie lowered her head into her hands and breathed deeply. When she looked up, she said, "It's going to be a shock to her and everyone else. What is your family going to think?"

He stood, took hold of her hand, and pulled her to her feet. Wrapping his arms around her, he said, "Once they get over the shock, I don't think anyone in my family will be too surprised. Except for the color red in her hair, Autumn doesn't look a whole lot like you. In fact, now that I think about it, she looks something like a cousin of mine."

"I never questioned the difference in appearance between Autumn and me, because I don't have any idea what my parents looked like. And I've never met Kenton's mother. But, of course, now that I know you're her father, I notice some similarities. And because I've never even seen a picture of Cami's father, I had no way to judge her features." Lettie shook her head. "It's all been a case of hidden identities. I just hope no one gets hurt by it."

"Agreed." Rafe took her hand. "Let's go look at my

grandchild. God! I can't believe it! Maria and I wanted children, and all this time I already had one." His eyes grew shiny. "I hope Autumn won't be disappointed that it's me and not Kenton who's her father."

"She'll love you, like I do. Let's take it one step at a time." Though Autumn had always claimed no interest in working at Chandler Hill, she liked the idea of being a member of the family that owned it. She still would inherit it, but she would always know she wasn't a true Chandler.

CHAPTER TWENTY-FOUR

Lettie and Rafe tiptoed into Cami's room and stood looking down at the little girl who resembled a rosy-cheeked cherub with soft, light-red curls. Those curls, Lettie knew, came from her.

"She's so beautiful," murmured Rafe. "Knowing she's carrying my blood makes it all so special." He trailed a finger against Cami's cheek, causing her eyelids to flutter before becoming still again.

"We'd better leave her," said Lettie. "If she doesn't have enough sleep, she gets cranky."

They shut the door to the nursery behind them and faced one another.

"May I spend the night?" Rafe asked.

Lettie's lips curved happily. "Of course. I hoped you would."

Rafe took hold of her hand. "I want to be with you."

"Yes, me too." Now that their true relationship was revealed, Lettie felt the need to show Rafe the love that had connected them forever.

They went into her bedroom and quietly undressed, comfortable enough with one another that words were not spoken.

Standing naked before Rafe, she couldn't help wondering what he saw. Still in her forties, she was in good shape for her age, but like all women, she was aware of her flaws.

Rafe seemed to sense what she was feeling and drew her up against him, making it clear that this was what he wanted.

"Every time I look at you, I see the young girl who took my breath away. I've loved you for a long time, Lettie, but now I love you more than I ever thought possible."

His lips came down on hers, gentle at first and then more demanding with desire.

In moments, all she could think of was pleasing him.

Later, sated and lying next to him, Lettie fingered a tear from the corner of Rafe's eye. "What's the matter, sweetheart?"

"I guess I'm overwhelmed by the events of today," he said honestly. "Suddenly I have a family." He reached over and caressed her stomach. "I can't believe you had my baby. I wish I'd known. I would've been there for you. You must have felt so alone with both Rex and Kenton gone."

"Yes," she admitted. "It was a difficult time for me. Paloma was here to help, thank heavens."

"Well, you've had the baby, so now it's up to me to make her mine." His sad smile pricked her heart. "I've missed so much of her life. What is Autumn really like? I heard you've had some issues with her in the past."

Lettie couldn't hold back a sigh. "Autumn wasn't an easy child and became even more difficult as a teenager. But she's beautiful, bright, stubborn, and caring—on her own terms. She claims I loved the inn and vineyards more than I ever loved her. I can't deny her accusation that I spent more time working there than either she or I wanted. I loved her, but you know how committed I was and still am to Chandler Hill."

He squeezed her hand. "You've done a wonderful job with it."

"I wanted to do a good job with Autumn too. I just didn't know how. With Cami, I take great delight in every little detail.

I know I didn't always do that with Autumn. She's right. I wasn't the mother she needed."

Rafe lifted her chin. "Look at me, Lettie. Don't beat yourself up over the past. You were just a kid."

"Autumn is a good person. She's done so much for her people in Africa. She really loves them. That's where she met Cami's father. She won't tell me or anyone who he is. She claims he's in politics now, and it would ruin his career."

"Interesting. So, she's loyal too. I wonder how she's going to react to me, a Spanish grape grower."

"Well, I'm a grape grower too, so who knows?" Lettie said, attempting to put some levity into the conversation.

"I'm going to be nervous about meeting her," Rafe admitted.

"Don't be. You're a wonderful person and you've made an enormous success of Taunton Estates Wines."

"Guess we'll just have to wait and see," Rafe said. "Meanwhile, I'm going to enjoy my granddaughter. God! It feels so good to say that. I still can't believe I have a grandchild."

"More importantly, that we share her," said Lettie, both pleased and relieved by his enthusiasm.

Lettie wrung her hands as she waited inside the Portland airport for Autumn's arrival. She'd landed earlier in L.A. and was taking a short flight up the coast to Portland.

Aware Autumn would be tired from the travel and she would once again be forced to hold off telling her about Rafe, Lettie couldn't stop tension from squeezing her shoulders.

As a group of recently deplaned passengers headed her way, Lettie searched the crowd for her daughter. A tall, striking woman stood out in the crowd as she strode forward with confidence. Wearing sandals and a bright-colored muumuu, she tossed a long braid behind her back and shifted the knapsack on her shoulder. Looking at her tanned skin, the cleft in her chin, the way she moved her shoulders when she walked, Lettie was stunned by how many features of Rafe she now saw in Autumn.

"Over here!" Lettie waved her hand wildly until Autumn finally caught her eye.

Smiling, Autumn rushed over to her. "Hi, Mom! I'm so glad to see you. Where's Cami?"

"She's at home. It's her naptime. I thought we'd all have a better evening if I let her sleep in. She'll be so excited to see you."

"Let's hope she remembers me." Autumn shook her head. "I've been so busy working, too much time has gone by."

Lettie was tempted to say something about that and decided not to.

They grabbed Autumn's two bags from the rotating baggage belt and carried them to Lettie's Volvo wagon.

As they were stowing the bags, Autumn looked at the baby seat and exclaimed, "I can't wait to see Cami! Tell me what she's like. Emails, letters, and photos don't do justice to all I want to know about her."

Lettie smiled at her. "I've got lots of stories to share with you. Let me get out of the airport traffic and I'll tell you. I'm still not used to city driving."

"Still a country mouse, huh?"

Lettie laughed. "Guess I'll always be one."

As they drove out of the city, Lettie turned to Autumn. "Cami is an amazing child. She's bright and curious and already says a remarkable number of words for someone her age. I've read that girls often talk before boys, but she's incredible. Of course, I'm always chatting to her."

"You are?" Autumn's eyes rounded.

"Oh, yes," said Lettie. "I carry her in my backpack as I walk the fields and vineyards. She's going to grow up knowing an awful lot about grapes and wine." She smiled at the memory of Cami toddling beside the rows of grape vines.

"I see."

"She loves being outdoors," said Lettie.

"Good. She'll love South Africa. I've agreed to go there and help set up a teaching program. With Nelson Mandela as president, so many good changes are taking place inside the country."

Heart pounding with dismay, Lettie pulled over to the side of the road and stopped. "You're really going to take Cami away from me?" She couldn't hide the tears that sprang to her eyes.

"Oh, Mom, I'm sorry." She reached over and patted her hand. "I should have waited to tell you."

"Oh, but ..." Lettie couldn't finish.

Autumn gave her a sympathetic look. "She's my daughter. I want her with me. She'll be safe in South Africa. It's time I took her back. It'll be okay, Mom. We'll come back for vacations. I promise."

Lettie clamped her teeth together, so she wouldn't say something she might later regret. Her daughter hadn't kept her earlier promises to come home. Why should she believe her now?

Feeling as if she was driving into a tunnel with no light at the end, Lettie pulled back onto the highway. The sun, so brilliant a moment ago, seemed as dim as a fading light bulb. The light puffy clouds in the blue sky now held a distinctive dark gray.

"Mom?"

Lettie glanced at her daughter.

"I'm sorry, I really am. But I want to raise my daughter. You knew her being with you was supposed to be only temporary."

Lettie's sigh was long and unhappy. "I understand. I just don't know how I can bear to let her go."

"Let's not worry about it now. We've got two weeks together." Autumn settled back in her seat.

"Yes, you're right. Let's enjoy the time together. There are several things I need to talk to you about."

"How's Abby?"

"She's fine. She and her new partner love their work at the inn. Abby is in charge of all the retail at the winery and at the inn. Her partner, Lisa Robbins, is into healthy food and products. She makes her own soap and maintains an unbelievable herb garden from which she makes all kinds of products to sell in the barn. They work well together and are happy."

"I'm glad," Autumn said. "I still think of Terri. I could always count on her to understand what I was going through." She gave Lettie a weak smile. "I know I wasn't the easiest kid around. She made that clear to me."

"She did?"

"Yes. She's the person who urged me to travel and see the world and see how other people lived. She thought that would settle a lot of issues for me. It was the best advice I've ever received. I've found my niche helping others."

"Your work is very admirable," Lettie said. "I try to keep up on the news, so I understand more about where you are and what you're doing."

"I want Cami to have the same kind of freedom to be herself that I have," said Autumn earnestly.

"She's awfully small to take on the world," Lettie said softly.

"Mom, she'll love Africa. I just know it."

Lettie managed a nod, but inside her heart was breaking.

CHAPTER TWENTY-FIVE

When they arrived home, Cami was outside on the front lawn playing with Ellie Rodriguez, Paloma's niece acting as the nanny. Lettie had laid out a pink sundress for Cami to wear, and now, looking at her run around the grass like a pink butterfly, Lettie's heart filled.

At the sight of the Volvo pulling into the driveway, Cami stopped running and stared at them.

"Oh my! She's so big and grownup," whispered Autumn, getting out of the car.

Lettie climbed out of the car and stood as Cami raced toward them crying, "Nonnee! Nonnee!"

Autumn held out her arms, but Cami raced past her to Lettie.

Lettie picked Cami up and hugged her to her chest. "I've got a surprise for you! Your Mommy is here. Let's say hi."

"'Kay." Cami beamed at her mother. "Hi."

Autumn held out her arms. "Want to come to me?"

Cami stared at her and shook her head.

"Give her time," Lettie said softly. "She'll get used to you."

Lettie set Cami down on the grass. "Go get the ball to show Mommy."

Autumn turned to Lettie and snapped, "You let her call you Mommy?"

"What? No. She's saying Nonnee. That's what she calls me." Lettie placed a hand on Autumn's arm. "Everything will get straightened out. We'll work on it together."

"I'm sorry." Autumn sighed. "Guess I'm overanxious."

"And you're tired, no doubt. Let's get the suitcases inside and you can relax for a bit. I can't imagine it's been an easy trip." Lettie had wanted to fly to Africa for a visit but after realizing how long she'd be in the air, she simply couldn't do it.

"The trip wasn't too bad, but it was a long one. Thanks, Mom."

Later, after she was settled, they sat in the living room observing Cami play with the building blocks Lettie had given her.

"She *is* bright," Autumn commented with pride. "And creative."

"Oh, yes. She already can point to certain letters. I think she'd going to be an early reader. Of course, I spend a lot of time with her. Her nanny, too."

"Did I have a nanny at this age?"

"Paloma and her mother were the ones who cared for you," said Lettie, unable to keep regret out of her voice. She wished now she'd spent more time with her daughter at this young age. But exactly as she'd been accused of doing, she'd spent more time on running the inn and growing grapes than she had on her growing child. But then, like Paloma and others had told her, she'd done her best with all she'd been given to do.

When Cami began to fuss, Lettie rose. "Why don't you take care of Cami while I get her supper ready." Before Autumn could object, Lettie left the room. When Cami called for her, she kept going. Lettie would have just two weeks to get Cami ready to leave her.

While Cami ate her meal, Lettie and Autumn sat at the kitchen table. Cami was doing a good job of feeding herself with her fingers, though she had to be helped with larger pieces of cheese and fruit.

Though Lettie was heartsick at the idea of Cami leaving her, she did her best to hide her feelings. She didn't want Cami to be upset.

"Okay, bath time," said Lettie. "I'll clean up here while you get started on her bath. I've left out a towel, pajamas, and diaper for her. Later, I'll show you where I keep everything."

"All right. Thanks." Autumn lifted Cami from her highchair. "Let's go."

Cami burst into tears and held out her arms to Lettie. "Nonnee!"

Autumn sighed unhappily. "Here. Do you want her?"

Lettie was tempted to say yes, to sweep Cami into her arms and hug her tight, but she resisted those maternal feelings. "No, you carry her. I'll walk alongside you. It'll give me a chance to show you our normal routine."

"Okay." Autumn's eyes filled. "Thank you for being this understanding and kind."

"Of course, honey. I remember how you insisted I take over for you when you first brought Cami here, so we'd both be comfortable. Now, I guess it's my turn to do the same for you."

"Thanks." She gave Lettie a look of gratitude.

Lettie stood by as Autumn placed Cami in the tub and began to play with her in the warm water. Watching them together, it seemed only right that Cami be with her mother. But that didn't stop pain from filling every part of Lettie's heart. She'd heard being a grandparent was the gift for surviving your own children. After being with Cami, she knew how real it was.

After Cami was in her pajamas, Lettie showed Autumn the blanket Cami used to settle down, the music box that she listened to, and the exact way the door to the nursery should be left.

"Whew! I think I have everything straight," she said.

Lettie couldn't help laughing. "I'm sure you'll have your own routine in Africa, but for now, let's keep to one that makes Cami comfortable."

"Yes, I think that's a good idea," Autumn agreed.

After everything had been done according to normal procedure, kisses were exchanged, and then Cami was placed in her crib. Lettie showed Autumn how she rubbed Cami's stomach and then stood aside as she took over. When Cami was finally asleep, they tiptoed out of the room together.

Lettie had hoped she'd have a chance to talk to Autumn about Rafe, but those thoughts disappeared when Autumn turned to her and yawned. "I'm going to bed. I'm exhausted." She gave Lettie a long hug. "Thanks for everything, Mom. See you tomorrow."

"Glad you are home." Lettie returned the embrace with an extra squeeze.

After she left the room, Lettie collapsed on the couch feeling like a rag doll whose stuffing was being pulled out of her piece by painful piece. She wondered if she could convince Autumn to stay in Oregon. Important work could be done right there in the state. Poverty and the need for help existed everywhere. Besides, Lettie wanted her to grow to love the land, the vineyards, the inn as much as she did, because the day would come when she'd have to take it over. Besides, Rafe deserved the opportunity to get to know his own daughter, didn't he?

After a restless night, Lettie awoke to the smell of coffee. For a moment she thought Rafe might be in the kitchen, then she remembered Autumn's presence and sat up with a start. Today was the day she'd be able to tell her about her heritage. It was a gift, really, because it was something that Lettie had never known. Rafe came from a good, hard-working, well-respected family in the valley and was a wonderful person.

She climbed out of bed thinking that after a leisurely breakfast, she'd take Autumn on a walk through the vineyards to the grove of trees that was so special to her. There, they could share the truth. After she'd quickly showered and dressed, Lettie hurried into the kitchen. It was empty. She looked out at the deck. Autumn was sitting in a chair watching Cami in the play area Lettie had set up there. She grabbed a cup of coffee and went outside to join them.

"Nonnee! Nonnee!" Cami cried, holding out her arms to her.

Lettie set down her coffee cup and went to her.

"Please don't pick her up," Autumn said. "She'll never learn to know me if you're always going to her rescue."

Lettie bent over and kissed Cami on the top of her head. "Hi, baby! Mommy and I want to see your baby doll. Will you show us Izzy?"

Distracted for the moment, Cami concentrated on picking up her stuffed doll.

"Izzy is Cami's baby," Lettie explained as she took a seat in a chair. "I'm hoping you'll take a walk with me. There's something I want to talk over with you."

"Okay," said Autumn. "It will feel good to move around. Give me time to get my shoes on and I'll meet you out front."

"I'll bring Cami," said Lettie. Receiving a stern look, she added. "If you'd like."

Autumn studied her. "Okay, thanks."

Lettie lifted Cami out of the play area and gave her a long hug. She knew she'd have only a few days more of hugs with her sweet girl.

###

Out on the front lawn, Lettie set Cami on the grass and laughed when the little girl immediately toddled over to the big, red rubber ball Rafe had given her.

Autumn had just stepped out of the front door when Rafe pulled up in his truck and got out.

"'Afe! 'Afe!" Cami cried, running over to him.

Grinning, he picked Cami up and swung her around in the air before giving her a hug and setting her down.

Autumn looked askance at Lettie. "Who is that?"

"That's what I wanted to talk to you about," said Lettie.

"Are you dating him,? He's handsome, but, Mom ..."

As Autumn's voice trailed away, Lettie studied Rafe. His dark hair, still wet from the shower, was combed away from his rugged features, and a touch of gray gleamed silver at the temples. His body was muscular and trim. For a man in his fifties, he was, as Autumn had mentioned, a very handsome man. His questioning look settled on her. She shook her head, indicating she hadn't told Autumn yet.

His gaze swung to his daughter. A look of pride crossed his face before he quickly covered it with a more neutral expression.

"Hi, Rafe," said Lettie, "What's up?"

He bent down and kissed her on the lips.

Lettie ignored the frown on Autumn's face and kissed him back.

When they broke apart, they turned to her.

"This is Rafe Lopez," Lettie said.

Autumn smiled politely. "Hello." Her gaze lingered on the two of them.

"Up! Up!" cried Cami, clinging to Rafe's legs.

He laughed and ruffled her hair. "Maybe later. Right now, I need to talk to Nonnee."

"Excuse us." Lettie led Rafe over to the truck.

"She doesn't know about us," Lettie said quietly. "I was about to take her for a walk to tell her then."

"Sorry to interrupt, but I needed to speak to you about my father. We had a long talk last night. The doctor is telling him he must slow down. Because of his heart, he's not able to continue working for you full-time. He's going to speak to you about it."

"Oh, no. I'm so sorry to hear this. I hope he'll be okay. He's been such an asset to the winery. He doesn't know it, but a retirement fund was set up for him a long time ago."

"Ah, nice of you. I know of someone looking for a vineyard job. Sam Farley is in his thirties, is a hard worker, and comes highly recommended. I was thinking he could work for both of us. Would you like to set up a time to interview him together?"

"Yes, as long as it isn't today," Lettie said. "I need this time with Autumn." Tears came to her eyes. "And, Rafe, in two weeks, she's returning to Africa with Cami."

"Aw, I'm sorry, Lettie. I'd hoped we'd have more time with her." He reached over and thumbed a tear from the corner of her eye.

She quickly stepped away, knowing if he continued to touch her, she'd rush into his arms and sob. Today, of all days, she couldn't allow herself that luxury. She had to navigate the time with Autumn with an inner strength she'd be forced to summon.

He shuffled his feet, stared at his daughter in the distance, and said softly, "She's a beautiful woman. I can't believe she's part mine."

"I'll arrange dinner for the three of us, and then maybe you can have some time alone with her."

"I'd like that," he said. "I'll call you tonight to see how the day went."

"Why don't I call you when I know we'll have privacy," Lettie countered.

"Good idea. Love you." The look of longing in his eyes when his gaze turned to Autumn was heartbreaking to see.

"Love you too." Lettie lifted on her toes and kissed him.

As they parted, Lettie noticed Autumn entering the house with Cami.

"Our daughter isn't always the easiest person to get along with," said Lettie. "We may have to give her time to get used to the idea of you as her father. But, Rafe, I love you, and I always will."

"I know. Guess I'm a little anxious for it all to work out."

"It will be fine," Lettie said with more conviction than she felt.

CHAPTER TWENTY-SIX

Lettie entered the house and walked into the kitchen. Cami was in her highchair and Autumn was sitting at the kitchen table.

Lettie reached into the cupboard for crackers for Cami and turned to Autumn. "What are you doing?"

"Trying to figure things out." Her dark eyes flashed. "What is this man to you?"

Lettie drew a deep breath and let it out slowly. The time had come for the truth. "He's your father and Cami's grandfather."

"Whaaat?" The look of horror on Autumn's face was hurtful. She jumped to her feet. "Is this some kind of joke? Why would you let me believe Kenton Chandler was my father?"

"Because I thought he was," said Lettie. "Until your skiing accident, I had no idea Kenton wasn't your father. But when I saw your blood type as O positive, I knew he couldn't be. Kenton was AB positive and I'm A positive. I'd met Rafe about the same time I met Kenton."

"Is that the only possibility?" Autumn asked, standing with her hands clutched at her side, looking as if she was about to cry.

Lettie gave her a steady stare. "I loved them both."

"Sorry," said Autumn. "I'm just so confused right now. The person I thought I was no longer exists."

"The Lopez family is well respected in the valley. And Rafe has done very well for himself."

"You've always told me you wanted me to run Chandler Hill Inn one day. Now, there's no way I could change my mind and think of doing it. Not with what I know now. I would feel such a fraud."

"I'm a Chandler which makes you a Chandler too."

"But my father ..."

"Rafe and I knew how we felt about one another, but he had commitments to his family, which he honored. And then Kenton and I fell in love. Kenton and I loved each other very much. He never knew about my pregnancy. He died before I could tell him. The father you never knew was not Kenton, but Rafe. As you never had with him, you now have a chance to know Rafe as your father. I think you'll like him. He's smart and generous and kind. Cami loves him."

"How could you let Cami get close to him when I never even knew about him?"

"It's not something I could tell you on the phone or in a letter. I wanted you to be here with me to meet him, to see him for the great person he is. Autumn, he's thrilled to think he has a daughter. You see how he is with Cami. He adores her, and she loves him."

Autumn lowered her head into her hands.

Lettie went over to her and rubbed her back. "I know it's a lot to take in, but I hope you'll see how important it is for you to talk to Rafe, learn more about him, give him the chance he deserves to be in your life. His parents know and want to say hello, too. They remember you as a child, but I think they'd like to meet you as the young woman you've become."

Autumn jumped to her feet. "I can't even think now. Will you watch Cami? I need to take a walk."

"Sure." Lettie was pretty certain she knew where her daughter was headed. She herself intended to visit the grove of trees as soon as Autumn was able to have a private moment.

###

Later, Lettie put Cami in her carrier and swung it up on her back. Used to going on walks with her, Cami clapped her hands with glee. "Go!"

On this June day, puffy clouds floated in the blue sky like dollops of whipped cream waiting to be scooped up. *A good growing day*, thought Lettie. She hoped it would also be a good day for helping Autumn find some inner peace.

As she walked past the rows of vines, Lettie thought of all she'd been given. She owed so much to Kenton and his father. They'd taken a chance on her—a young, unsophisticated girl from nowhere—to help them with their dream. Though she occasionally felt trapped by the weight of her commitment to them, and sometimes wished she could leave, she knew how lucky she was. Without them, who knows where she would've ended up. Lettie wanted Autumn to be grateful to them, too, but also to be willing to accept the relationship between Rafe and her.

As she neared the grove of trees, she noticed Autumn's stiff-shouldered posture as she sat on the stone bench there.

At the sound of Cami's excited "Hi," Autumn turned to them.

"Mind if we sit with you for a while?" Lettie asked her. "We can leave if you want."

"No, no, it's all right," she said, waving them forward.

Still wearing the baby carrier, Lettie sat down beside her. "I've always loved this spot. It's where I can sort through my problems. There's something special about the peaceful sound of pine trees singing in the breeze among the hardwoods, the smell of their needles, and the memories surrounding the two Chandler men."

"I'm confused," said Autumn. "You say you loved my fa ...

Kenton, but you were with Rafe."

"Rafe and I were immediately attracted to one another, and yes, we were intimate briefly. But when we realized that the relationship could go nowhere, we didn't pursue it. Within days, Kenton asked me to go with him to the beach for a relaxing time before Christmas and his induction into the Army. Kenton had been my sweet, best friend, so I agreed to go. Alone together, we realized we wanted to be much more than friends. In a whirlwind of just three weeks, Kenton asked me to marry him, and we eloped to Las Vegas. We were both as happy as we could be about it. And we were happy together, Autumn. Even though it was a time of free love and all that, both relationships were sincere."

"Didn't you suspect you were pregnant before ... Kenton left for the Army?"

Lettie shook her head. "We were under so much pressure to abide by Rex's will, to set up our own wills, and to learn from experts, I attributed any of those symptoms to stress and grief."

"Why don't I remember Rafe from my childhood?" Autumn asked.

"He and his wife lived in California. He might have met you briefly when they came back home. I didn't spend much time with them. It was best that way."

Lettie reached over and clasped Autumn's hand. "I want you to get to know Rafe. He actually cried when he learned he had a daughter."

"I'll be kind, Mom, but there's not going to be any big celebration that signifies he's suddenly my father. He has to earn the right to that."

"As you must prove you're worthy to be his daughter," Lettie gently reminded her.

Autumn's surprise was telling. "Fair enough. We'll take it

from here. Help me put Cami on my back and I'll carry her over to the inn. I want to see Paloma and Abby and some of the others."

"Sure," Lettie said. "They'll be anxious to see you both."

Together they transferred Cami and the carrier to Autumn's back.

Left alone in the grove of trees, Lettie took in several deep breaths and let them out again.

Back at the house, Lettie went about straightening it. When she stepped into the guest room where Autumn was staying, she saw that little had changed over the years. The bed was unmade, clothing was scattered on the floor, and a laptop was plugged in on top of the bedside table.

Lettie picked up the clothes and set them on the overstuffed chair in the room, then quickly made up the bed. The house was small enough and open enough that it was important to have everything at least tidy.

Glancing out the living room window, she saw Autumn and Cami get out of Paloma's car and breathed a sigh of relief. Of all the people who knew her, Paloma knew her best. She'd help Autumn see how precious the love was between Rafe and her.

Lettie hurried outside to greet them.

"Hi, Paloma," said Lettie. "Come on inside. It's about time for a glass of wine."

"Thanks," said Paloma. "I wanted to tell you about an incident at the inn today. I've taken care of it, but I think you should know about it before our usual weekly meeting."

"Okay. I should be back to my normal routine next week, but I want these first few days with Autumn to be special."

"Understood," said Paloma. "You work too hard as it is."

"Nonnee! Nonnee!" cried Cami.

Lettie reached for her, then checked her motion.

"Go ahead, Mom. She loves you," said Autumn.

Lettie took Cami from Autumn's arms and gave her a growling bear hug. "Love you, little one!"

Cami gazed at Lettie with wide eyes and planted a wet kiss on Lettie's cheek.

Fighting tears, Lettie kissed her back. Too soon, she'd lose the opportunity to do so.

They went inside.

While Autumn fed Cami her supper, Lettie and Paloma took glasses of wine out to the deck.

"It's been a beautiful day." Paloma took a seat in one of the deck chairs.

"Yes," said Lettie. "The weather has been cooperating. Hopefully it will be a good year for our grapes." She sat in a chair and faced her best friend. "What happened at the inn?"

"You know how we have a policy to protect our more famous guests from being exposed? One of the new maids was overheard telling a friend on the phone that she was going to make a lot of money, that she'd taken a photo on her phone of Kimberly Cassidy at the pool.

Luckily it was reported to me. I made sure the photo was deleted from the phone and fired the maid on the spot. As you've said many times, we can't ruin our reputation by stuff like that."

"Totally right," Lettie said. "Are we going to have any repercussions from the firing?"

Paloma shrugged. "Who knows? I don't think so. She signed our agreement that clearly states if caught doing anything like it, the staff member will be fired immediately. For the moment, I believe the problem is solved."

"Is the event recorded in case we need it in the future?"

"Yes, a full report was made."

Lettie smiled at her. "What would I ever do without you? You're the best."

"Let's just say we make a good team. If you hadn't stepped in to help me, I'd probably be on the streets or dead."

They sipped their wine quietly for a moment.

"Seems like a long time ago, doesn't it? So much has happened since then," commented Lettie.

"Some things don't change," said Paloma. "I told Autumn how it was between you and Rafe all those years ago and how happy you both are now. Not to take away anything from your relationship with Kenton. That was sweet too. But sometimes things have a way of working out like they might've all along."

"Rafe's so thrilled to have a family of his own. I hope Autumn understands how important it is for her to make time for him."

"Yeah, I talked to her about that, too," said Paloma. She laughed softly. "Being part of the Lopez family will be a whole new experience for her. All those people, all those kids. Cami will love it."

Autumn stepped onto the deck with Cami in her arms.

"I hear you're going to get a new tractor man," said Paloma in a loud, clear voice. "It's about time Joe retired. He and Rita are thinking of moving to Arizona. At least for the winter months."

"That'll be nice for them." Lettie decided to set up an interview with Sam Farley as soon as possible. That would give Joe time to begin training his replacement before winter.

"Always talking business, you two," said Autumn, smiling at them. "I'm going to set Cami down in her play area while I grab a glass of wine. Will you watch her?"

"Sure," said Lettie. "Let me hold her. It's been a while."

Autumn laughed. "A few hours, anyway."

They exchanged smiles.

Paloma stood. “I’m sorry. I just realized the time. I have to get home. Isabel is stopping by with the kids.”

“Tell her I’ll give her a call,” said Autumn. “I’d love to catch up with her. It’s been a long time. Maybe I’ll even ask her for some advice on raising girls. She has two, right?”

Paloma’s smile lit her face. “Two little angels, two and four.” She turned to Lettie. “Thanks. See you later.”

Still holding Cami, Lettie rose and gave her friend a quick kiss on the cheek. “See you tomorrow.”

Autumn gave Paloma a hug. “Thank you for talking with me today.”

“I’m so glad to have the time with you. Love you.”

As they smiled at one another, tears stung Lettie’s eyes. Through Autumn’s infancy and pre-school years, she’d relied heavily on Paloma to help her. She was glad to see they still had a bond.

After returning to the deck with a glass of wine, Autumn plunked down in a nearby chair and let out a long sigh. “What a day this has been!”

“Stressful, I’m sure,” Lettie said, commiserating with her daughter. “Let’s just have an easy meal tonight, and you can relax. I’ll take over Cami’s routine if you want.”

“Thanks, I’ll give her an early bath. She’s getting used to me, but I’ve decided she should call me Mama instead of Mommy. Mommy is too close to Nonnee, and it’s confusing.”

“Good idea,” said Lettie, pleased that she wouldn’t be asked to give up the beloved name Cami had given her.

While Autumn bathed Cami, Lettie prepared a simple salad of greens, cold shrimp, sliced eggs, and tomatoes topped with a King Louis dressing. The tartness of the dressing added a nice touch to the salad’s ingredients. On this warm evening, that salad, garlic bread, and a crisp pinot grigio would be perfect, Lettie decided.

Autumn returned to the kitchen with Cami. "Something smells good. Garlic?"

Lettie laughed. Her garlic bread was known for having a lot of garlic, but she liked it that way.

"I have a nice, light, summer meal prepared, including the garlic bread. Sit down and I'll be glad to wait on you. I love having you home. Are you sure you can't stay and do some of your charity work here?"

Autumn shook her head. "I can't let the government in South Africa down. Not after all the country has been through."

Lettie couldn't hide the pain in her voice. "I wish Cami could stay."

"I know you love her, Mom, and I'm grateful for all you've done for her, but I need her with me. It's essential that we form a bond."

"I understand. Let's put her in her highchair with some toys while we eat. She's usually good for ten minutes or so."

As they ate, both Lettie and Autumn watched Cami, exclaiming now and then how smart she was.

"I think she has Rafe's mechanical aptitude. See how she balances those blocks?" Lettie said with pride.

Autumn set down her fork and gave her a steady look, worry in her eyes. "What do you think I inherited from him?"

"Well, though your chin isn't exactly like your father's, you have a small cleft like his. And I noticed earlier when you walk you move your shoulders like him. You're both smart and there's something about your eyes that reminds me of him. Remember, I don't know what my own parents looked like, so it's hard to know for certain."

Autumn glanced at Cami. "She has a little dimple-like

indent on her chin. Do you think that comes from Rafe?"

Lettie smiled. "He and I both would like to think so."

"After talking with Paloma, I'd like to get to know Rafe better. As a person, if nothing else."

"I've been hoping you'd say that. Why don't I arrange for him to come for dinner tomorrow night? And if things go well, you can spend more time together. You might want to visit his place. He's changed the old Taunton vineyards and winery into something that's spectacular."

"You both know I have no real interest in becoming a vintner, right?"

"But someday you might have to take over the business end of Chandler Hill. We can't let it go to someone outside the family."

"Mom! That's exactly why I'm so confused. You talk as if I'm a Chandler, not a Lopez."

"Sweetie, you're both. You're young. Do your thing in Africa and then come back home."

Autumn's eyes flashed with hurt and indignation. "My work in Africa is a *thing*? You don't have any idea how valued my work is."

Remorse filled Lettie. "I'm so sorry. I didn't mean it the way it sounded. Of course, I'm proud of you and your work, but at some time you'll be needed at home."

She waved away Lettie's suggestion. "The way things look now, that's not going to happen for a very long time. You're young yourself, Mom. The winery and inn are in great shape. I'm not ready to live a life here in the valley doing something I don't really want to do."

Rather than argue, Lettie let the subject drop. She and Autumn would need to sort out the winery another time. They had more important issues to deal with—namely, giving Rafe a chance to know his daughter.

CHAPTER TWENTY-SEVEN

Lettie's nerves tingled as she raced home from the inn to prepare for the evening ahead. To take some of the strain away, dinner from the inn was to be delivered to her house at eight o'clock, giving Autumn, Rafe, and her enough time to say goodnight to Cami before her bedtime and then giving the adults time to talk. Though she wouldn't have the burden of preparing the food, Lettie wanted the table set nicely. She planned to serve one of the vineyard's best bottles of wine, along with hot cheese puff appetizers that Rafe especially liked. She'd also serve some chilled, marinated mushrooms. They'd always been one of Autumn's favorites.

Anxious to see how her day had gone without her, Lettie entered the house full of questions. They died on her lips when she found Autumn in the living room talking to Rod Mitchell.

"Rod? What are you doing here?"

Wearing a smile that was more like a smirk, he rose to his feet. He knew she didn't want him at her house.

"Autumn walked onto my property, and I decided to accompany her back here. It's been a while, Lettie. I understand you and your other neighbor are seeing one another. I tried to tell Autumn what a mistake that might be. I hear he's having some financial troubles."

"Nonnee!" cried Cami, running over to her from the kitchen where she had been playing alone.

Lettie swung Cami up in her arms and faced Rod. "I don't know what you're talking about."

"A banker friend of mine said that Rafe Lopez has been

looking to refinance his mortgage. He said the bank was reluctant to do that for him considering his lack of equity." His look of satisfaction was infuriating.

"Which property are you talking about?" Lettie asked. "If it's the one over by Salem, he's trying to set it up for a friend of his. Which bank was it?"

"Now, Lettie, you know I can't tell you that ..."

"I think it's time for you to go, Rod. We're about to have company." She let the edge in her voice shine through. The man was a first-class jerk, and she couldn't stand the sight of him.

"Mom ..." Autumn began. "Why ..."

Lettie cut her off. "Not now."

Autumn closed her mouth and stared at her wide-eyed.

Lettie led Rod to the front door. "See you around town, I'm sure." She couldn't hide her sarcasm. Rod seemed to be everywhere.

Rod gave her a hard stare. "You're going to be sorry you never worked out something with me. Rafe Lopez is an interloper who's only after your money and land."

"No, Rod, that was you. Remember?"

Lettie slammed the door behind him and leaned against it. "What a slime!"

"I'm sorry, Mom. He asked if he could walk me home, and I said yes."

"I know how charming he can be," admitted Lettie. "But he's one of the worst—a smooth talking guy who will lie and twist the truth to get ahead. Spanish crews won't work for him, and nobody in town wants anything to do with him after he's pulled a few underhanded stunts against other growers."

Autumn's body sagged. "I should have seen him for what he was. God! I'm so stupid about men!"

"Cami's father?"

"Yes, he was a smooth talker too."

"It just occurred to me that you grew up with a bunch of women around you, but no men. We should have taught you better."

"Yeah, but I'd better smarten up. I don't want to live alone all my life."

"True," said Lettie. "C'mon! Let's get ready to meet a really great guy. By the way, did you see Abby?"

"I stopped into the gift shop to say hello. Tomorrow, I'm meeting her for lunch."

"Good." Lettie hoped Autumn would see how much these people loved her and would, one day, count on her for her support.

When Lettie opened the door to welcome Rafe, she was touched to see how much care he'd taken with his appearance. He'd shaved, and his hair was slicked back away from his face. His plaid, short-sleeved shirt appeared brand new, and his khaki pants looked like they'd just come from the laundry.

"Hi, sweetheart," Lettie said, giving him a kiss on the cheek. "C'mon in. Autumn is changing Cami and getting ready to put her down for the night, but she'll be right out."

"I'm a little nervous," Rafe admitted, swiping a hand through his hair. "It's like an adoption in reverse."

"You'll do just fine," Lettie assured him. "I love you enough for both Autumn and me."

He chuckled, but she knew he wouldn't relax until he'd had a chance to spend some time with Autumn.

Rafe followed her into the kitchen.

"Mmm, my favorite cheese puffs?"

Lettie smiled. "Made just for you. I'm having dinner sent over from the inn—the Beef Wellington you like so much. It's one of Autumn's favorites too."

"What's a favorite of mine?" asked Autumn coming into the room.

"The inn's Beef Wellington."

"Is that what you ordered? Yum!"

"Yes, it's one of your father's favorites too," said Lettie, the words slipping out easily.

Autumn and Rafe stared at each other, and then Rafe laughed. "A surprise, huh?"

"Yes, indeed," said Autumn pleasantly.

Lettie allowed the breath she'd been holding to escape. "Well, then, maybe you'll pour the wine, Rafe. I've got a nice syrah to sip before we change to a cabernet for dinner. Let's go out to the deck."

Outside, the sun was just beginning its descent. Though it would be a while before it was dark, the colors that spilled from the western sky onto the earth below cast a warm glow around them as they sat on the deck.

"Rod Mitchell was here with Autumn this afternoon," Lettie told Rafe. "He implied that you were having financial problems because the bank didn't want to give you a loan."

Rafe shook his head with disgust. "Why do people like him fail to get all the facts before they spread nonsense? A group of friends wants to buy a nice piece of property over by Salem. I'm trying to help them work out a deal with one of the local banks. The recession of the early 1990s changed so many banking rules. Now, it's not so simple to set things up."

"How is that going to work? Several people owning a property?" Autumn asked. "It sounds a little like a type of socialism."

Rafe shrugged. "I hadn't thought of it that way, but I guess you're right. Three different men will own the property under a business name. They all plan to live and work there, so each will have to do his share."

"In my village in Africa, I saw how important it was to work together. But the leader had a lot of authority. That was important too."

"Tell me more about your work in Africa. For someone who hasn't traveled much, I find it fascinating."

Autumn began describing her work in detail.

Lettie listened carefully, realizing she hadn't previously shared information to this extent. As Autumn spoke, Lettie's respect for her grew.

"I can see why your mother is so proud of you," said Rafe. "If you will allow me to say it, I'm proud too."

Autumn studied Rafe somberly.

At the sound of someone at the door, Lettie rose. "That must be our dinner. Go ahead and enjoy yourselves while I get everything set. Rafe, perhaps you'd pour the dinner wine?"

He turned to Autumn with a grin. "I'm good at that."

As she left the room, Lettie heard Autumn's laughter behind her. She felt a wave of happiness, pleased Rafe was using his charm to get to know his daughter.

At dinner, once everyone had commented on the delicious beef, Lettie steered the conversation toward history of the valley. "Rafe's family has lived and worked legally in the valley for many years."

"Yes," said Rafe. He went on to explain that those who hadn't been able to receive citizenship prior to 1986 when the Immigration Reform and Control Act was passed were given permanent residence then. He smiled at Lettie and turned to Autumn. "Like your mother, my family and I love the land."

"Nice. Now you know how I feel about Africa," said Autumn. "I love the land and the people there."

"I hope you'll come to love Chandler Hill," Lettie said. "And I hope you'll give Cami the chance to love it too."

"Maybe she can visit now and then," Autumn said.

Rather than speak through a throat thickened with tears, Lettie remained quiet.

"Autumn, I'd like my parents to have the opportunity to talk with you, get to know you a little before you leave," said Rafe. "Are you willing to do that?"

"Yes," she said. "I want Cami to know her family and her heritage."

"And you?" Rafe said.

"I'm trying to get used to the idea," she said. "I'm still a little confused about where I fit in."

"Good enough. We'll go from there." Rafe's smile of encouragement was heartwarming.

Coffee and the inn's special flan were served and eaten as talk continued about various members of Rafe's family.

When conversation ebbed, Autumn rose. "Thanks for dinner. Rafe, nice to get to know you a little better. Mom? I'll do the dishes later. If you don't mind, I'm going to my room. I have a few things to take care of."

Lettie waved away her concern. "Don't worry. We'll do the dishes."

Autumn started to leave the room and then stopped. "Maybe I can meet your parents in a day or two, Rafe. Please let me know when they're free."

The look of excitement on his face was touching. "Sure thing. I'll get right back to you."

After she left, a long sigh escaped Lettie's lips. "Well, that wasn't so bad. She seemed genuinely interested in hearing about your family."

"Considering her life has been turned upside down, she's been very kind. I really appreciate that."

"I think she was surprised to learn that you have a college degree in viticulture and oenology."

Rafe shook his head. "Fancy names for grape growing and winemaking, but it's a fascinating business."

"Yes. Funny, in some ways, I feel as if I were born to do it. Obviously, Autumn doesn't."

"She'll come around," said Rafe. "After all, she's likely to inherit not one, but two big properties. Even if she doesn't do the work, she'll need to know the business."

"Maybe when Cami is older, Autumn will let her spend the school breaks here. I'll even pay for her college education."

Rafe laughed. "One step at a time, *Cariño*."

She joined in the laughter. "*Si, Señor.*"

The next afternoon, Lettie held a birthday cake on a plate in front of Cami. The cooks at the inn had made it especially for her. Pink flowers and one pink butterfly adorned the chocolate icing. Two flickering candles were set into the cake at the top.

"Happy Birthday, Cami! You're two!" said Autumn.

"Two!" Cami repeated holding up four fingers.

The three adults laughed.

"Four will happen all too quickly," Lettie said, sobering, wondering how many times in the next two years she'd see her beloved granddaughter.

Rafe placed a hand on Lettie's shoulder. "Let's have Cami blow out the candles."

"Okay. Ready, Cami? Blow hard! Mama can help you."

Cami's attempts at blowing out the candles were touching. At the last moment, Autumn discreetly helped snuff the flames, and they all clapped.

Delighting in the attention, Cami clapped too.

Lettie tucked that moment of pure joy into her memories. Later, when Autumn and Cami were gone, she'd need moments like these to treasure.

"Mom? Did you hear me?"

Jerked away from her thoughts, Lettie sent Autumn a questioning look.

"I say we let Cami dig into the cake on her own. Do you agree?"

"Why not? It's a toddler's dream come true."

Lettie set down the cake in front of Cami.

When Cami realized what was happening, she shrieked with glee, plunged her plump hands into the gooey mess, and lifted some to her face.

Autumn grinned at Lettie. "Shall we?"

Lettie didn't hesitate. She swooped a pink flower off the cake and put it in her mouth.

"How about me?" said Rafe, snatching his own piece of what was now a mess.

Autumn, her lips edged with chocolate icing, grinned. "Perfect. The four of us celebrating together."

Cami looked at them with rounded eyes. "Mine."

That set off more laughter.

"She's two all right," said Autumn. "It's a birthday I'll never forget. Thank you both."

Lettie and Rafe exchanged satisfied looks.

The next day, Lettie pulled her car to a stop outside Joe and Rita Lopez's home. At Autumn's insistence, Lettie had agreed to accompany her and Cami on a visit to Rafe's parents. Lettie understood Autumn's nervousness about meeting them as their granddaughter. She'd heard the story about how they'd opposed a relationship between a young Rafe and Lettie.

Lettie got out of the car and waited for Autumn to extract Cami from her car seat. Glancing around, she noticed the care that went into the lawn and plantings around the house. Now that Rafe and his siblings were grown and many of the grandchildren too, Rita spent a lot of time outside gardening both flowers and vegetables. The gray-clapboard, two-story house with a red-painted front door appeared as welcoming now as the white house had been the first time Lettie had seen it. Maybe because it had always been a place where family and friends of theirs gathered.

Before they reached the front porch, Rita opened the door with a smile. "Ah, there's little Cami!"

Cami squealed with excitement and held out her arms to her. With a shy smile, Autumn handed Cami over to her great-grandmother.

Laughing, Rita jiggled Cami in her arms. "Such a pretty baby." She turned to Autumn. "Life is full of surprises, eh? And some, like this one, are special."

Autumn glanced at Lettie and smiled.

Rita waved them inside. "Come in! Come in! I've made fresh lemonade and a few little things to eat."

Lettie hid a smile. Rita's "few little things to eat" were a feast to others. But she was glad that she had fussed for this meeting. It was a good sign.

Rita led them to the kitchen where Lettie knew from past experience most of her social meetings took place.

She turned to them with sparkling eyes. "Please sit down and help yourself to food. May I get you each a cup of my special cinnamon coffee?"

"Yes, please," said Lettie. "Wait until you taste it, Autumn. It's delicious."

Rita set Cami down on the spotless kitchen floor and handed her a couple of wooden spoons, several plastic bowls, and opened a small bag of wooden blocks for her.

"With the birth of Sophia's baby, how many grandchildren

and great-grandchildren do you have now?" Lettie asked.

"Twenty-two," Rita replied with a sense of pride. "And I love them all." She cast a warm glance at Cami. "Especially this little surprise."

"It's nice that she has you. I never had any family around in my life," said Autumn.

"True, but a lot of other women were there for you—Paloma, Abby, Terri, and, now, Lisa," Lettie quickly said.

"Yes," Autumn agreed, "but they were more like mothers."

"Good women. All of them," said Rita with conviction.

After serving each of them mugs of coffee, Rita took a seat opposite Autumn. Smiling at her, she said, "You are a surprise too. I knew you as a baby when I used to cook some meals for the inn before it became so big. Since then you've grown and traveled and become a mother. And now you're a Lopez. A surprise for you too, no?"

Lettie could see how startled Autumn was by Rita's directness, but she was glad to have the issue addressed right up front. Rita was a woman who had a lot of pride. She was loyal and loving to friends but was a fierce defender to those who dared to disrespect her or a member of her family. As she waited for Autumn to respond, Lettie held her breath. Her daughter could be very blunt at times.

"It was more than a surprise," said Autumn. "It was a total shock. I thought I knew who I was and suddenly everything I believed about myself was wrong. In a way, it was as if someone had died in the family. But after talking to my Mom and to Rafe, I realize I come from a good family on my father's side." She gave Lettie a sympathetic smile and turned back to Rita. "Of course, we don't know much if anything about my mother's family. So, it's nice to have *some* information on my background."

"Yes, I can imagine how you feel," said Rita quietly. "In

your case, you've lost something. And for my family, we've gained from it. You mean everything to my son, and he means everything to me. I pray you don't hurt him. You have it within your power to do so."

Autumn shook her head vehemently. "I don't ever want to do that. I see how much he loves Cami and how devoted he is to my mother."

Rita nodded with satisfaction. "You came from their love. Rafe has loved your mother for years. It's too bad we wouldn't acknowledge it. Then, who knows what might have happened?"

Lettie's vision blurred when Rita squeezed her hand. She was saved from responding when Cami let out a cry and threw down the wooden spoon onto the floor. Rising to her feet, she walked over to Rita and stood facing her. "Cuck?"

"Cookie?" said Rita smiling. She turned to them. "Okay with everyone if I give her a cookie?"

"It's fine with me. Just one," said Autumn. "I can see she's got both of you wrapped around her little finger."

Rita's smile was bright. "One of the joys of being a great-grandmother is the ability to do a little spoiling."

"Oh, yes," said Lettie. "And I love being a grandmother."

Rita got to her feet. "I'll be right back. I want to get the photo album."

After Rita left the room, Autumn turned to Lettie. "She's so nice, and I'd forgotten how pretty she is."

"Good genes," Lettie said, arching an eyebrow at her.

Autumn laughed and shook her head. "I'm glad you insisted I come here today."

"Me, too," said Lettie, happy her daughter was finding her family.

Rita returned carrying what looked like a large, very thick book.

She plopped it on the table and said, “Prepare yourself.”

“Exactly,” said Lettie rising. “I’ve already been initiated into the family history. Now, it’s your turn.” She spoke to Rita. “If you don’t mind, I’ll leave the two of you to it. I need to get back to the inn.”

“Of course. I understand,” said Rita, starting to rise. “Thanks for coming.”

Lettie waved her back in her seat. “No need to walk me to the door. I’ll let myself out.”

“Thanks,” said Rita, already opening the book.

As Lettie later told Rafe, things could not have gone better. An only child, Autumn was loving the idea of a large family.

CHAPTER TWENTY-EIGHT

The time came for Autumn and Cami to leave. As Lettie drove them to the airport, she couldn't stop tears from rolling down her cheeks. She loved her daughter and adored her granddaughter. She would miss them more than either of them knew. Though she should have been aware of it long ago, it seemed a cruel twist of fate to have been given the care of Cami and then have her taken away.

"I'm sorry, Mom, but you know it's best for Cami to be with me, right?"

Lettie reluctantly nodded. "I just wish you lived closer. After that trip to and from Vail, I've become even more terrified of flying. I honestly don't think I can ever get on a plane again."

Autumn gave her a look of sympathy. "We'll visit as often as we can."

"I know, but it won't be the same as if you were living nearby. And the coming and going will be heartbreaking."

"It's the best I can do. I have a rewarding life of my own doing for others," said Autumn with a quiet firmness.

At the finality in her voice, Lettie winced. She told herself to pull it together, vowing to be brave, even if it destroyed a part of her heart forever.

Lettie pulled up to the terminal. They'd already agreed she would not go inside with them. She did, however, get out of the car to help with the suitcases.

"Here, hold her while I get someone to take the luggage." Autumn handed Cami to her.

Lettie held on tight to Cami. Feeling her eyes fill with tears, she hastily blinked them away to keep from frightening the little girl she loved with all her heart.

"Nonnee loves you. I'll send you pictures of 'Afe and me and the inn. I don't want you to forget us, hear?" Her voice broke. "Love you, little one."

Cami looked at her with concern. "Nonnee," she said, touching the tears at the corner of Lettie's eyes.

Lettie grabbed Cami's hand and kissed it.

"Time to go!" Autumn said, approaching them, breaking the magical spell of the moment. She swept Cami out of Lettie's arms.

"I know you don't like goodbyes, so we won't linger." Autumn gave her a quick kiss. "Love you, Mom. I'll let you know when we can come for a visit." Her eyes filled. She turned away and hurried into the terminal with Cami, who looked over her mother's shoulder and stared at Lettie.

Lettie stood for a moment, frozen by shock and horror. Cami was gone.

Blinded by the tears she couldn't hold back any longer, she stumbled to her car and got in. A policeman motioned impatiently for her to move, and she pulled away from the curb feeling as if the world had come to an end.

On the ride home, Lettie's mind was crowded with memories of Cami's first few teeth, her first steps, her first words. *How, can I live without her?* Fresh tears spilled down her cheeks in painful streaks.

When Lettie pulled into the driveway of her house, she was relieved to see Rafe's silver truck parked there. He, of all people, would understand the pain ripping her apart and would comfort her as only he could.

She got out of her car and headed toward the front door.

Rafe appeared from the side of the house shouting, "Babe! Stop!"

But the little golden puppy kept running straight toward her, and then suddenly reversed course and ran back toward Rafe.

Laughing, Rafe caught the puppy in his grip.

Approaching her with the dog, Rafe grinned. "Thought we could use another baby around here. What do you think?"

He placed the squirming puppy in Lettie's arms. The bright-eyed pup looked into her eyes and then a warm, pink tongue licked the salty trail of tears from her cheek. Lettie hugged the puppy tight. It momentarily laid its head on Lettie's shoulder, and then, bursting with energy, it squirmed to get down.

Lettie set the puppy on the grass and smiled up at Rafe. "It's a girl. Where did you get her? She's a yellow lab, right?"

"Yes. She's a nice puppy, ten weeks old. I contacted a kennel outside of Portland a while ago. She's a cuddly one, so I've been calling her Babe. But it's up to you to name her."

"No, no. I like Babe. It's close to Baby, which I sometimes used to call Cami." Her eyes filmed over with the tears she tried to hold back.

Rafe opened his arms, and Lettie hurried into them. There, in the comfort of his embrace, she allowed her tears to flow.

When she quieted, Rafe tipped her face up. "It's going to be all right. I've taken the rest of the afternoon off. It looks like rain. Let's go inside."

They called to the puppy, who, curious as ever, bounded over to them and stood wagging her tail at them before following them inside.

Lettie was surprised to see that a doggie cage had already been set up in the kitchen. A bag of puppy food, several toys, a soft, pink blanket, and puppy pads sat on the counter.

"You really planned this." Lettie gave Rafe a grateful smile.

"Yeah, I knew you'd be upset when Cami left."

She caressed his cheek. "I love you."

He grinned. "I know."

"Do me a favor, please" she said. "I want all the furniture removed from the nursery. I don't think I could bear to see that empty crib. I'm giving it and the rest of the furniture to a staff member. And someday, when I'm feeling a little better, we can pick out furniture for an older child. Autumn promised she'd bring Cami for a visit as often as she could."

"I understand. I miss Cami already."

With a quiet sadness, they placed the baby furniture in the garage to be picked up later.

Standing in the empty room, Lettie's shoulders slumped. "It seems like a bad dream to have her gone. In so many ways, Cami seemed like my baby, not Autumn's."

Rafe put an arm around her. "That's natural. You had the care of her for most of the first two years of her life."

"I wonder if she'll remember me when I see her next."

Rafe gave her an impish grin. "Haven't I told you, you're unforgettable.?"

Her lips curved. "Many times."

His lips met hers. The warmth of his kiss filled a tiny bit of the hollowness inside her and sent a frisson of need through her.

As if he sensed what she was feeling, Rafe pulled away and said in a hushed voice, "Let me love you."

"Yes, please." Having felt such loss, Lettie wanted to feel life at its best—making love with Rafe.

Babe trotted after them into the bedroom.

Lettie went back to the kitchen, took the doggy blanket from the counter, and placed it in the far corner of the room.

The exhausted puppy lay down on it and was soon fast asleep.

Nodding toward the dog and then giving her a devilish grin, Rafe said, “That pup better get used to this.” He pulled his T-shirt over his head and tossed it aside.

Studying his next movements, Lettie took off her pants and blouse and watched him undress. At the sight of his naked body, excitement wove its way through her and settled in her core. She needed this act of life when a part of her was dead inside.

Rafe swept her up into his arms. “I love you!”

She smiled at him. “And I love you.”

He placed her on the bed, and she opened her arms to him.

Later, her thoughts turned to Cami. “Do you suppose Cami will miss me?”

“I’m sure she will, but we’ll keep in touch the best we can.” Rafe gently twined his fingers through her curls as she lay against his broad, muscular chest.

“I bought Autumn a new computer and had it shipped to her,” said Lettie. “She promised to keep in touch that way. I also bought her a new camera, a Canon. She’ll be able to send us pictures with it.”

“Okay, Nonnee, you’ve done what you could. Autumn knows how much we love our grandchild. I believe she’ll keep us informed.” He kissed her. “Let’s go for a walk through the vineyard. That always makes you feel better.”

Lettie got out of bed with a smile. Rafe knew her so well.

Outside, they walked hand in hand over her land. Babe raced in circles around them.

“Who’s going to get up at night to let the dog out?” Lettie gave Rafe a pointed look.

He raised his right hand. “As long as I get to sleep with you,

I'll do my share. I promise."

She gave him a playful push. "You'd better."

As they walked along the rows of grapes, they automatically checked the canopy to make sure sunlight could reach all the grapes evenly.

"I think it's going to be a good year," Lettie said. "Scott thinks so too."

"Scott Kurey is a good winemaker. So are you. The two of you will make something spectacular."

"You make some pretty wonderful wines yourself." She loved that Rafe appreciated all she'd learned. She remembered the first time she'd tried wine with Rafe and Kenton. Even back then, Rafe had thought she had a good palate for wine.

"I'm anxious to meet Sam Farley," she said. "I'm sorry I wasn't able to do so earlier, but with Autumn and Cami gone, I can once more concentrate on Chandler Hill."

"I've set aside tomorrow morning to be with him. Even though our properties are next to one another, there are slight nuances to the growing of the grapes. I figure I'll meet with him first and then bring him over here. Let's have lunch together at the inn, and then he's all yours."

"Sounds good. Ready for dinner?"

"Sure. Let's go back. If you want, we can go into town for some Italian food at Nick's."

"That sounds nice. I've been so busy with Cami, I haven't had the opportunity to be social."

At the house, Lettie changed into a simple, sleeveless cotton sheath in her favorite light pink. McMinnville was not a fancy place, and although the food at Nick's was excellent, the atmosphere was super casual. Still, Lettie wanted to look her best. Though the town was filling with more and more tourists, it was still the place where old friends could meet.

###

When they walked into Nick's, she waved to Rafe's cousin, Elise, who was a waitress there, and quickly moved away from the tables in the front of the restaurant by the window. She had no desire to have any conversation with Rod Mitchell. He was sitting at a table with a blonde who looked like a starved "wannabe starlet" from California.

She was grateful when Mark Pierce called out to them. A fellow vintner, he'd established his vineyard in the mid-'80s and was doing very well. Lettie had always liked him and his wife, Jeanne.

"How are you doing?" Mark stood as they approached his table. "We just ordered. Want to join us?"

Lettie cast a glance at Rafe. At his smile, she said, "That would be nice. I've been a bit isolated by the care of my granddaughter."

"I heard she was due to go back soon," said Jeanne.

Blinking away the sting of tears, Lettie said, "Autumn and Cami left this morning."

"But Lettie has a new little one to care for," said Rafe, giving her an encouraging smile.

"Oh?" Jeanne's eyes sparkled with curiosity.

Lettie grinned at her. "A puppy. A little yellow lab. We're calling her Babe."

"Labs are good dogs," said Jeanne. "I'm sure it will seem lonely with Cami gone, but maybe the puppy will help. I know how attached you were to Cami."

"Yes. It's distressing because she and her mother live so far away."

Jeanne shook her head. "Kids today think nothing of traveling all over the world. Me? I'm content to stay right here unless it gets nasty in the winter. Then, we like to spend a couple of weeks in Arizona."

The conversation stopped when Rod approached the table. "Thought I'd say hi. Given any more thought to selling some of your acreage?" he asked Mark.

Mark's smile didn't reach his eyes. "As I told you, I'm not interested. Things are going well, and I need all the land I have to increase production."

"How about you, Rod? How are things going?" Rafe said.

Rod's face contorted with dislike. "Unlike you, I didn't grow up here working in the fields for someone else. So, it's taking me a while, but I'll get there."

"Yes, it's hard for some newcomers to understand the land and how it works," Rafe said smoothly. "If you ever want to sell, let me know." He turned to the waitress. "How about bringing your best bottle of pinot from Taunton Estates."

Lettie hid a laugh at the look of dismay on Rod's face.

He frowned at Rafe. "How'd you get them to carry your wine?"

Rafe shrugged in a nonchalant manner. "Some of us old-time field workers know how to make a good wine and sell it to our friends."

Rod grimaced and walked away.

"Good job of setting him straight, Rafe," said Mark. "I've never liked the man."

Lettie sat back in her chair, glad they had such good friends. Living and working in the valley, she'd come to understand that a certain amount of cooperation between vineyards was essential. Degrading others would hurt Rod in the long run.

After a delicious meal and good conversation, Lettie and Rafe headed home. The ride to Chandler Hill wasn't long, but drivers had to be careful on roads that wound their way from the valley through farmland to the rolling hills of the vineyards.

Rafe brought his truck to a stop in her driveway and turned to her. "I've been thinking of renting my house to my sister Sophia and her husband, Paul. They live in a small place, and with the birth of their new baby, they need more room. I trust Paul to take as good care of the house as he does the farm. Sophia is thrilled with the idea. What do you think?" His finger trailed down her cheek.

"Are you asking if you can move in with me permanently?" He already knew she wouldn't leave Chandler Hill to move in with him, and she'd told him that though she loved him, she wouldn't marry him or anyone else.

"Yes," said Rafe, giving her a steady look. "As long as you won't marry me, the best I can do is to live with you."

"Oh? I would love it." She threw her arms around him and hugged him tight. When she pulled away from him, she paused. "You understand my position, don't you? Marriage would complicate things between us."

"I wish I didn't understand, but I do. And I respect you for it. But that doesn't mean I don't want us to be together. I'm tired of traveling back and forth from your place to mine. And I don't give a damn what some of the more conservative people in the valley might think. I want to shack up with you, as some would say."

Lettie warmed at his earnestness. They'd talked around and around about marriage and where their relationship was going. This sounded like a good solution.

"Come on inside and let's figure out how we're going to make this work."

When they walked into the house together, Lettie heard the sound of frantic yipping and hurried into the kitchen. They'd used Cami's old baby gates to pen in the dog. The puppy pad they'd put on the floor was in shreds. A puddle of pee pooled nearby.

"Ach! Babe, come. You need to go outside." The puppy galloped with her as Lettie rushed her outside. "Here. You get busy here. Outside. Understand?"

Babe cocked her head at Lettie's words and then trotted over to Rafe and wagged her tail.

"Oh no, you don't. I'm going to tell you the same thing." He looked over at Lettie. "It's going to take a while, but she's a smart pup. We'll get her trained."

"*We'd* better," grumped Lettie.

Rafe put an arm around her. "Just one happy family."

Lettie leaned into him. That sounded good.

CHAPTER TWENTY-NINE

For Lettie, having Rafe move in with her was the beginning of several good years. The inn, the vineyards, and their relationship thrived. And though Autumn and she weren't as communicative as some mothers and daughters were, Autumn dutifully kept them informed of Cami's growth and activities. Photos of her showed a beautiful little girl with dark eyes and light-red hair. Lettie couldn't quite define it beyond the chin, but there was a bit more of Rafe in Cami's features, and that made her happy for him. Then, after the Y2K new year, Autumn finally agreed to bring Cami for a visit. Lettie could hardly wait to see her. According to email reports from Autumn, Cami was a bright, determined, six-year-old.

On this early-April morning, Lettie stood with Rafe in the Portland airport, her heart starting and stopping in nervous beats at the thought that Cami might not want anything to do with her. Emails, photos, and phone conversations weren't the same as actually being with someone. And Lettie's memories were of a little girl who'd clung to her with affection.

Rafe put an arm around her. "Relax. It'll be okay."

Lettie forced a smile, but she couldn't chase her worry away.

Passengers from the San Francisco flight started entering the waiting area. Lettie grabbed hold of Rafe's hand.

And then suddenly Autumn and Cami were heading toward them.

Autumn smiled and lifted her hand in greeting.

Lettie rushed forward to greet them. As she did, Cami hid

behind her mother.

"Welcome home!" Lettie cried, hugging Autumn hard. She glanced over at Cami, who stood back, staring at her wide-eyed.

Lettie knelt before her. "I'm so happy to see you, Cami. Nonnee has missed you terribly. And look! Here's Rafe. You used to call him 'Afe. And then when we asked you to call him Grandpa you said, 'No, Rafe'. You probably don't remember because you were just a toddler when we saw you last, and now you're a grown-up six-year-old. May I give you a hug hello?"

Cami nodded and allowed Lettie to give her a hug. Though it wasn't the enthusiastic one she'd wished for, Lettie was glad for even that.

"How are you?" Rafe asked Autumn, beaming at her.

"Anxious to get home. It was a long trip," said Autumn, returning his smile.

Lettie got to her feet and offered her hand to Cami.

Cami hurried to her mother's side.

Patience, Lettie reminded herself. As she accompanied the others to the baggage claim area, she kept a watchful eye on Cami. She walked beside her mother, gazing around with interest. Lettie remembered that same curiosity in Cami as a toddler and drew a satisfied breath. She would use Chandler Hill to connect with Cami again.

While they waited for the bags, Lettie turned to her daughter. "You look wonderful! Even better in person than the pictures show you." At twenty-nine, Autumn was a striking woman. The sun had burned her long limbs a pleasant brown and exposed the red tones in her dark hair. Her dark-brown eyes snapped with intelligence.

"You look good too, Mom," said Autumn. "Living with Rafe must suit you. You seem so happy."

"Thanks." Lettie shot a quick look at Rafe standing nearby. They had a good life, and maybe because they both enjoyed the land, they were content to live and work at home together. Once, to please Rafe, she'd tried counseling for her fear of flying. But rather than help her, it only intensified her deep-rooted anxiety of being caught in the sky with no option to save herself. A control issue, the counselor had suggested, offering further counseling sessions—sessions Lettie turned down.

"How about you? Are you seeing anyone special?" Lettie asked. "You never say anything about it in your emails, and our phone calls are usually rushed."

Autumn shrugged. "I'm friends with a few co-workers, but I haven't found any man I'm willing to marry."

When the luggage belt began to move, Rafe waved her over to help identify the bags, leaving Lettie with Cami.

"I wonder if you'll remember the vineyards," Lettie said. "I used to carry you on my back and walk with you through the rows of grapevines. You loved it."

Cami looked up at her. "I did?"

"Yes. And now we have a dog to go with us. Her name is Babe. Remember me sending you pictures of her?"

Cami studied her. "I like dogs."

"Do you have a dog at home?"

"No," Cami shook her head. "Mama doesn't want one."

Autumn rolled a large suitcase over to them. "What doesn't Mama want?"

"A dog," said Lettie.

"Cami, I've told you that with my long hours and my traveling for the job, it doesn't make sense to have a dog. Maybe later, when you're a little older."

"Who stays with Cami when you're gone?" Lettie asked. There was so much she didn't know about their everyday life.

"We have a housekeeper who will stay over. She's great," Autumn replied.

"Her name is Karabo," said Cami.

"Cami gets along really well with her, which is a big relief to me."

Rafe walked up to them rolling a second large suitcase behind him. "I think we're set. Ready to go?"

They loaded the bags into Lettie's new Lexus RX and headed out. "That old Volvo wagon finally quit on me, so I had to replace it earlier this year," Lettie explained to Autumn.

"I'd forgotten how green everything looks," Autumn commented. "And the trees are so tall."

"Oregon's rain will do that," said Lettie. "It's good for the crops though. Bud break has just happened."

"South Africa is making some good wines now," Autumn said. "It's fascinating."

"Yes, I've read about it. I'm so happy you're taking an interest in it." The idea pleased Lettie. Though Rafe had warned her against it, she kept hoping Autumn's dedication to her job was only until she could take over the winery.

"I'm interested in South African wines as a consumer, not as someone involved in the actual process of making it. I'm sorry, Mom. I know it's a disappointment to you, but I haven't changed my mind about it."

"I understand," Lettie said, not understanding at all. Didn't Autumn realize what an opportunity awaited her? She quickly changed the subject. "You'll be staying with us at my house. We've added a guest wing since you've last seen it, so you'll have all the privacy you want."

"Sounds great. This will be a nice break for the two of us. Right, Cami?"

From the backseat, Cami glanced at Lettie shyly and nodded.

By the time Rafe pulled the car into the driveway, Lettie was feeling better about things. Though Autumn wasn't ready to take on family responsibilities, she might one day.

As they got out of the car, Babe bounded toward them.

"It's Babe!" Cami cried, embracing the dog. She laughed when the yellow lab licked her hand.

After Babe greeted all of them with wags and kisses, she stayed at Cami's side as they got the luggage and carry-ons inside.

"Welcome," Lettie cried, leading her guests to the guest wing.

Standing in the middle of one of the guest rooms, Autumn said, "Very pretty. I love the openness."

"Thanks." A sliding door led to a small deck off the room. But it was the view overlooking the rolling hills that gave the room a sense of space.

They stood together on it looking out.

Autumn placed a hand on Lettie's shoulder. "You've really made this house special. It's hidden away from the inn, giving privacy to everyone here."

"The changes have been good. Wait until you see what we've done at the inn. We've recently done an upgrade to the rooms, as well as the common areas. It's a nice improvement." Lettie gave Autumn an impulsive hug. "I'm so glad you're here."

Autumn smiled. "Me too."

Lettie drew Cami to their sides. "You too, little one."

Cami looked up at her with somber eyes, then her lips curved, sending a surge of love through Lettie.

Lettie spent every spare moment she could with her family. As the days went on, Autumn left Lettie and Cami to do things on her own. The bond between them deepened as they walked the hills, swam in the pool at the inn, and shared treats and stories. Babe shadowed them whenever she could.

Watching Cami run through the rows of vines with the dog one day was like seeing a dream of hers come alive, thought Lettie with satisfaction. There was something so right about it—as if the land she loved was enfolding Cami in its embrace.

And when Rafe, Lettie, and Cami were together, the look of pride and joy on Rafe's face was equally satisfying. It seemed only fair for him to be able to enjoy the child and grandchild he thought he'd never have.

Sitting in the living room, reading books together, Lettie held her breath as Cami asked Rafe, "If you're my Grandpa and Nonnee is my grandmother, why don't you have the same name? Nonnee is a Chandler like me. Your name is Lopez."

"It's not so much the name that matters, but the love we share," Rafe said smoothly. "Because my name is different from yours doesn't mean I don't love you. In fact, I think I love you more because of it. Right, Nonnee?"

Lettie smiled her agreement. "You're a very, very special granddaughter to both of us. We love you so much."

"Okay." Cami studied him and turned to Lettie. "Can we go to the inn now?"

Rafe and Lettie laughed together. *Oh, to be six,* Lettie thought, wishing life was that simple.

Too soon it was time for Autumn and Cami to leave. As they packed their bags, Lettie worked hard to hold her emotions in check. She and her daughter had spent enough time together that the edges that had previously existed between them seemed to have disappeared. And Cami? Lettie loved her. Both she and Rafe did.

After a quiet trip into Portland, Lettie stood outside the airport terminal wishing she could be like the other passengers about to take a flight. But she was as landlocked as a sparrow with clipped wings.

Autumn hugged her. "Thanks for such a nice visit, Mom. We'll try to make it back here much sooner next time."

Lettie wrapped her arms around her daughter and rocked her back and forth, unwilling to let her go. "Thank you for coming and bringing Cami with you. It means so much to us."

"I'm glad I got to know Rafe better. He loves you."

"And we love you." Lettie forced herself to step away. "Have a safe flight. Please let us know that you got home safely."

"'Bye, Nonnee," said Cami. She held onto the stuffed bear that contained a recording Lettie and Cami had made together at one of the stores outside Portland.

Tears stung Lettie's eyes as she embraced the girl she loved like no other. "Remember to write to me and Rafe. And we'll send you emails in return."

As agreed, Autumn and Cami entered the terminal on their own. Autumn didn't like emotional scenes, and Lettie knew the longer they lingered, the more emotional she would be.

The next few months were difficult. Lettie, still missing her family, turned to the business of growing grapes, making wine, and keeping a careful eye on the inn. Well-established as *the* place to go in the valley, the inn continued to be busy with small groups, weddings, and more and more themed weekends involving wine tastings, musical concerts, and even mystery dinners.

Receiving emails from Cami was the highlight of any day. And when Autumn and Cami called on the phone, it was even better.

They'd just completed the harvesting of grapes in October when Lettie realized she hadn't heard from Autumn in a while. In her office, she picked up the phone to call her.

After several rings, a voice said, "Hello?"

"Karabo? Is that you? It's Lettie Chandler calling for Autumn. Is she there?"

A sob came over the phone. "Oh, God! You don't know?"

Lettie's blood turned to ice in her veins. "Know what?"

"Oh, I'm so sorry. Autumn was hit by a car and killed this morning." Karabo began to cry in earnest.

The room spun around so fast Lettie thought she might be sick. Gripping the edge of her desk, she tried to hang onto the thought that was too terrible to bear. Karabo must be talking about someone else, she told herself. Autumn was young and beautiful and healthy.

"No," said Lettie firmly. "I need to talk to her. Please get her for me."

The sobs through the phone became even louder. "Mrs. Chandler, I'm with Cami now, but I think it's best if you come here. She needs to be with you."

Lettie dropped the phone, ran into the adjacent bathroom, and threw up. After emptying her stomach, she stood on shaky legs and washed her face with a cold cloth. Her strong, fiercely independent daughter was gone. And though Cami needed her, she couldn't deal with the thought of flying to Africa. For that, she would never be able to forgive herself.

She stumbled back to her desk and picked up the receiver. "Karabo, are you still there?"

The buzzing line was her answer.

Lettie grabbed her car keys and purse and ran to her private parking spot at the inn. *Rafe! I have to get to Rafe!*

She was halfway to his house before she realized she could've just called him. She kept driving, aware she needed him, not a voice at the other end of the phone.

As she drove through the entrance to his property, she saw his truck parked alongside the road to his house, pulled up beside it, and slammed on her brakes. Climbing out of the car, she called his name.

He looked up with surprise.

Sobbing now, she started running toward him.

He hurried to meet her. "Lettie! What's wrong?"

"It's Autumn. She was killed by a car. Just found out she's dead," she sobbed between gulps reaching for the oxygen that had escaped her lungs.

Rafe steadied her and looked at her with alarm. "Breathe. Now tell me everything."

"I don't know much except what I already told you. Karabo said I need to come for Cami."

"I'll do that," said Rafe. "It's something I feel I should do as her grandfather." He took hold of her arm. "C'mon. Let's go find out exactly what's going on. I'll drive."

They both got in her car. Lettie sank against the cushions of the passenger seat feeling as helpless as she'd been as a child trying to make her future bright.

Rafe reached over and patted her knee. "Steady. We'll get through this together. Our daughter was precious to both of us, and so is Cami. We'll do right by both of them."

Lettie thought she'd never loved him more. He was her rock, her strength.

They made the call to South Africa together. Lettie spoke to Karabo and then turned the phone over to Rafe, who put it on speaker. His face flushed, his eyes awash with tears, he asked the hard questions for which they needed answers.

Lettie sorted the information in her mind. Autumn had

been jogging along the road outside of town when a car veered out of control on a curve and instantly killed her. Her body was at the morgue and would be held until Lettie made arrangements to have it buried or cremated. As for Cami, she knew her mother was not coming home, but needed Rafe or Lettie to come to her as soon as possible.

Rafe was given the number of a lawyer, and after thanking Karabo, he said, "I'll call you with my flight information as soon as possible."

He hung up and covered his face with his hands. When he looked up, grief had distorted his features into lines of sadness.

Lettie went to him and wrapped her arms around his shoulders. They clung tightly to one another, shaking with emotion as their tears blended.

"I should have called more often, made a better effort to be in touch, been a more loving mother," said Lettie, regret eating away at her insides.

"Don't do that," said Rafe softly. "Let's remember the good times." His look was so full of sadness, her heart twisted.

They worked to find the quickest, easiest flights to and from Johannesburg. As soon as the arrangements were made, Rafe called Karabo and gave her the flight information.

When he was through, Lettie said, "I need to speak to Cami." How she wished she could magically transport herself there.

"Nonnee?" Cami's voice sent tears streaming down Lettie's cheeks.

"I'm here, sweetheart. Rafe is coming to bring you home."

"Mama isn't coming back. Mama's dead," said Cami. "I want Mama here."

"Yes, sweetheart," crooned Lettie. "We all want Mama here. While you're waiting for Rafe to pick you up, you listen to our special Teddy bear, the one with the song inside. Remember how we sang to one another? I want you to feel as if I'm right there. All right?"

"Okay," said Cami, beginning to cry.

Karabo took the phone from Cami and spoke into it. "Don't worry. I'm not leaving Cami's side. I'll be right here with her."

"Thank you. I appreciate that more than you'll ever know."

Lettie hung up the phone with a sigh that came from the heart. Life could be so unfair.

Once again, Lettie stood outside the Portland airport, heartbroken.

"You and Scott are set to do the winemaking?" Rafe asked her. Lettie nodded. Scott Kurey and she had been in charge of winemaking for both her vineyards and his for some time, but Rafe had always been on hand to lend a hand and offer an opinion.

Rafe wrapped his arms around her. "I need to do this. I'll call and give you as much information as I can, whenever possible. Karabo said she'd help me pack up personal items, and the lawyer has agreed to quickly process legal matters. One of Autumn's co-workers will go through work papers. It's the best we can do with just one week's time."

Tears stung Lettie's eyes. *She* should be the one going to Africa, not Rafe.

"I'll miss you," she managed to say before giving Rafe a kiss that told him just that.

As Rafe walked into the terminal, a sob caught in Lettie's throat. She started forward and stopped. It was too late to make a change. She knew each day of the next week would be her punishment for not being able to conquer her fear of flying.

###

With all the work involved in the processing of the grapes, the days flew by. Nights were another matter. She lay in her empty bed unable to stop thinking of Autumn, reliving moments she wished she could live again. And like so many mothers, she knew she'd do some things differently. She imagined Cami calling for her mother, calling for her, and couldn't wait to be able to hold her in her arms.

And when Lettie allowed herself a few hours off one afternoon, she drove to a mall to purchase pink pillows and stuffed animals for Cami's bed. Later, when things were more settled, they'd decide together on what other items might make Cami's room more comfortable for her.

On the afternoon of Cami and Rafe's arrival, Lettie paced inside the terminal waiting for passengers to disembark from the San Francisco flight. A number of people emerged from the walkway before she saw Rafe walking toward her. Beside him, Cami looked so small, so fragile.

Lettie called out to them and waved.

Clinging to the Teddy bear she and Cami had picked out together, Cami rushed forward into Lettie's waiting arms.

Fighting tears, Lettie hugged Cami tight while she worked to gain composure.

Rafe came up to them. "How are you?" he asked Lettie, giving her a kiss on the lips.

"Glad you're here." Smiling, she saw how fatigue had formed shadowy blotches under his eyes and deepened lines across his brow. "I'll get you home and you can rest up there."

"Sounds good." He turned to Cami. "Babe is going to be happy to see you."

Cami's lips curved slightly. "She's my dog now."

Lettie and Rafe exchanged looks.

"Sure," said Lettie. "She loves you, like Rafe and I do."

Though the ride home wasn't even an hour, both Rafe and Cami shut their eyes and napped. Lettie kept glancing at the two, drinking in the sight of them.

As she pulled into the driveway at her house, Babe's barked greeting awakened them. "We're home!" Lettie announced.

She helped Cami out of her seat and stood by as Babe greeted her with pink-tongued kisses. Cami wrapped her arms around the dog and held on tight. "You're mine now, Babe."

As if the dog understood, Babe barked and wagged her tail. When Lettie took Cami's hand to lead her inside, Babe followed.

In Cami's room, Lettie fluffed the pillows and showed her the pink lamb and fuzzy blanket she'd chosen for the bed. "I know your favorite color is pink. When you're ready, we can fix up your room any way you want. "

Wide-eyed, Cami nodded.

Lettie unpacked Cami's suitcase, placing her clothes in the bureau or hanging them in the closet. Most of the clothes were suitable for fall, but come winter, she'd need warmer ones.

Lettie had almost finished her task when she noticed a wrapped package tucked into a corner at the bottom of the suitcase. She lifted the small but heavy item out of the suitcase and held it up.

"What's this?"

"It's mine," said Cami, reaching for it. "Karabo told me I could pick one thing of Mama's to bring with me."

"May I see it?" asked Lettie taking a seat on the bed. "Why don't you and I open it together?"

Cami slowly began to unwrap the brown-paper cover. As the wrapping fell away, Lettie saw the object was an elephant carved out of some kind of stone.

"I miss Mama. I want her to come back," said Cami, breaking into tears.

Her own eyes filling, Lettie pulled Cami onto her lap and rocked her gently. "I miss your Mama too."

"She's not supposed to be in heaven! She's supposed to be with me!" Tears slid down Cami's cheeks.

"I'm sure Mama would like to be here with you. She loved you very much, and I loved her."

Babe put her head in Lettie's lap and whined.

Cami reached out and stroked the dog's head.

"Let's try to remember all the good times with Mama. Then it will feel as if she's with us. I remember when she was a little girl about your age, she tried to make brownies with Abby. They mixed the batter, put them in the oven, and guess what? They burned! Your Mama was so upset! They tried again, and this time they were better."

"Karabo says Mama isn't a good cook. That's why she cooks for us."

"Guess who does a lot of the cooking here?"

"You?"

Lettie shook her head. "No. Rafe. He likes to work in the kitchen. Maybe you'd like to cook with him."

"Brownies?" Cami's eyes rounded. "Can I? Karabo let me help too."

She climbed off Lettie's lap and ran out of the room, calling, "Rafe! Rafe!" protective as always, Babe trotted at her heels.

Lettie watched them go, knowing there'd be other times when they'd need to talk about Autumn and her death. Lettie had already started to put together a photo album of pictures of Autumn and the rest of the family for Cami to use at those moments when she missed her mother.

She stood and looked out through the sliding-glass door at

the rolling land below. Her gaze automatically swung to the grove of trees that was so special to her. If Rafe approved, Autumn's ashes would be buried there.

CHAPTER THIRTY

With Cami's presence, life for Lettie took on a whole new dimension. She tried to time her day around Cami and her activities. It was one of the things she wished she'd done more of with Autumn. She didn't want Cami resenting the inn as Autumn had.

To her joy, Lettie found her eager to learn about grape growing and making wine. She also loved listening to Lettie and Rafe talk about it at dinner, and when Lettie went to the inn to check on things, Cami loved going with her.

After a rough beginning at school for being the new girl and having a bit of an accent, Cami settled in and made friends. Her favorite was Olivia Sanchez, one of Rafe's nieces. Lettie loved the idea because it made it seem as if her granddaughter was part of an extended family.

Dropping Cami off at her friend's house on the afternoon of her first sleep-over party, Lettie watched the ten-year-old sprint for the house with a sense of satisfaction. Cami was a popular girl who'd made friends through her kindness.

Lettie was heading for the inn when her cell phone rang. She smiled at the sight of Rafe's name and picked it up.

"Yes?"

"When will you be home? I have a special evening planned for us."

At the sexy tone of his voice, Lettie immediately changed direction. In their fifties, they both enjoyed a satisfying sex life. With Cami living with them, the spontaneity of the past had been lost to Cami's schedules and needs. An evening like this, she thought, would bring back a spark to their lovemaking.

Rafe greeted her at the door holding a tulip glass of bubbly champagne. "Come in, my dear," he said with an exaggerated leer.

She giggled and accepted the glass of wine. The delicious aroma of garlic and butter met her nose.

"I'm preparing a special shrimp dish for your pleasure. But first, let's sit in the den with our drinks. It's been a while since we've had the opportunity to have a quiet, late dinner."

Lettie eagerly followed him into the room that had become their retreat in the house. A fire glowed in the stacked-stone, gas-lit fireplace, flanked by white-painted wooden shelves loaded with books and keepsakes. Lettie took a seat in her usual green-leather chair at one side of the fireplace, and Rafe settled in the same-style chair opposite her.

He lifted his glass. "Here's to us! Do you realize today is the anniversary of the first day I met you thirty-four years ago?"

She clasped a hand to her chest. "I didn't know you were such a romantic. My word, it's been a long time, and so much has happened. I'm glad we're together."

He set down his glass on the table beside him and came over to her. Leaning down, he kissed her on the lips.

A familiar tug of desire filled Lettie. He'd always had that effect on her.

When they parted, Rafe's eyes shone with affection. He got down on one knee in front of her.

Lettie's heart bumped to a stop. They'd discussed marriage many times and had agreed, for business reasons, it would never happen.

"I need to give you something that shows how I feel about us. Lettie, will you accept this token of love from me?"

He opened a flat, black-velvet box. Inside, nestled against

cream silk, was a necklace. At the end of a gold chain, a pendant in the shape of a grape leaf gleamed at her. In the center of the leaf a cluster of diamonds, designed to look like grapes, sparkled.

Tears came to Lettie's eyes. "It's gorgeous, Rafe. What a perfect way to show our devotion to one another. Without the love of our land and the grapes, we would never have come together." She flung her arms around him. "I love you, Rafe, and always will." He pulled her down on the carpet with him. In minutes, they had their clothes off and were celebrating in the best way they knew, their bodies working together to bring pleasure to one another.

Later, lying together in front of the fire, Lettie stroked Rafe's strong chest, curling her fingers through the chest hair that was beginning to show signs of gray.

"Mmm, nice. Amazing what you've learned in thirty-four years!"

Rafe laughed. "The last ten years with you have been the best of my life."

"For me too," said Lettie, filling with love for him. She rose up on her elbows and looked into his handsome face, a face she loved like no other. "Thank you for being such a good man, a good grandfather."

He gazed at her with love. "You make it so easy." He sat up. "Now where is that necklace of yours? I want to see it on you right now."

"Don't you want to wait until I get dressed?"

He gave her a wicked grin and shook his head. "Nope. I want to see just you and that necklace." He found the box, lifted the necklace out, and hooked it around her neck. "There!"

She looked down at the pendant nestled against her bare breasts. It was the perfect gift from the perfect man.

By the time Cami returned from her sleep-over the next day, Lettie felt a new sense of commitment between Rafe and her.

As Cami grew into her teens, Lettie remembered how difficult Autumn had become and grew tense at the idea of the same disconnect happening between them. But compared to Autumn, Cami was an easy child, willing to listen. And even though Cami didn't hesitate to disagree with her, she did it in a less-combative way than her mother. There were no crude accusations, no temper tantrums, just a quiet determination to win any argument. Lettie couldn't help but wonder who Cami's father was. There was nothing in all of Autumn's personal papers to indicate who it might be, and the name of the father on Cami's birth certificate remained blank. It seemed ironic to Lettie that one small family could have so many unanswered questions.

The matter didn't become an issue until Cami was involved in a tenth-grade biology project that focused on genes and how they are passed down from one generation to the next.

"Why didn't my mother ever tell you about my father?" Cami asked, plopping down at the kitchen table and giving Lettie a plaintive look.

Lettie shook her head. "I don't know. She made certain no one else knew anything about him because she said it would hurt others. After she died, I went through her personal papers. There wasn't any mention of him."

"They met before Mom moved from Zaire to South Africa, right?"

"Yes." Lettie brushed the worried wrinkles from Cami's

brow with the tips of her fingers. "It's hard not knowing about your parents. I don't know anything about either one of mine. Can you imagine being dumped off at a foster home with no records, nothing? I sometimes resented my mother for what happened to me, but then I didn't know what was going on in her life. Maybe she did me the greatest favor she could."

Cami's eyes glistened with tears. "I love you, Nonnee."

Lettie drew her into an embrace. "And I love you, Camilla Chandler, with all my heart."

They held onto each other until Cami's cell phone rang, and the moment was lost.

Lettie and Cami remained close. And when she chose to go away to college to study viticulture and then to live in Europe for a few years, studying winemaking there, Lettie was content to let Cami go because she'd promised to eventually come home for good.

CHAPTER THIRTY-ONE

With Cami away, and Babe now gone, Lettie and Rafe settled into a quieter existence. Their wines were becoming sought after. Rafe took particular pride in participating in various wine shows and contests. He even traveled to France on business and spent two glorious weeks with Cami in the Côtes du Rhône wine region of France.

During this time, Lettie made a decision on her own to take her new financial manager's advice to invest in a start-up company in international sales. Things were going well at both the winery and the inn. Lettie wanted to leave Cami plenty of money to run things when she could convince her to come home and take over the operation. It would, she decided, be a secret surprise, proving once and for all that her life at Chandler Hill was not only a big success, but a tribute to Kenton and Rex Chandler's generosity.

As a part of her slowing down, Lettie brought in a new manager to oversee the inn. A graduate of the Hotel School at Cornell, he was an eager young man who said he was genuinely interested in learning all he could about the wine industry. With him on site, she enjoyed having more time to herself for reading and other projects. She even added vines to a block of land, hoping to add something new to their wines.

The fact that she wasn't feeling well was something she tended to ignore. At sixty-five, she was still agile, active, and involved in life and work. She was determined not to let the aging process get her down.

When she couldn't ignore the changes in her body, she

made a doctor's appointment for a day when Rafe would be at a wine show in California.

Dr. Simonson's empathy when he told her she had just a few months to live did nothing to stem the shock that went through her in waves of horror. She had no intention of dying this young.

She drove home in a stupor. Surely such a diagnosis belonged to someone else, someone who'd lived longer, she told herself. She wasn't ready to give up. There was so much more for her to do. She'd recently helped design a new label for wines coming from a new section of grapes that she was calling the Camilla Block.

Still shivering from the news, she entered the empty house. Rafe was in San Francisco and wouldn't be home for another two days. Alone in her kitchen, she allowed herself the relief of tears. The hot trail of them down her cheeks did nothing to lessen the pain of her new reality.

She picked up the phone and called her best friend.

Paloma arrived within twenty minutes. "*¡Ay, Dio mio!* What is it, Lettie?" She grabbed hold of Lettie's hand and gazed deeply into her eyes, studying her.

Tears filled Lettie's eyes.

"No," Paloma whispered. "I know you've been sick, but not this."

"It's true," said Lettie. "I talked to the doctor today. It isn't good. Six months or less is all I have."

"No!" cried Paloma. "It is too soon."

Sighing, Lettie wondered why her life had always seemed to proceed on a time schedule labeled "Too Soon". She'd been born too soon, had her family too soon, and was now dying too soon.

Crying softly, Paloma wrapped her arms around Lettie. "I'll be here to help you. I love you, Lettie."

"I love you too." Lettie laid her head on Paloma's shoulder. "I'll need you to help with Rafe and Cami. They don't know yet. It isn't something you tell someone over the phone."

"It's a beautiful day. Go sit on the deck, and I'll bring us some tea. We can talk there."

"Thanks." Lettie got to her feet wearily and went outside. Sitting down in a rocking chair she stared blankly at the scene in front of her, too shocked to notice what was there.

Paloma stepped out onto the wide, wooden deck and stood behind the chair. Placing a comforting hand on Lettie's shoulder, the faithful friend who'd always been her support asked, "Are you okay?"

Lettie patted Paloma's hand. "Just trying to come to grips with reality."

"You're a good woman, Lettie," Paloma said with conviction. "Think of it as going home. Going home to Jesus."

"What if I'm not ready?" Lettie said softly. She had so much to take care of before that time came. And she and Jesus weren't exactly on speaking terms.

She looked out at the rolling hills she loved so much. Her gaze swung to the grove of trees where the ashes of Kenton, Rex, and Autumn were scattered and buried. Soon she'd join them.

Below her, in the foliage softening the edges of the deck, a hummingbird hovered at the edge of a broad rhododendron leaf. Lettie watched as the hummer, spying a bit of moisture on the leaf's surface from a recent rain, dipped its wings into the water and fluttered them, taking a bath with such exhilaration it brought tears to Lettie's eyes. Suddenly, she was weeping—for all she'd been given and all that she'd lost.

###

That night, Lettie was surprised to see Rafe's truck coming up the driveway. Wondering if something had gone wrong at the wine show in San Francisco, she went to the front door to greet him.

He got out of the truck and hurried toward her. "Paloma called me and told me to come right home. What's going on?"

Lettie opened her mouth to speak and was as surprised as he by the wail that left her mouth. She collapsed in his arms, crying so hard she couldn't speak.

White-faced, he picked her up in his arms and carried her inside to the living room couch. Sitting down beside her, he drew her into his lap and let her cry. "What is it, Lettie? Tell me."

She gave him the grim news about her health.

"We'll do everything we can to fight it," Rafe announced with determination. "So many people beat cancer these days. You'll be one of them."

Lettie shook her head. "I already talked to the doctor about it. He was very honest with me. Chemo would only prolong the agony. The cancer is too far spread, the disease too severe. Besides, I told him that I don't want to make my last days full of my being sicker than I already am."

"Good God! I knew you weren't feeling well, but this?" Rafe's shoulders slumped. He covered his face with his hands. The sound of his sobs filled the room and the corners of her heart.

When he lifted his head, his cheeks were wet with his tears. "We'll have to tell Cami."

"Not yet," said Lettie. "Remember how awful it was going through your mother's death with cancer? Watching her linger, the waiting, the agony, the helplessness of seeing her like that? I want to avoid as much of that as possible for Cami. Understand?"

"Okay, but we can't hide it for too long. She'll need time to get used to the idea of taking over for you."

Later, after Rafe brought in his suitcase and got settled, he climbed into bed with her. Drawing her into his arms, he held her tenderly. Stroking her back, he whispered, "I love you, Lettie. I don't want to let you go."

"I'm not quite ready," she said. "The thought of leaving you and my life here is too painful. Paloma says I'm to think of it as going home to Jesus. But my home is here with you and Chandler Hill." She wiped her eyes.

"Let me love you now," he said. "No sex, just love." He began by fingering her ears, cupping her breasts, trailing his hands down her body, moving down to the curves of her hips, following the lines of her legs, reaching her toes.

"What are you doing?" Lettie whispered.

"Memorizing you," said Rafe, beginning to cry.

His gentle hands on her felt so good, so real. "We'll take it one day at a time, enjoy what we can," he murmured.

She nodded, but she knew her time would come too soon.

CHAPTER THIRTY-TWO

Lettie lay in bed waiting for Rafe to show up with Cami. The disease was the winner of every battle she'd fought in body and mind. She'd wanted to avoid having Cami suffer through this with her, but now she'd run out of time. Her final days had arrived with frightening speed.

At the sound of Rafe's truck in the driveway, Lettie tried to rise, but fell back against the pillows, too weak to get to her feet. It amazed her that her body, so strong, so healthy for most of her life, had turned into a fragile shell of her former self.

Lettie heard the front door open and then the sound of feet running toward her.

Cami burst into the room. "Nonnee! Nonnee! Why didn't you tell me? I would've been here for you."

Lettie fought to smile. "I know, sweet girl. And now you are."

Crying softly, Cami threw her arms around Lettie. "I love you so much!"

Lettie patted the bed beside her. "Have a seat. There's so much I have to tell you."

Her words hollow with regret, Lettie told Cami about turning Chandler Hill over to her. "I've left behind some funds to help you, but it will be a challenge. However, with your background, I'm counting on you to beat it. After all, you're both a Chandler and a Lopez." She forced a smile. "You can't beat that combination!"

"Oh, Nonnee, it's the best combination ever." Tears flowed

down Cami's cheeks.

Lettie hugged Cami to her chest and let her cry tears for them both.

Thoughts of all she'd accomplished flooded her mind. The inn of today would be unrecognizable to Kenton and Rex. The vineyards were a spectacular sight—row upon row of healthy, cultivated grapes. And the wines? A delight to nose and tongue. She'd been given a challenge she'd often thought she'd never meet. But sometimes, at her lowest, the spirits of the Chandler men had carried her through.

Sudden panic seized Lettie. She grabbed hold of Cami's hand. "I want you to promise you'll come home."

"Yes, Nonnee, I'm coming home. I'm not sure how I'll succeed, but I'm going to try."

Lettie smiled at her and echoed the words Rex has spoken to her. "Good girl."

A ray of sunlight entered the room and hovered above them, spreading a lemony shade across the ceiling, shedding its light on them, like a blessing from above.

Time passed in moments of wakefulness amid bouts of sleep. Past memories wove through Lettie's thoughts. She recalled the first time she'd seen Chandler Hill, remembered Rex's astonishment at her poetic description of the hills, recalled Kenton's rescue of her in San Francisco. Other memories appeared and then faded—memories of Autumn as a baby, Abby and others working at the inn, images of Rafe as a young man, and finally, Cami as a baby.

Lettie opened her eyes to find Rafe sitting in a chair beside their bed, Cami on the other side. She loved them so much.

"I've had a good life thanks to both of you," she said clearly, meaning it with all her heart.

Tearful, Cami squeezed her hand.

Lettie closed her eyes. It was time to go home.

She felt Rafe's lips on her cheeks.

Then, moments later, she was in a field of flowers running toward three figures crying, "Kenton! Rex! Autumn! I'm here!"

Thank you for reading *Going Home.* If you enjoyed this book, please help other readers discover it by leaving a review on Amazon, Goodreads, or your favorite site. It's such a nice thing to do.

Enjoy an excerpt from my book, *Coming Home–* A Chandler Hill Inn Book (Book 2 in the Chandler Hill Inn Series, which will be out in mid-2019.

CHAPTER ONE

Camilla Chandler walked through the vineyards at Chandler Hill in the Willamette Valley of Oregon toward the grove of trees that meant so much to her. The ashes of her grandmother, Violet "Lettie" Chandler, now resided there along with the ashes of her mother, Autumn, Lettie's husband, Kenton, and Rex Chandler, Lettie's father-in-law and the original owner of the inn and winery that Cami had just inherited.

The gray skies of this cool fall morning held a promise of rain, which suited her mood. The raindrops slated to fall would match the tears she'd somehow managed to hold onto after weeping for days at the loss of her grandmother, a woman beloved not only by Cami, but by all who knew her. For eighteen months of Cami's first two years, Nonnee had raised her, forming an early, loving bond between them. And then, when Cami was only six, Lettie stepped in to take the place of Cami's mother after Autumn was hit and killed by a car while jogging one day.

Cami lifted her face to the sky and watched as a red-tailed hawk circled in the air above her and then glided down to perch on the limbs of a tall white oak, part of the collection of trees that was her destination. As her grandmother had done, Cami sought refuge and answers among the pine and hardwood trees that rose from the earth in a sturdy cluster—sentinels keeping watch over the vines that lined the hillsides like promises of good things to come.

Cami entered the inner circle of the trees and sat on the stone bench that had been placed there long before her birth.

"What a mess," Cami blurted before she could stop herself. Wrapping her arms around herself, she wished she had worn her sweater. The crisp fall cold seeped into her bones as she began to cry. If Nonnee were here, she would hug her and tell her everything would be all right. But at the moment, nothing seemed all right. Especially after receiving the email from Bernard. Cami rocked in her seat, wishing there was an easy way to get rid of the pain. "Bernard Arnaud is a ... a ... jerk!" Her angry cry filled the air and bounced off the branches and boughs of the trees, making it seem as if their echoes confirmed her opinion of him.

She could hear her grandmother's words in her head. "Take a deep breath, darling, and begin at the beginning."

Following those silent instructions, Cami drew in air, straightened, and spoke aloud. "Nonnee, I thought he loved me. I thought he understood I had to come home to Chandler Hill, that I owed it to my family to be here. After our many months of being together, he called those days ... and nights ... a fun romance. And now, he doesn't want to see me anymore! After I helped to bury you, he told me this in an email ... an email for God's sake!"

Cami fisted her hands as fresh tears rolled down her cheeks. "I feel so ... so ... stupid!"

A sparrow landed on the ground not far from her and peered up at her with dark eyes, like a messenger sent by her grandmother. How she missed her!

Cami bowed her head. As strange as others might think of it, sitting in the grove, giving up her secrets brought answers. Though all of her Chandler relatives were deceased, they still spoke to her in memories and in stories others shared about them. They were fine people—her mother, grandmother, and the two Chandler men who'd given Nonnee the challenge of making the Chandler Hill Inn and Winery what they were today. Now, it was up to Cami to keep the enterprise healthy and strong. She knew it was an inheritance some people would love to have, but with the breakup with Bernard, it had already cost her dearly. And at twenty-three, Cami wondered how she could ever meet the challenge Nonnee had passed on to her.

The cool breeze blowing through the pines filled the air with whispers. Cami cocked her head to listen. No answers seemed clear but one. Somehow, she'd have to find the courage and strength within her to keep things going. If Nonnee, all five-feet-three inches of her, could do that, then so would she.

Cami stood to leave. Hearing a noise behind her, she turned to see Rafe Lopez walking toward her. Her lips curved, and she lifted a hand in greeting. Her grandfather was a striking man in his early seventies who was struggling with Nonnee's recent death. Cami and her grandfather, Rafe, had always had a close bond, and now that it was just the two of them living in Nonnee's house, they'd grown even closer.

She'd always called him Rafe, even as a child. When it was suggested she call him Grandpa, she'd stamped her toddler foot and said, "No! My Rafe!" He loved it then, and he loved it now.

"Thought I'd find you here," said Rafe. "Get a few things settled in your mind?"

She smiled sadly. "There are no simple answers, are there?"

He shook his head. "Life is anything but simple. May I sit with you?"

"Sure." She sat and indicated a place for him next to her. "What's up?"

"I just talked to Paloma. She's decided to leave Chandler Hill to live in Arizona with her daughter and her family."

Cami's eyes widened. "But Paloma has been almost as big a part of Chandler Hill as Nonnee."

"Yes, but now that her best friend is gone, and with her new inheritance, Paloma is free to leave." The sadness in his eyes reflected her own. "A lot of things will never be the same."

"I heard that Abby wants to retire by the end of the year." Cami let out a worried sigh. "Sometimes I feel so alone."

Rafe put an arm around her. "You've always got me. But I think it's time for me to move. I'd like to take over the cabin after Paloma is gone. What do you say?"

"You don't want to stay in the house with me?" Cami asked, genuinely surprised.

"Too many memories there. And the cabin is a special place for me. It's where I first spent time with Lettie. Of course, after all the renovations we've done, it's not a simple cabin anymore, but a very nice place for an old man like me."

Cami hugged him. "A very special old man. I'll miss you, but I agree. It's right for you to be on your own without worrying about me." She studied him with tenderness. "But I'll always be there for you, Rafe. A woman couldn't have a better grandfather than you."

He cupped her face in his broad, strong hands. "You'll never know what a gift you are to me, my granddaughter. I never suspected your mother was my child. When I found out, I cried with joy. And now I have you."

Cami had heard this story many times. It was a sweet one. She couldn't help wondering who her own father was. It was something her mother had refused to divulge. But someday, maybe when things were in better shape at the inn, Cami intended to find out. She needed to know.

Some families were complicated, she thought as she got to her feet once more. She held out a hand to her grandfather.

He took it and rose. "Ready to go home?"

"I guess so." *Home was as complex as her family.*

Cami sat in the office within the inn and stared out the window. The room and its history weighed heavily on her shoulders. She'd met with lawyers regarding the transfer of ownership of the inn and vineyards from her grandmother to her, but when she'd asked to see information from the financial advisor, he'd sent her an accounting of Nonnee's investments and requested that the meeting she wanted with him be postponed for two weeks while he dealt with some other issues. Overwhelmed by all the new information thrown at her, Cami had readily agreed.

Now, it was time to decide which of her available funds she'd use for the upgrades to the guest rooms the inn manager, Jonathan Knight, was insisting be done. Jonathan, the young manager Nonnee had hired just before she was diagnosed with cancer, was not one of Cami's friends. He'd all but sniffed his disapproval when Cami told him he would now report to her.

"But you have no experience in the hotel business," he'd protested. "I understand you studied Fine Arts in college. That certainly doesn't qualify you to run an operation like this."

"Nevertheless, I own the entire business," said Cami sweetly, though inwardly she was seething at the insulting tone of his voice.

"Cami? Mr. Evans is here to see you," announced Becca

Withers, her assistant, startling her out of her memory of that encounter.

Cami smiled. "Thanks, Becca. Please ask him to come on back." Cami had had a couple of telephone conversations with him. Dirk Evans had sounded very smart, very polished, very cocky.

Becca showed Dirk into the office and, standing behind him, waved a discreet hand in front of her face to indicate she thought he was a hottie.

Tall, with sun-streaked brown hair and fine features, he swept into the room and beamed at Cami. Through lenses in black eyeglass frames, his blues eyes surveyed her.

From behind the desk, she rose to shake his hand. "Hello, Dirk. We meet at last."

"My pleasure. Photographs Lettie had of you on her desk don't do you justice."

"Yes, well, have a seat and let's get down to business, shall we?" Cami said briskly. "I want to talk to you about my grandmother's portfolio. We're about to start a renovation project at the inn, and I'm going to need to sell some more stocks."

All confidence seemed to evaporate from him. He sank into a chair and faced her with a look of despair. "We've had some disappointments. One in particular."

A niggling feeling crept through Cami like a python, squeezing her insides. "You're not talking about the Montague Fund, are you? I directed you to sell that two weeks ago."

"Yes, I know. I tried to do that for you and all my clients, but there's a problem. It turns out that the Montague Fund was basically a Ponzi scheme. Most of the money is gone. I'm working on getting back what I can. I've already begun filling out claim papers, but it's going to take time for the Feds to sort through it." He pushed his glasses further up on his nose. "I was given reliable information on the fund, so I'm not sure what went wrong."

Cami's mouth went dry. She gripped the arms of her desk chair so tightly her fingers turned white. "What went wrong? My grandmother was a very conservative woman. I don't believe she would have wanted you to invest her money in something like that. Was she aware of what you'd done? Did she approve?"

"She told me to go ahead and do whatever I could to ensure you'd have enough money to carry on with the inn. The fund promised exceptional returns ..." his voice trailed off.

She narrowed her eyes and studied him. "So Nonnee didn't know?"

He looked at her and then away. "Not exactly."

"I could have you reported and perhaps have your license taken away," said Cami, "but then I guess I'm not the only client of yours who feels that way."

"I did nothing wrong," Dirk countered. "I got the information for the fund from a very reliable source. Believe me, you're not the only person who has been hurt by this."

Cami's lips thinned. "So that makes it all right?"

He shifted in his chair and looked away from her.

"Did everyone in your office suggest their clients invest in this fund?"

He shook his head. "Mr. Berman didn't like it, warned his clients against it."

Cami leaned forward and gave him a steady stare. "I want this entire portfolio transferred to him immediately. Understand?"

"But ..."

"Stay right here. I'm calling him now."

Dirk let out a snort of disgust. "You don't have to do that."

"But I do," she said, with a calmness she had to force.

Cami scrolled through her contact list and tapped in the number. She was immediately put through to Russell Berman. He listened to her and then said, "I'd be honored to work with Lettie Chandler's funds, and now yours. I suggest going over everything, making sure that the remainder of the money is placed in safe, conservative funds."

"But Mr. Berman, what am I going to do? I need money to pay for the renovation of rooms." Cami felt like crying, but she refused to break down in front of Dirk.

"The market is volatile right now. Hold off on spending any money until I get things sorted out. Then, you and I can talk about the renovation of rooms."

"Okay, but the hotel manager isn't going to be happy about it," sighed Cami. As she hung up, she wondered why she felt as betrayed by Dirk as she had been by Bernard.

"Okay, Dirk," said Cami, getting to her feet. "I think we're done here."

He rose and turned to go, then turned back to her. "Maybe we could have dinner sometime."

Hysterical laughter bubbled inside her. *He'd ruined her future and was asking for a date?*

"Really? I don't think so. Goodbye, Dirk."

Later, repeating that conversation to Becca, she said, "Can you believe it?"

"Yes. Have you taken a look at yourself? Thin, but with curves any guy would go for, you're a stunning woman with that strawberry-blond hair and dark eyes. I'd kill for your looks."

Cami wrapped an arm around Becca. "You're adorable. Being short isn't bad, you know."

"And being a little round?" Becca said with an arched eyebrow.

"Cuddly and warm. I've seen the looks Jonathan Knight

gives you."

Becca made a face. "Jonathan is in love with himself. Haven't you noticed?"

The two of them looked at each other and laughed. Tall and broad-shouldered, Jonathan carried himself with confidence. His dark hair, green eyes, and strong features were undeniably attractive. His attitude, not so much.

"For the time being, I've given up on men," said Cami with feeling.

"Not me." Becca grinned. "And you have to admit that Dirk Evans is one hot guy."

"Yeah, but looks aren't everything, Becca." Cami recalled how handsome she'd thought Bernard was. Now, the memory of his face as he leaned down to kiss her made her stomach fill with acid.

Cami's meeting with Jonathan went no better than her talk with Dirk.

"You can't tell me the renovation program I've planned is kaput," he groused, sitting in the office he'd assigned her. "The timing of it is perfect. Cold winter months are slow at the inn. And if we're going to raise rates, we need to refresh the rooms."

"I don't have any answers yet," Cami said. "But give me time to come up with a plan."

Jonathan's lip curled with derision that matched his tone. "How can we work things out if we don't have the money to do it? It'll take a miracle."

Cami held up a hand to stop him. "I'll get back to you as soon as I can, Jonathan. That's all I can promise right now."

His silence screamed his anger as he stormed out of the office.

Cami watched him leave, determined to show him just who she was. A Chandler and a Lopez.

About the Author

Judith Keim enjoyed her childhood and young-adult years in Elmira, New York, and now makes her home in Boise, Idaho, with her husband and their two dachshunds, Winston and Wally, and other members of her family.

While growing up, she was drawn to the idea of writing stories from a young age. Books were always present, being read, ready to go back to the library, or about to be discovered. All in her family shared information from the books in general conversation, giving them a wealth of knowledge and vivid imaginations.

A hybrid author who both has a publisher and self-publishes, Ms. Keim writes heart-warming novels about women who face unexpected challenges, meet them with strength, and find love and happiness along the way. Her best-selling books are based, in part, on many of the places she's lived or visited and on the interesting people she's met, creating believable characters and realistic settings her many loyal readers love. Ms. Keim loves to hear from her readers and appreciates their enthusiasm for her stories.

"I hope you've enjoyed this book. If you have, please help other readers discover it by leaving a review on Amazon, Goodreads, or the site of your choice. And please check out the Hartwell Women Series, the Fat Fridays Group, the Salty Key Inn Series, and The Beach House Hotel series. ALL THE BOOKS ARE NOW AVAILABLE IN AUDIO on Audible and iTunes! So fun to have these characters come alive!"

Ms. Keim can be reached at **www.judithkeim.com** And to like her author page on Facebook and keep up with the news, go to: **https://www.facebook.com/pages/Judith-Keim/184013771644484?ref=aymt_homepage_panel.**

To receive notices about new books, follow her on Book Bub - **http://bit.ly/2pZBDXq**

And here's a link to where you can sign up for her periodic newsletter!
http://eepurl.com/bZoICX

She is also on Twitter @judithkeim, LinkedIn and Goodreads. Come say hello!

Acknowledgements

Because I had an idea for a new series, my husband, Peter, and I traveled to the Willamette Valley in Oregon to get a feel for the area and to learn more about grape growing and winemaking there. The fact that pinot noir is my favorite wine may have been a factor. In selecting a place to stay, I wanted to experience something that I could envision in a book. We chose Youngberg Hill. Situated at the top of a hill overlooking rolling landscape below, this inn was the perfect place. Chandler Hill Inn is based on our experiences there.

I wish to thank Wayne Bailey and his wife, Nicolette Nickolau, for being so gracious to us, as they are to all their guests. Wayne patiently answered my many, sometimes foolish, questions. Some of his ideas about organic farming were incorporated as part of Rex Chandler's thinking in the book. Any things I didn't get right are my fault, but I hope I've given readers a true sense of the valley and, more specifically, Youngberg Hill.

Made in the USA
Lexington, KY
08 March 2019